REFLECTION

BOOK TWO IN THE CHRYSALIS SERIES

ELENE SALLINGER

Published by Xcite Books Ltd – 2013

ISBN 9781909520769

Printed and bound in the UK

Praise for *Awakening*

'I love romance novels with an extra added spice and this was perfect for me.'

- Stressed Rach, Blogger

'A fantastic read. I really enjoyed reading about both of the main characters and found them very rounded and I could totally understand why they were drawn to one another. I whizzed through page after page of this book, desperate to know what happened next and how things would resolve themselves.'

- Lucy Felthouse, Blogcritics.org

'To sum up this book it will keep you hooked till the last page wanting to know what they will do next, it's a brilliantly written book which will make you fall in love with both Claire and Evan two really solid main characters. It will tug on those heart strings and some may even shed a tear at the depth of emotions within these pages which keeps you reading till the end... I found myself willing them to just go for it.'

- Midnight Boudoir

'*Awakening* is anything but a typical BDSM story. It is refreshing, as it concentrates on the emotional side of the relationship, instead of simply jumping to sex scenes Characters are realistic and likable.'

- Rain Hart, The Romance Reviews

'Ms Sallinger has the perfect combination to make this tale exquisitely beautiful, touchingly heart-wrenching and hedonistic enough to keep your body on fire.'

- Danielle, Coffee Time Romance

Acknowledgments

No book is accomplished without the help of others. In particular, I'd like to thank J for being willing to debate plot points and help me see where I was running off the rails. I'd also like thank my daughter for being patient when her dad and I debated said plot points.

Additionally, I'd like to thank the women of Mercer County Aware who talked with me, counselled me, and helped me see how abuse of all kinds can translate so heavily into the mental baggage we carry.

I'd also like to thank everyone in the kink community who has welcomed me with open arms. You're too numerous to name, I'd hate to leave anyone out, but your feedback and open communication has been invaluable.

To my beta-readers … you're all awesome. Thank you for catching all my mistakes!

Finally, I'd like to thank everyone at Xcite Books for making my entrance into the world of writing so painless.

This book is dedicated to everyone who thinks that what they desire is shameful. Sometimes, accepting ourselves is the hardest, scariest thing we do.

Chapter One

Curled in the foetal position, Bridget Ross fought the agonised pleasure wracking her body. Every muscle clenched as she denied her body the release it sought. She would not allow this. She would not succumb.

Intentionally, she bit the inside of her cheek, drawing blood. Anything to distract her from the sensations her dreams had fed her. Slowly, the pleasure faded only to be replaced with the throbbing sting in her cheek. That pain she could deal with. The other –

Stop! Don't think about it.

Horror flooded her body at the realisation of how close she'd come to falling off that ledge. One she'd vowed she'd never stand near again. It had been *too* close. Tears ran down her cheeks and her limbs became leaden with shame.

At her back, her pit bull terrier, Daisy, whimpered and whined and nuzzled her, but Bridget couldn't find the will to comfort her. Not when she herself was beyond comfort.

Could a person will themself into non-existence? Simply lie there and wilfully deconstruct their cells so they merged with the universe and ceased to exist?

On the side table, Bridget's alarm clock began to

chime, informing her it was now 5.30 a.m. and time for her run. She ignored it. Eventually it cut off.

She stared into the darkness, blanking her mind deliberately. If she didn't think, she didn't feel and then she could tolerate this. If she allowed herself to feel in this moment, she'd be lost.

Bridget willed herself to be empty. She lay there; a lump of flesh. The only indication of life was the rise and fall of her chest and even that she would have traded if she could.

It was futile. She knew it, but still she wished for it. Memories were funny. They had a way of sticking with you no matter how deep you thought you'd buried them. She could no more escape her memories that she could will herself to stop breathing.

As if to test the notion, Bridget blew out all her breath and held herself still. She refused to inhale until her lungs screamed for air, and then she waited longer. Finally, conceding defeat, she sucked in a breath forcefully.

Despite herself, her body lightened. The clenching of her muscles relaxed. Her tears dried. Today was not the day that she gave up. Today she was not able to die.

Too bad that wasn't the same as living.

Dragging herself from the bed, she made her way to the bathroom. She began her usual routine, going through the motions just as she did every morning. Turning the knobs on the shower, she undressed and waited for the water to reach the correct temperature.

Whorls of steam billowed out from behind the glass walls of her shower before she finally stepped in. The water scalded her creamy skin, turning it

2

tomato red, but went unnoticed.

Drenching her loofah in Dial, Bridget wielded it the way a carpenter wields sandpaper. She scrubbed relentlessly, taking off layers of skin. Tears ran down her cheeks – whether from pain or lingering shame she didn't know. Didn't truly care. She ignored them. Ignored the burn and scratch as the scalding water failed to rinse away the slime she felt along her skin.

It wasn't enough.

She became frenzied in her need to cleanse herself. She knew the stain would never be washed away. It marred her spirit as permanently as if it were tattooed on her skin. But it didn't stop her from trying.

She reached for the soap again, only to have it slip through her cramped fingers and clatter against the tiles spilling the bright, orange liquid.

Staring in dismay at the soap running down the drain, defeat settled into her body and the loofah slipped from her fingers. Collapsing in on herself, Bridget huddled in the corner of the shower sobbing and wishing she could rinse her crimes down the drain as easily as she could the soap.

Dressed in running gear, an iPod strapped to her arm, she waited for the sky to lighten sufficiently so she could commence her run. Standing pressed against her front door, she watched the sky through the small window cut-out in the heavy, wooden door.

Clouds dyed the colour of cotton candy swirled in the sky and patches of robin's egg blue poked through the early morning dawn cloud cover. Its beauty wasn't lost on Bridget, but the ants crawling under her skin were winning the competition for her attention. She needed to get out of this house. She needed to get away from the memories. She needed to *run*.

As if on cue, a ray of sunlight broke through the clouds illuminating her street. She knew a sign when she saw it. Unlocking all four deadbolts on her door, she walked briskly down the block. When she felt sufficiently warmed up, she began to jog. Daisy trotted happily at her side, her tongue lolling out.

The music in her ears set the pace as it always did, starting out slow, building in tempo as she ran so that she would have to focus all her attention on the beat and her pace in order to match it.

Each choice in the playlist was deliberate. Each drenched and pulled her in. The music absorbed her consciousness, taking her away from her memories, burying them down deep once again. It never failed her. It allowed her to fool herself into thinking she could outrun the past.

Absolutely gorgeous.

Connor Reynolds was riveted by the sight in front of him. Perfection personified. Damn, he wanted his camera in his hands. There was no better subject. The composition took care of itself. No need to do any fancy lens work, or fiddle with too many settings. Framed by the trees lining the running trail, it was all taken care of, just point and shoot.

Without warning, he was yanked hard to the right. All thoughts of adding the sunrise to his growing portfolio flew from his brain as his ankle wrenched sharply and he went down on the path. Skin shredded against the asphalt and white daggers of pain lanced along his wrists and into his elbows as he barely saved himself from getting a massive case of road rash along his face.

'Stop!' a feminine voice cut through the silence. 'Dang it! I said stop!'

Connor dragged himself up off the park trail and scanned for Lotus, his Rhodesian Ridgeback. She was responsible for this current debacle. Well, at least that was his story and he was sticking to it. Not his inattention. No, not at all. She'd clearly decided she'd had enough of running by his side and was now more interested in the dog that was currently wrestling with her. The problem, however, was that unlike his leash, which he'd quickly released once she'd yanked him, that dog's owner was being dragged and bounced around like a leaf on the wind at the moment. What in the hell had possessed her to wrap a leash around her waist?

Forgetting his injuries, Connor dashed across the trail to where she was vainly trying to get the dogs to stop. Wading in between them, he reached for Lotus' collar and yanked her to the side with a sharp, 'Relax!' To the strange dog, he put up a hand and said, 'Stop!' He didn't know the proper command for her, him, whatever, but his tone should get the job done. Thankfully, the dog stopped.

Turning his attention back to Lotus, he ordered, 'Sit.' She turned her root beer-coloured eyes up to his. The plea of "let me play" screamed at him, but he ignored it. Patiently, he repeated the command. She was so stubborn when she wanted something. This time, she sat.

Confident he had about 30 seconds before she ignored him, he spun to help the dishevelled owner.

Much to his amusement, she was on hands and knees grumbling curse words that would make a sailor blush. Facing away from him, she presented a very lovely, lush ass for his perusal.

Her jogging clothes hugged her body and he was mightily impressed with her equipment. Her running equipment, of course, not the wiggle in that gorgeous ass as she struggled to her knees. Not the shapely curve of her waist or the lightly muscled arms set off by her black runner's tank. Her headphones were dangling around her wrist and her coppery red hair was falling out of the simple band where she had it tied up in a sloppy knot.

'Daisy!' Her voice was smoky and tinged with an accent he couldn't place other than Southern. 'You little bitch! What have I told you about running off like that? Y'all damn near broke my ankle.'

Her vowels were long and her consonants soft and silky. "Running" lost the "g" and "you all" didn't even exist for her. He grinned at her use of "bitch" in its one and only appropriate usage as the pit bull terrier – he was guessing, anyway – was clearly a female with a name like Daisy.

'That's my fault, I'm afraid.'

She whirled to face him stepping backward and catching her knee on her dog's leash. He reached for her arm to steady her and a look of terror flashed across her face. She jerked up her hands and pushed one hard into his chest. With the other, she slammed her forearm against his, batting him away.

'Shit!' he hollered, tucking the aching limb under his armpit in a vain attempt to curb the throbbing. 'What the hell is wrong with you, lady?'

'Don't touch me!' she gasped, her breath ragged and her chest heaving.

'Don't worry,' he snapped, 'I don't plan on getting anywhere near you.' His arm still throbbed. 'I was just trying to help. You were about to fall and it was clear I'd startled you.' He shook his wrist, trying to flick away the pins and needles.

'I didn't know you were there.' She placed her hands on her knees and visibly brought her breathing under control.

Connor remained wary. Gorgeous or not, she'd already proved volatile and he wasn't at all sure she wouldn't flick off again. 'Look, it was my dog that caused the problem. Well, it was me, really. I was distracted and she got away from me.' Taking in the dogs casually sniffing each other, he gestured toward them, saying, 'They seem no worse for wear.'

Glancing at her dog, she said, 'Daisy will take any opportunity to play. I guess it was bound to happen.'

'That leash isn't your best choice if you want to be able to keep yourself on your feet when your dog decides to get rambunctious.'

'But it keeps my hands free.' Her voice dropped and her gaze turned distant as she spoke and Connor wasn't certain he'd heard her.

'Huh?' he prompted, wanting her to clarify.

As weird as this encounter had been, he found he wasn't looking to leave yet either and he really should since he had things to do.

'Nothing.' Her voice turned sharp and cool. 'Your knee is bleeding. Are you injured?'

She reached out as if to touch him, only to pull back like she'd been burned. Something was way out of kilter with this one. Now that she'd mentioned it, he noticed the burn of the shredded skin on his knees and the ache in his palms. Examining both, he determined that all the damage was superficial and told her so.

With a brisk nod she said, 'I'd keep a better eye on my dog if I were you.' She jerked lightly on the leash and set off down the path away from him.

'Hey!' he hollered after her. 'What's your name?'

She ignored him.

He stood, rooted to the spot, watching her until she disappeared from sight. Crazy. She was certifiable. Definitely.

Looking down at Lotus, he stroked her silky head and shrugged. 'You can't win them all, huh, baby?' Taking up her leash, he continued on his way, leaving all thoughts of that strange encounter on the trail behind him.

Chapter Two

Bridget idly tapped her fingers on the battered top of the small bistro table as she waited for Claire to arrive. Around her, Bean There Done That was alive with the energy that only a college town coffee house can have. Small groups of students clustered around laptops that competed for space with encyclopaedic textbooks which overflowed the tables. The huge tomes crowded out their cappuccinos and macchiatos while they debated the merits of lives they hadn't yet begun to live.

Several of her own students were currently huddled around a table in the far back. Hopefully, they were studying for the exam she'd dropped on them for the following day. They'd waved to her as they'd come in, calling out a "Hey, Professor Ross, you drink coffee?" as if it were completely alien for their teacher to actually do something human like drink coffee.

Unfortunately, her "Of course, coffee's the single best chemical reaction in the world" had fallen on deaf ears. The blank look she'd gotten let her know that she needed to step up her Chem 101 classes if they hadn't understood the apparent, albeit bad, joke that it was.

Still, they were good kids. It warmed her heart to see the group included Jack Rigby, who was a great guy, but a very poor chem student. Skyler, her best student, was also in the group and it looked like she was taking a special interest in helping him. More than likely that interest had less to do with altruism and a lot more to do with Jack's baby blue eyes and well developed body, but hey, if it helped him pass she was all for it.

Her eyes danced restlessly around the café as she waited for her best friend. The pale green walls were unexpected in a coffee shop where so many went for mocha shades that matched their primary cash crop, but they worked here. Mona Van Hove, the owner, was not your usual sort of person and there were significantly more comfortable, overstuffed chairs arranged around low tables than there were bistro tables.

The artists' work adorning the walls was for sale. Mona took a special interest in displaying local works and showcasing aspiring unknowns. The fireplace that dominated the back wall was always in use during the frosty Vermont winters and during the summers she filled the area with candle displays that created a cosy atmosphere no matter the temperature.

The vibe was one of bustling energy. Conversation was lively, but muted enough that you didn't have to raise your voice to be heard. The clink and tap of dishes as coffees and espressos were made to the accompaniment of the hiss and spit of the machine frothing milk was a comfort on a day like today.

Despite herself, she'd been unable to get the unfortunate encounter with the strange jogger out of her head. She'd been barely civil to him and that wasn't like her. She was polite to everyone. It had been bred into her from the time she was old enough to walk. No Southern woman worth her salt lost her manners regardless of the situation. However, she had definitely done that this morning.

She'd wanted to put it down to the fact that he'd startled her. That she'd had the dream *again* when she'd gone so long without it she'd thought she might actually have gotten past it. But the reality was that her own reaction had startled her more than anything else.

Yes, he'd absolutely frightened her, but she'd learned years ago to clamp down on the terror and panic that hit her like a Mack truck every time a man caught her by surprise. But no, this time she'd actually pushed him. She'd physically assaulted a man who was guilty of simply startling her. Making it even worse, once she'd recovered her composure she'd found that she'd wanted to reach out and touch him for very different reasons than fright. And *that* was not like her at all.

Bridget Ross of the Charleston Rosses did not run around touching strange men just because she found them attractive. The weirdest thing about it all was that he wasn't a stunning individual. If he'd been gorgeous she could rationalise her reaction. His features, however, were relatively nondescript. His hair was a deep, chocolate brown cropped extremely short in one of those styles that said a man just couldn't be bothered with it. His chin had been strong, with the morning's stubble still present as if he'd gone jogging before shaving. His nose had clearly been broken at some point in his life as it sported a distinct bend.

His eyes, well, *they* had been extraordinary. She would give him that. He had the greyest eyes she'd ever seen. A pale shade of charcoal, they were almost the colour of the ash left in the grill after a good barbecue. He'd towered over her, but only because she was five feet tall on a good day and he was probably just under six feet. She'd had to look up at him and the lack of equilibrium she'd felt had a lot more to do with the way her heart had begun to race and her body had responded to him.

He'd looked at her with those ash-coloured eyes and she'd felt as if she was on fire. As if she was being consumed from the inside out and she wanted nothing more than to continue to burn.

That was unacceptable.

She had panicked. Unable to comprehend her reaction, she'd resorted to rudeness to gain control. Her loss of discipline rankled her. That wasn't like her and now she didn't even know where to find him to apologise.

The bells on the door tinkled, drawing her out of her thoughts. Claire entered with Wade Stalls, a native of River Rock and the owner of Stalls General Contracting. He was doing some renovations on the townhouse Claire and Evan shared a few blocks away. Bridget tensed as Wade approached the counter, where Mona was preparing the order of an elderly gentleman. Unfortunately, this was as predictable as the fact that mixing Mentos with Coke would be explosive.

She watched with a mixture of sympathy and pain

as Mona caught sight of Wade approaching with Claire and promptly dropped the coffee she'd been about to hand to the old man. Porcelain shattered and hot coffee spilled all over the counter, thankfully missing both Mona and the customer. Mona's skin, normally a lovely shade of cinnamon, turned crimson and her caramel-coloured eyes went wide with mortification. She looked down and shook her raven hair across her face as if she could hide the physical evidence of her shame. Mona's hands shook and her friend, normally so together, witty and sharp, literally began to trip over herself. She lost all composure whenever Wade was in the room.

For his part, Wade seemed embarrassed by her distress. He was solicitous to the old man and helped clean up the mess, grabbing a handful of napkins and wiping up the counter after making sure the man was OK. He was abrupt and clipped with Mona, treating her like a criminal. Obviously unable to take it any longer, Mona fled after asking one of her baristas to take over. Bridget went after her with a quick stop to let Claire, who was ordering for herself, know where their table was.

She ignored the "Employees Only" sign on the swinging door next to the restrooms and knocked gently before letting herself into the office. Mona was slumped in her chair, a tissue crumpled in her hand and her arms wrapped around her body as if only sheer will was holding her together.

'Oh sugar, don't be so hard on yourself!' Bridget exclaimed as she hurried over to Mona and wrapped her friend in a hug.

'Bridg –' her voice was watery '– why can't I get

myself together whenever he's around?' The question was more of a wail.

'Because you refuse to realise that he's just a man, darlin'. He's not this god you've put on a pedestal. Hell, he's friggin' stupid as far as I can tell. He can't even see such a phenomenal catch right in front of his face. Now, do you really want a stupid man?'

Mona snorted at Bridget, considering they both knew Wade was anything but stupid, but it had the desired effect as Mona took several deep breaths and swiped at her eyes.

'Bridget, I have loved that man since I was in high school and, frankly, I'm sick to death of feeling this way. I'm wasting my best years pining for a man who doesn't want me.'

'I know, Mona.' Bridget hugged her friend again, unwilling to lie to her. She stroked her hair and said, 'But I completely disagree that you've wasted your life. You have a wonderful business, gorgeous friends who love you –' She flicked her hair and got the laugh she'd hoped for at her obviously self-aggrandising words. Capitalising on the moment, she said, 'Come on, sugar. Come take a break and have a coffee with me and Claire.'

Mona shot a panicked glance in the direction of the café. 'I don't want to go back out there, Bridg.'

'Mona, don't make me go there.'

Mona gasped and pulled back from Bridget. 'You wouldn't!'

'I absolutely would.' Bridget pulled her best stern look. 'Now, what are you going to do?'

'Well –' she drew herself up to her full five feet six inches and pushed her chair back under her desk '– I

14

guess you leave me little choice.'

'Indeed.' Bridget barely contained her grin as Mona pushed past her, grumbling about how she'd be damned before she'd let Bridget ruin another espresso machine making her own coffee.

'Caramel, vanilla, and a hint of cinnamon.' Bridget licked her lips unconsciously as she swallowed the silky brew Mona had set before her.

'Yup.' Mona grinned, clapping as Bridget guessed the flavours in her latest find. Turning to Claire, she said, 'Your turn.'

Claire sipped carefully and closed her eyes, a look of pure bliss passing over her features as she swallowed. She took another sip and repeated the process before saying, 'Almonds and chocolate.' She set the cup down with a satisfied grin.

'You guys are so good!' Mona was jubilant and, now that Wade was gone, the successful, smart, and gregarious woman was back in charge rather than the insecure mess she always reverted to in his presence.

'Well,' Claire said, 'I can't speak for Bridget, but I take my coffee very seriously, especially now.' She rested an unconscious hand on her swelling abdomen.

A pang of deep envy shot through Bridget that she quickly stamped out. She wasn't going there either. The spell was broken, however. As Mona and Claire discussed the merits of decaf coffee in satisfying her cravings yet protecting Claire's unborn child from the effects of caffeine, her mind wandered back to the morning's encounter with the jogger.

'Care to share?' Claire's voice cut through her ruminations and she was surprised to see her two friends looking at her quite intently.

'Pardon?' She stalled for time.

'Exactly what has got you scowling?'

'I don't know what ya'll are talking about.' Pretending a deep interest in the material of her skirt, she smoothed the napkin over her lap even as she blushed.

'Spill, Bridget.' Claire was looking at her with one eyebrow raised and worry colouring her hazel eyes.

Remorse flooded Bridget and she sighed deeply before saying, 'I ran into someone this morning and it's thrown me off.'

'Who?' Claire and Mona asked in unison.

'I don't know.' She picked at her napkin before grabbing it and balling up in a fist. 'I mean, I literally ran into him, or his dog at least. And then he frightened me, I pushed him, and then nearly tore his head off I was so rude.' She was tripping over her words and not making an ounce of sense, and she knew it.

Taking a deep breath, she looked at her friends who were patiently waiting her out and started over. She filled them in on the encounter, her reaction, and her remaining disquiet. When she'd finished, Claire and Mona sat quietly, their sympathy evident in their faces. They knew her history. In that, at least, no explanation was required.

'So,' she said on a breathy sigh, 'I behaved like a bitch. I can't even apologise and it's nagging at me badly.'

Claire reached out and squeezed her hand. 'Stop being so hard on yourself. There isn't one thing that happened that wasn't a natural response. Both the

16

fright and the attraction. You're still a functioning woman, Bridget. You're going to respond to men.'

Hot tears flooded Bridget's eyes. It wasn't the attraction she had a problem with, it was the stupidity that giving into attraction led you to. That was something she would never allow. The lesson she'd received had imprinted on her like indelible ink. Once was enough.

Mona took her other hand and began making soothing noises to her which only made Bridget laugh given the role reversal she now found herself in.

'You guys are good to me, but stop. Seriously. I'll be fine.' She gently disengaged her hands and stood, reaching for her handbag. 'Listen, I have to get to class, but I'll see you guys this weekend, right?' Their book club was meeting at Bibliophile as usual.

'Yup,' Mona said smiling.

'Wouldn't miss it.' Claire grinned, considering her husband was the proprietor of the shop.

'Good.' She forced a grin. 'I'll see you ladies then.' With a wave, she forced all thoughts but the upcoming lesson out of her mind as she stepped into the afternoon sunshine.

Pinewood University was the heart of River Rock. The city itself had grown up around the school and its economy was highly dependent on the university. The grounds were stately and looked very much like they must have looked when the school first opened in 1867. The verdant campus was surrounded by the trees of its namesake. The quad, so named for the four, expansive areas of manicured grass intersected by wide sidewalks that looked more like narrow roads, was crowded and thrumming with energy.

Groups of students clustered on the grass, studying or just hanging out. Their laptops and MP3 players were out of sync with the classicism of the campus and created a surreal feeling at times. Remove the students and you could have been in a Sherlock Holmes novel.

Connor was oblivious to the mystique as he hot-footed it across the quad, trying to get to the auditorium before he was any later. A quick glance at his watch told him it was pointless.

Dammit! He had to do better than this. He really did. But he hadn't been able to resist the afternoon sun and the treasures he'd found in the local parks to sketch and photograph. Mothers and nannies with children at play. Dogs and their owners playing in the park. The shot he'd gotten of a Border Collie mid-flight with a Frisbee in her teeth and a look of pure adoration on her face as her owner clapped with joy had been awesome.

But it had also happened when he should have already been on his way to work. Sam, his boss, put up with his lateness because he was a hard worker and he stayed until the work was done. Truth be told, Connor liked his job. It afforded him solitude and time to think. For all that he was an observer and documenter of humanity he didn't enjoy spending a tremendous amount of time *among* people. He liked to be on the edges, watching and recording. He didn't like to be interacting.

Hence, his job was perfect for him. As a custodian for the university, Connor had plenty of solitude to think and observe. People never noticed the help. A janitor was invisible until there was a mess to be cleaned up.

Still, Connor loved the campus and the work. He'd finish whatever task was at hand, only to be caught by the play of light on the mosaic tile lining a hallway. He'd instantly be transported and have to dig into his ever-present backpack and grab either his camera or his CleanSlate in order to capture the image.

Today, though, Sam had asked him to come in on his day off and help set up for a concert that was taking place on campus. A popular up-and-coming group, C Note, was giving a concert, requiring the small sports arena to be arranged and the stage set up and prepped for the evening's entertainment. In fact, sound check was in just under an hour. He'd better get a move on.

Connor picked up the pace and was so focused on making his way across the small campus that he almost didn't register the voice calling out to him. Turning, he saw the crazy jogger from this morning headed his direction.

Shit! He had nowhere to go.

'Hey there! Hold on.'

The redhead was still cute, but he remained wary as she hurried in his direction hampered by a clinging, pale green skirt and cream silk blouse that gave her a sexy, professional look.

He really didn't want to stop. Well, he wanted to look, but he didn't want a repeat of this morning. Still, his own sense of manners had him waiting for her to catch up to him. He must be a glutton for punishment.

She was breathless when she finally reached him,

which of course brought out his inner Neanderthal because he couldn't resist the sight of her heaving breasts. They were absolutely gorgeous. Full, and nicely showcased by her blouse. Just enough cleavage showed without making her appear slutty or undermining her professionalism. With a supreme force of will, he pulled his gaze away from her spectacular bosom and up to smirking green eyes.

'Really? The once over?' she said, but there was no heat in her voice, only that silky drawl that made him want her rubbing against him like a cat. His body certainly liked that idea and he had to put a major clampdown on the stirring in his groin.

'You are *incredibly* gorgeous.' He didn't bother to hide his appreciation of her body which caught her off guard by the surprise that passed over her face at his words. 'But you're also dangerous for someone as tiny as you.' He grinned and rubbed the spot on his chest where she'd pushed him.

A flush of embarrassment coloured her skin, tinting it a sweet shade of pink, before she replied in that smoky, Southern lilt, 'I am so sorry about that. I don't normally respond so aggressively to being startled. I don't have an excuse, but I wanted to apologise.'

He grinned down at her, enjoying her obvious discomfort.

'And why exactly did you grace me with such an enthusiastic response?'

She squirmed and looked away from him, gnawing on her lower lip. It was absolutely adorable and had him imagining much more explicit things she could be doing with those lips. They were as full and voluptuous as the rest of her and – get a grip on yourself, Connor! He forcefully brought himself back to the present.

'You startled me, and I reacted instinctively. I apologise again.'

She looked up at him and saw his grin.

'You're enjoying this, aren't you?' She was clearly affronted but being a good sport.

'Yes, yes I am.' Again, he didn't bother hiding. 'You have a heavy hand, Miss ...?' The obvious question hung in the air.

'Ross. Bridget Ross.'

She held out her hand to shake. It was tiny and delicate with perfectly manicured nails painted a deep shade of burgundy. His own hand engulfed hers and he liked the feel of her skin against his. So much so, he didn't let go.

'I'm Connor Reynolds, Bridget Ross.' He grinned again as she tugged gently on her hand; only when she tugged harder did he let it go.

'Well, Connor. I'd like to make it up to you, if you'd let me.'

He raised an eyebrow as he waited.

'Would you let me buy you a cup of coffee?'

'Coffee?' He pretended a pout. 'I'm going to be wearing a bruise for at least a week.'

She laughed at his obvious acting. It was a lovely sound, light and tinkling and made with her whole body. Not one of those weak, simpering laughs. This reached her eyes and made her face shine.

'OK, how about coffee and a pastry of your choice? I have a bit of pull with the owner at Bean There Done That.'

'Hmmm.' He pretended to think it over when he already knew he was going to say yes. 'OK, but it will have to be tomorrow. I have somewhere to be at the moment.'

'Are you a photographer?' She nodded in the direction of his equipment.

'What I am is late.' He dodged the question, but softened his words with a smile. 'Is 11 a.m. good for you tomorrow?'

She shook her head saying, 'I have a class at 11.30. How about after lunch, say 1 p.m.?'

'One it is.' He smiled again.

'OK then, good.' She smiled back and turned saying, 'I'll see you tomorrow.'

'Yup.' He waved as she moved off, taking a good, long look at her shapely ass which he'd admired so much that morning. His hand itched to cup it. He watched until she turned into the faculty parking lot before finally heading to the stadium to find Sam.

He didn't even try to wipe the grin off his face.

Chapter Three

What in the hell had possessed her to ask him out for coffee? She'd only planned to apologise, not ask him out. She seemed to lose the ability to think straight when it came to that man.

Connor. She liked the name. It fit him. He looked like a Connor, like something straight out of one of those *Highlander* movies. His grey eyes had been laughing the whole time. What a smartass. She snorted at the memory, but found herself grinning just the same.

'Something funny, Professor?'

Bridget snapped out of her thoughts as Skyler dropped her exam on Bridget's desk. She looked up at her student and nodded.

'Yeah. Well, to me anyway.'

She noted that the rest of the class was already gone. Skyler was always the last to turn in her exams. A brilliant student, she nevertheless agonised over tests. Many a time, Bridget had to remind her to relax and breathe. That she either knew it or she didn't. She wasn't going to learn it while taking the test.

Once, Bridget had found her sobbing over a B that she'd gotten on an exam. She'd refused to open up when questioned as to why this was an earth-shattering event, but Bridget had seen this type of thing before. Students who pushed themselves so hard for one reason or another, but who all had a common thread of feeling like they had something to prove, whether to a parent or friend.

'How are you doing, Skyler?' She worried about this one. She seemed very close to a breaking point some days.

'I'm good, Professor. Never better.' The words were bright but she didn't meet Bridget's eyes.

'I'm always here if you want an ear, Skyler.'

Wary brown eyes met Bridget's green ones.

'What makes you think I need someone to talk to?' Her entire body went rigid as she spoke. Her chin jutted up in the air and the muscles along her jaw stood out in stark relief as if her teeth were clenched.

'Nothing in particular. You simply seem a bit more tense than usual. I'm just making myself available.'

Skyler visibly relaxed at those words, confirming Bridget's suspicion that there really was something troubling her.

'Everything's OK, Professor. Promise.' She threw a shaky grin at Bridget and, with a quick hitch of her shoulder to adjust her backpack, left the classroom, leaving Bridget alone once again to ponder her stupidity at arranging a date with Connor.

No, not a date. An apology. One that happened to involve coffee and pastry. She was a grown woman. And she didn't pick up men, or chase men, or *anything* men any more. She'd had enough disastrous attempts to learn that it just wasn't worth it.

She'd given up men and had even gotten past her reservations enough to have a vibrator. Well, more like Claire had made sure she got past her inhibitions and got a vibrator.

She smiled at the thought of the unusual friendship she'd struck up with Claire. They'd met through the romance book club sponsored by her now husband's bookstore, Bibliophile. At the time, it had been Claire who'd been in need of a shoulder and some unfettered friendship. They'd become close, closer than Bridget had been with anyone in a very long time. She'd been happy to see Claire and Evan get past their respective baggage and find happiness with each other. A year later, they were solidly married and had a baby on the way.

Pain stole through Bridget at the thought of Claire's unborn child. Oh, she was happy for her best friend. Ecstatic. She knew she was going to be the best damn godmother ever put on the face of this planet, but how she wished a baby was in the cards for her.

But, just as the deep, intimate relationship Claire had was not destined for her, neither was motherhood. For just a second, tears threatened, but she refused to give into them. Bridget Ross didn't sit and wallow in self-pity. This was the hand she'd been dealt and she was going to make the best of it.

A glance at the delicate, pearl-encrusted watch that adorned her wrist told her it was time to get a move on if she was going to be on time for her meeting – not a date – with Connor.

Connor was early, but he didn't mind. He'd been to the coffee shop before, but never hung out there. He'd always grabbed a cup of the daily brew and been on his way. He wasn't a "hang out" kind of guy. He liked his solitude, and bustling coffee shops always made him feel conspicuous. But if this is where Bridget wanted to meet, then so be it. He was happy to put up with the crowd for a chance to be with her.

He passed the time by people-watching along the small main street that hosted River Rock's downtown. He wasn't being very successful at his usual game of creating instant back stories for the people he saw. His thoughts continued to stray back to Bridget.

She'd dominated his thoughts since their encounter on campus yesterday and not in an innocent way at all. He'd had some very, very vivid dreams of her, to the tune of waking up with a raging erection that he'd had to handle himself in the shower since she wasn't there to sink into. It hadn't been nearly as satisfying as he'd hoped, considering how his dick wanted to rise up every time he thought of her or how it just ignored him altogether at the sight of her. Even now he tingled when he spotted her coming towards him down the street. As they made eye contact, she smiled and raised a hand in greeting.

Those coppery waves hung down her back today and he bet they'd feel silky wrapped around his hand. She was dressed conservatively at first glance. Simply cut black trouser pants and an emerald green sleeveless top that clung to her body and showed off her toned arms. The clothes were elegant and smart, hugging her body in a way that drew your eye to every lush curve. She held herself with the grace of a dancer and moved with the same litheness.

He wanted her.

Wanted her on her knees in front of him, those lips

wrapped around him and her green eyes locked with his. He wanted her bent over with that round ass turning pink under his hand as he plunged into her. He bet her nipples would be lovely, clamped in metal, swollen and red.

His cock stirred, and once again he resorted to reciting the great masters to get it to settle down. Thankfully, he got himself under control. Not an easy thing where Bridget was concerned. He wanted her in a way that he hadn't wanted a woman in a very long time. His own proclivities made deep relationships few and far between. Few women could handle what Connor liked. After the last disaster, he'd stuck to the basics and kept his darker side hidden.

She made him want to swing the closet door open and shine the light on all the dark shadows inside. It wasn't just her beauty; it was something behind her eyes. It hinted of depths that she kept hidden and it made him want to explore and expose them. Made him want to watch her gasp as he showed her the limits of her body and her pleasure.

She really needed to get a hold on herself. This was not even a date and it was certainly not something to be losing control over. But her traitorous body wasn't listening to her at the moment. She didn't even really know how to react to the fact that her nipples had gone hard and she'd grown damp when all he'd done was look in her direction and smile that crooked grin he seemed to always wear. She'd felt like lightning had struck right through her pelvis. She tingled in a way that reminded her she had to be careful and she willed her body into submission.

She'd never experienced reactions like this. After That Day, she'd thought she'd never respond physically to a man again. Certainly, the few relationships she'd had over the years hadn't sparked this type of reaction in her. They'd been caring relationships that had ultimately ended disastrously for everyone because she'd tried to make lovers out of friends. Never once had she been honest with any of them about why she was so inhibited. The sex had been perfunctory and controlled. She'd made sure of it. She wouldn't allow them to touch her in any way that might cause her to lose the strict control she maintained.

In the end, they all had the same complaint and she really couldn't blame them. It probably wasn't very fun when a woman wouldn't allow you to do much more than stick it in and pump. They'd all called her frigid. Ice queen. Or, more colloquially, bitch.

She shook her head to clear it. No good came in dwelling on what couldn't be changed.

Shaking off the shame that wanted to surge from dredging up the past, Bridget took a deep breath, mentally pulled up her big girl panties, and smiled in greeting.

Chapter Four

'Hi there.' Bridget held out her hand to Connor and had to school her expression when her heart went berserk as his much larger hand engulfed hers. 'You been waitin' long?'

'Nope, just a few minutes. But I was people-watching, which is always fun.'

He bent to gather up his backpack and Bridget took the opportunity to look her fill. He was dressed casually in jeans and a T-shirt. The late spring weather was just hot enough that a jacket wasn't necessary in the midday sun. She'd left her own in the car. His sleekly muscled arms were set off nicely against the deep, midnight blue of his T-shirt. His dark brown hair was slightly wind-blown.

Her hand itched to touch him. Would his hair feel as soft as it looked? The trail of her thoughts caused her a moment's pause since she didn't usually spend time thinking about touching men, or wondering what they smell like or if his skin would be warm or cool to touch.

He caught her mid-stare when he straightened and the smile he sent her way was smug with a hint of heat. She flushed but refused to look away. Bridget was no coward ... well, at least with most things.

Lifting her chin, she met his gaze directly and saw his ice-grey eyes warm to charcoal as his grin widened.

With a nod in the direction of the door, he said, 'Shall we?'

'Thank you,' she replied, tearing her gaze away from his and entering the shop.

Familiar smells of coffee and pastry, along with the sounds of conversation, set her at ease. Her friend Mona's voice rang out as she made the rounds of the regulars, stopping by their tables and chatting with them about the weather, their families and such. With a deep breath, she put her awkwardness aside. This *wasn't* a date. It was an apology. Nothing more.

They took their place at the end of the line and she studied the menu. She'd basically memorised it, given how much time she spent there, but it gave her some time to compose herself. Tasha, one of Mona's baristas, was running the counter and the line was moving swiftly.

'What'll you have?' she asked Connor when they reached the register.

He was standing a bit too close due to the line behind them and she was doing her best to ignore the heat of his body. Her mind was on board with that game plan. Her body, however, was not listening. Her womb clenched and she felt an uncomfortable rush of moisture between her legs. This was *so* not happening.

'Hmmm.' He rubbed his chin and she followed the movement of his fingers, imagining it was her he was rubbing. Her nipples tightened and she ripped her gaze away, beginning to dig into her handbag for her wallet. 'I'll just have the daily brew, black.'

'That was an awful lot of thinking for "the daily brew, black".' She raised an eyebrow at him.

'*That* was an awful lot of letting you get an eyeful, gorgeous.'

Those grey eyes laughed down at her and she felt the heat suffuse her body.

Crap!

She was in trouble. Every moment he spent with her intrigued him more. From her resistance to the obvious attraction between them to the cool way her mind worked, he wanted to know more. They shared a lot of interests. Their passion for running and physical activity, they both were rabid readers, loved movies and good food. Though the latter was something he didn't get to enjoy very much. Meals for him were usually what he could microwave. It wasn't that he couldn't cook, he could hold his own. His grandmother had seen to that. His salary simply didn't support gourmet meals in trendy restaurants, but he knew all the best diners and hole-in-the-wall joints in town.

'I'm telling you, absinthe was a big part of the picture – pardon the pun – when it comes to the French impressionists,' she said as she took a sip of her macchiato.

She drank froufrou coffee, but she looked damn good doing it. Her full lips were tinted a shade of copper that almost matched her hair. Her green eyes were lively and sparkling under thick lashes. She wore make-up sparingly, which he was glad of, since she was beautiful in her own right. She didn't need help with her looks nor with that killer body. She was tiny, but she was perfectly formed. Large, full breasts, round hips, and a tiny waist. She was the image of fertility. And, as she licked a stray drop of coffee from her lip, the sight of her tongue sweeping along her lips had his cock jumping in his jeans and he was glad the table hid his reaction from her.

'I agree with you, but I still say, chemically enhanced or not, that period was my favourite in art.'

'Why?'

'Because impressionist art makes the viewer part of the piece. The details are fuzzy, and that leaves it to you, the viewer to fill in the gaps. It's like a piece of fiction that tells you the barest details about a character and you fill in the rest for yourself. In some ways that makes the story, or in the case of art, the painting, even more personal to you, because you're investing in the piece in your own imagination.'

That he was even having this conversation was unusual for him. He tended to be a loner. His life hadn't been the kind that lent itself to forming lasting friendships. His one friend, Marco, was back in his home state of Maryland. They kept in touch by email and phone, but Connor was basically alone here in Vermont. So, hanging out in coffee bars debating the merits of the French Impressionists over the surrealist art of which Bridget was a fan was not a part of his usual repertoire.

She put down her coffee mug and tilted her head in the most adorable way as she considered him. He laughed and ran a hand through his hair. He wasn't used to being under scrutiny. He preferred being the observer and, right now, he felt naked under her gaze. Like she was seeing something beyond the surface and he wasn't sure if it was meeting with her approval or not. Most surprisingly, he found that it mattered if she approved.

'You're very passionate about this.'

A smartass rejoinder of "You haven't seen what I'm passionate about" jumped to his lips, but he held back. This wasn't the time for corny pick-up lines. Frankly, she was too classy a woman for pick-up lines in general.

'I am.' He cupped his own mug and stared down into the black brew as if it would grant him the anchor he needed when he suddenly felt so off kilter under her regard. 'Art is the one area of my life that I'm completely at peace with. Watching an image come to life under my hands is like seeing a piece of my soul take form.' He avoided her eyes as he took a sip of the now cold coffee. He snorted. 'Corny, huh?'

'No.'

His eyes shot to hers. There was no humour in them; he saw interest and empathy, but not humour.

'That's beautiful, actually. The only time I'm ever completely at peace is when I'm running. I get lost in the music and the run and I stop worrying. So I think it's wonderful you have that calling and that passion.'

She'd leaned forward as she spoke, the vehemence in her voice adding an urgency that drew him like a magnet. When she placed her hand over his, a ribbon of heat trailed through his body. He didn't think she realised she'd touched him because she jerked her hand back like she'd burned herself as soon as she noticed.

Throughout their date, she'd kept herself under rigid control. His attempts at flirtation had met with a wall, but he sensed it was discomfort not disinterest. He'd seen her flush, seen her pulse jump, seen her nipples harden, but she stayed cool and remote. He wanted to get under her skin and find out what was making her pull back. She was a woman in her prime and the riddle she presented was one he wanted to solve.

'You in there?'

'Sorry, my mind wandered.'

His pulse leaped as she smiled and said, 'I asked if you've always been an artist.'

He looked away from her as his heart squeezed in his chest. This was not something he discussed. In general, it was something he tried to not even think about. It didn't matter that 15 years had passed. He felt the pain like it was yesterday.

Obviously, sensing his distress, she touched his wrist and said, 'Forget I asked. You don't have to answer that.'

It was her touch that loosened his lips. She knew she was holding his wrist; she squeezed it gently, connecting with him. In that moment, he knew he'd bare his soul if it would keep her touching him.

Covering her hand with his own, he told her his story.

'So, even though I have no formal training, I've always loved art. It's been with me since I was a child. I like to think that they'd be proud.' He was staring into his empty mug.

She didn't know what moved her more, his story or his touch. Being the only survivor of a car crash that killed his parents was bad enough, but having it happen as a child, on the night you received an award for winning an art contest, was just a cruel twist of fate. His grandparents sounded like lovely people, taking him in, giving him a home and a family, but their death when he was a teenager was just another kick in the nuts. But the thing that pulled at her heart the most was him being thrown into foster care. The family sounded as if they'd treated him more like an extra set of hands, someone to help around the house like a servant. He didn't seem bitter, but it said a lot that he'd left on his 18th birthday and hadn't spoken to them since.

'I bet they would. Have you ever shown your work?'

'No.'

'But you're a photographer? That must be pretty fulfilling.'

'Photography is its own pleasure, but it is nothing like painting.' He didn't look at her as he spoke. He seemed uncomfortable talking about this and she wondered how much it must hurt to have something you loved so deeply tied to such a tragic event.

Her hand was now clasped in his and she found she enjoyed holding his hand. There was a casual intimacy to it that she'd never experienced before, but that – after a few tense moments initially – she found she liked.

Just like she liked him.

She was uncomfortably aware of him, but she liked being with him and talking to him. She found she didn't want the date to end, but end it must. A quick glance at her watch informed her she had just half an hour to get back to campus and prepare for her next class.

'Do you have to?'

She grinned, knowing what he was asking. 'Yes, I do. I have a class to teach.'

'What if I said I wanted to see you again?'

She surprised herself by saying, 'I'd say the right offer might sway me.'

'How about a picnic? This weekend. I know a great spot. I've been wanting to get out there and snap some photos and paint. I'd love for you to be there. Hell, if you'd let me, I'd love to paint you.'

He took her hand again and rubbed the back of it with his thumb. The movement was both hypnotic and erotic and she felt it deep in her body.

Before she could chicken out, she agreed, giving him her number and entering his into her phone. Walking out together, she held out her hand for him to shake. Rather than shake it, he took it in his palm and kissed the back of her hand.

'Till Saturday. I'll pick you up at one. Text me your address.'

'No!' Her voice was sharper than she'd intended and his eyebrows shot up. 'Sorry.' She rushed to fill in the shocked silence. 'I don't allow men I've just met to come to my home. Even to pick me up. How about I meet you here and I'll follow you.'

'You're not even going to ride with me?'

'No. Not this time. I don't know you well enough.'

Curious grey eyes searched her face. She faced him resolutely despite the flush creeping along her skin and her desire to hide from the dawning knowledge in his eyes. Her own were burning, and the longer he studied her, the more scared she became that she'd burst into tears.

She opened her mouth to call the whole thing off only to be stopped short when he quietly said, 'OK. I'll meet you on Saturday, but not here. Let's meet at the library. It's closer to the end of town and we'll be headed out that way anyway.'

'No, here.'

Again, with the scrutiny.

'Here so that your friend sees us together and there's a trail back to me if anything happens to you?'

She almost squirmed at his insight, but she refused to back down and said only, 'Yup.'

'OK. I'll see you here on Saturday. One o'clock.'

Another quick kiss was dropped on the hand he'd never relinquished and then he tossed his backpack up on his shoulder, winked at her, and walked away.

She flopped on the bench outside the café as hot tears trickled down her cheeks. She really should just cancel. All the fun and camaraderie had been sucked out of their date at the reminder of her inability to simply be with a man in an unreserved fashion. He probably thought she was some kind of paranoid freak.

Sadly, he was right.

Chapter Five

Bridget stared at her iPhone in shocked dismay. He was refusing to let her cancel their date. She'd called him the night before and left him a voicemail when he hadn't picked up, saying that after some thought she'd decided to pass on the picnic. She'd had a moment of regret, but she'd let it go.

Fixing herself a light dinner of crab salad and toast, she snuggled on the couch with Daisy and completely missed every minute of her favourite programme as she'd rationalised her actions over and over. She'd spent the better part of her adult years alone and she was no lonelier than the next person. Right? She had a full and satisfying life with friends and activities. She loved her career. Loved her dog. Loved –

A quick glance at Daisy, who was eyeing her with one ear cocked and a look that said "Who are you trying to convince?", and she'd given up and gone to bed. At no time had she ever once considered that he'd refuse. *Could* a person refuse to let a date be cancelled?

Well, apparently he thought he could. She'd turned her mobile phone back on after class and seen the voicemail indicator. Checking it had turned up a few messages regarding work, then she'd heard Connor's voice. Unlike some people who sound differently over the phone, that deep, growly tone of his came through exactly the same as it did in person. It set her pulse racing exactly the same

way too. His message, however, had left her dumbfounded.

'Sorry, Bridget,' he'd said. She could almost hear him smirking. 'I know what you're trying to do and you're not getting away that easily. I will haunt that coffee shop until you show up. I remember where you jog too. So we can do this the easy way or the hard way. You can make me suffer the indignity of haunting you like a stalker or you can show up at one o'clock like we agreed and let me show you one of my favourite spots on the planet.'

There had been a long pause and she'd almost disconnected. When he'd resumed speaking, the smirk was gone and he sounded earnest instead.

'Bridget. I understand your caution. I respect it. I'll even give your friend, Mona, my social security number and driver's licence, just don't stand me up. Please.'

He'd disconnected at that point.

She had no idea how to react. He thought he understood, but he had no real idea. He thought it was the typical caution of a single woman with a new man. He had no idea what he was really getting into.

She smiled at his offer to give Mona his personal info. Little did he know that Mona was already his biggest fan. She'd joined them briefly during their coffee date and they'd had a discussion on the merits of Colombian coffee versus Robusta. Something

Bridget hadn't even realised existed. Coffee was just coffee to her, meant to be drunk with lots of cream and sugar.

Connor, however, took his very seriously. He gave Mona credit for not skimping. She only sold Arabica coffee, which they both agreed was more richly flavoured, and didn't sell out to simply give patrons a bigger caffeine shot. She thanked him and quite loudly informed Bridget he was a keeper before laughing at her friend's embarrassment and moving on to other customers and the duties of running her cafe.

'What are you thinking about, Ross? Me, I hope.' The low, elegant voice of her boss and Dean of the School of Sciences, Dale Whittier, scraped across her skin like nails. She instantly tensed as he continued, 'We do have your tenure review at the end of the semester, after all.'

Jerking her head around to face him, she controlled her instinctive shudder. From the moment he'd come onboard at Pinewood, he'd made subtle insinuations to her that skipped just to the edge of harassment but never quite crossed over. He'd hover a tad too close. Brush her in ways that if she addressed them would make her look over-reactive and paranoid.

To look at him, one would never suspect him of something as low as sexual harassment. He was handsome in a distinguished sort of way. Tall and lean, with salt and pepper hair. He dressed like the academic he was with lots of tweed and sweaters paired with cords, but he was never lacking in female company. Their department mixers often saw him with one beautiful female or another.

Rumours abounded of affairs with students as well as faculty members. He certainly wasn't so lacking in companionship as to make him desperate. Still, he rankled her. She was always left feeling as if she had a trail of slime over her body wherever his eyes had been. And they were everywhere, including her chest at this very moment. His scrutiny made her want to cover herself from his sight.

'Did you need to speak with me, Dean?'

She'd learned to be very careful in how she interacted with him. Remarks like "Did you need me?" or "Do you need to see me?" – simple things she would have said to anyone else – had been met one too many times with "Yes, very much so" and a lingering, implication-filled silence.

She'd learned to give him no openings.

His icy blue eyes met hers and she controlled the need to look away from him. You didn't show weakness to predators. Ever.

'Yes, Ross. I wanted to let you know I've called a staff meeting Monday morning at 8 a.m. I expect you there.'

'What's happened?' she asked, her curiosity getting the better of her.

'Just show up, Ross.' He raked her over one last time before turning and leaving her alone.

Feeling like she needed a shower, Bridget ran through all the reasons she stayed here at Pinewood when she felt like a mouse in the lion's den. Sure, she was only weeks away from gaining tenure, but was it really worth it when Dean Whittier was so repulsive despite the pretty package? Yes. She loved teaching chemistry, loved her students and the life she'd built, but how many more veiled suggestions could she really take?

'Professor Ross?' Her mental debate was thrust aside, however, at Skyler's timid greeting.

Lurching to her feet, she rushed to Skyler, practically pulling the girl into her office. She was dishevelled and looked stunned. Her blonde hair was falling out of the elastic band she'd used to pull it back and her brown eyes were almost vacant.

'Are you OK? Talk to me, sugar.'

Skyler fell into the visitor chair that Bridget guided her toward.

'Skyler?' Bridget knelt beside her and took her student's hand. It was ice cold.

For several moments, she just sat there staring over Bridget's shoulder and then it was like a veil fell down over her face. It hardened and her eyes snapped to Bridget's.

'Professor Ross, I need to know if I can take the mid-term on a different day. I'll take it early if necessary.'

'Why?' Bridget stood and moved to lean against her desk. Her Spidey senses were jangling a mile a minute and she knew in her gut there was more going on here, but it was up to Skyler to confide in her.

She looked directly into Bridget's eyes, replying, 'I have a medical appointment I can't change.'

'Skyler.' Bridget's tone was sharp. 'You can be honest with me.'

A wave of pain flowed across Skyler's face, distorting her features, but she schooled them quickly.

'I am, Professor.' Her words were tinted with a bitterness that made them crack.

At a loss, Bridget said, 'Bring me confirmation of the appointment and you can take the mid-term the day before.'

'That's fine.'

'Very well. I'll see you at 10 a.m. Don't be late.'

Skyler sat for several more moments before her eyes welled with tears. She nodded once and then left without another word.

Bridget watched her leave with a sinking feeling in her stomach.

Skyler Brooks couldn't believe she'd allowed this to happen. So much for a genius level IQ. She'd been as dumb as a fence-post and now she was stuck between the proverbial rock and hard place.

It *so* had not been worth it either. Sure, he'd been attractive and suave. He'd said all the right things and gotten into her head. But the sex had been mediocre at best. Could she be any more cliché?

A man with an ego that big had no room for anyone else in his bed. Initially, she'd been so flattered by his attention she'd practically thrown herself at him. Now, she couldn't get far enough away.

She had to stop and grab the wall, collecting herself as a wave of nausea so deep it almost knocked her to her knees ran through her. Leaning against the painted cinderblocks, she took several long, deep breaths. Saliva welled in her mouth and she tasted a bilious tang. She would be damned if she'd puke in the middle of the hallway. Swallowing frantically, she bolted for the nearest ladies' room.

Throwing open the door, she threw her backpack

to the ground and flung herself into one of the stalls just in time. Fortunately for her, there was nothing in her stomach to bring up, having already brought up the salad she'd had for lunch before Professor Ross's class. Her entire diaphragm clenched and held as she heaved and heaved, bringing up nothing but bile. By the time the spasms stopped, she was panting from the exertion. Hot tears sprang to her eyes as she hugged the cool porcelain, waiting to ensure no more would be coming up.

She'd confronted him, told him she was pregnant. She'd expected it would force him to finally let her go. He wasn't the sort who would want a child.

Nothing had prepared her for his response.

Rather than abandon her as she'd hoped, he'd picked up the phone and coolly arranged for her to have an abortion. There'd been no more emotion in his voice than if he'd been ordering lunch or hiring a rental car. When he'd hung up the phone, he looked at her with such disdain her skin had crawled.

'You *will* take care of this inconvenience. Do you understand?' His voice, once so provocative, was hard enough to cut glass.

She'd gaped at him, at a complete loss.

'Do you understand me, Skyler?'

'You can't force me to do this. What if I want to keep it?'

He'd stood then and moved over to where she sat slumped in the chair closest to the door. Leaning over her shoulder, he'd been close enough that she could smell the tang of coffee on his breath and the scent of his cologne. He'd grabbed her breast and squeezed hard, forcing her to arch. She cried out and he only squeezed harder.

'You don't get it yet, you little slut, do you?' He'd grabbed her ponytail and pulled her head back so that their eyes met. 'You're nothing but a piece of pussy to me, but I'll not have you ruining that pussy as long as I feel like using it. Nor will I have you trapping me with a brat. You *will* keep that appointment or I will make you wish you'd never been fucking born.'

Squatting in the stall of the ladies' room, Skyler began to laugh. Shows what he knew. She already wished she'd never been born.

Gathering herself, she stood on wobbly knees. She flushed and waited for a few more deep breaths before lurching to the sink. Her skin was flushed and her eyes were red-rimmed and swollen from crying. She looked like hell and felt worse.

After splashing cold water on her face, she ripped several paper towels out of the dispenser and blotted before balling them up and shoving them into the trash can. One more deep breath and she turned and shrieked.

'Professor Ross!' Her heart raced a mile a minute. She hadn't heard the professor come in. She'd probably been too busy crying.

Professor Ross was leaning against the door to the restroom. She held Skyler's backpack in her hand. A small frown crinkled her brow. Other than that she was the picture of calm. Skyler had always admired her. She was sexy and classy and funny and she always had a nice word for her students.

So many times she'd watched in awe as the professor had made complex chemical ideas sound fun and interesting. Skyler considered her a mentor and role model. Right now, though, she was the last person Skyler wanted to see.

'Skyler, sugar,' she drawled the way she did in that light Southern twang that made her sound like the classiest phone sex operator out there. 'You wanna tell me what's going on?'

'Professor. No disrespect –' Skyler held up a hand as if to ward the professor off '– but, no I don't.'

'Are you pregnant?'

Skyler didn't deny it, but she didn't feign outrage either. She was too damn tired.

'Professor, that's really none of your business.'

'Skyler, I just want to help. Please talk to me.'

More tears welled in Skyler's eyes and she could feel her lips wobble, but she wasn't going to cry now. Her tears wouldn't solve anything.

'You can't help me, Professor. No one can.'

Squaring her shoulders, Skyler walked to Professor Ross and held out her hand for her backpack. The professor hesitated; concern shone out of her green eyes, but she ultimately gave Skyler the pack and moved aside.

Skyler felt like a true shit for her attitude, but what could Professor Ross do for her? He was her boss, after all.

Bridget watched Skyler retreat down the hallway. She moved like she had the world on her shoulders. If the girl was pregnant, this wouldn't be the first time it had happened to one of her students. She only hoped whoever had knocked her up would step up and be responsible. She had a very bad feeling, however, that this "unchangeable appointment" was an abortion.

46

Not that Bridget was passing judgment. It was between each person's conscience and God whether they took that route or not, but the risks were so high if Skyler didn't take care of this the right way.

After all, she should know. Unconsciously, Bridget rested a hand on her lower abdomen. Yes, she should definitely know.

Chapter Six

She wasn't coming. Connor checked his watch for what had to be the fifth time. It was 1.15 p.m. and Bridget didn't strike him as someone who was anything other than punctual. She carried herself with the charm and class of a true Southern belle. With her sexy drawl and sensitivity, she was all gentility and refinement, but he sensed something in her. An eroticism that she seemed to keep under lock and key. That mystery, that enigmatic quality had kept her in the forefront of his thoughts ever since their coffee date. Hell, it had kept her the main star in all his fantasies as well.

He hadn't been so intrigued by a woman in a very long time. He liked that she was older too. Not that he was a baby, or she even that old. But he was 28 and, while she'd not admitted her actual age to him, he was guessing late 30s from some of the cultural references she'd dropped about growing up. The 80s was definitely her era.

Maybe it was growing up the way he had with his grandparents. They were in their late 70s when he'd gone to live with them. Maybe it was having to assume the role of caretaker when he was so young, but he'd never really fit with the girls in his age range. He was too serious. He wasn't enough fun.

Well, it was damned hard to be "fun" when you had to worry about Gran falling and breaking a hip while you were at school because she was too damn stubborn to ask for help. How could you not be "serious" when you had to rush home every day and make sure your grandfather was taking his medication as prescribed before going to your after-school job at the drugstore because from the age of 14 you'd been helping make ends meet.

His grandparents had loved him. So had his parents. Connor could honestly say he'd never been without love growing up. But when his grandpa had come down with lung cancer, the brunt of the responsibility had fallen to Connor. His grandmother simply hadn't been capable since senility had already burrowed in like a tick. Her moments of lucidity were too few and far between for her to be a reliable caretaker. So, Connor had done the only thing he could. He'd become a man at 14. He'd stepped in and filled the void as best he could.

Then, he'd buried them both when he was 16.

His chest clenched even now in grief. He'd loved them as much as they'd loved him. When his parents had died, they'd welcomed him with open arms. They'd kept his parents' memories alive and had encouraged him to be whatever he wanted to be. Some days, he wondered if they'd be disappointed with how he'd turned out.

He had a small sum of money put away; the little bit that was left after selling his grandparents' house. It was the only thing of value they had to leave him, but he hadn't wanted to go back there. After his two year stint in the foster system, he'd just wanted to get the hell away from Maryland. The neighbourhood the house was in had gone downhill and he'd had enough of depressing, rundown neighbourhoods. He'd sold everything, banked the money, and made his way north before finally settling in Vermont.

The decision to stay in River Rock had been a complete fluke. He'd landed in town because a photographer he admired was having a show and giving a lecture at the university and he'd wanted to sit in on it. It had been the height of spring when the foliage was new and the flowers were in bloom. After leaving the bus station, he'd walked for a bit to stretch his legs and had come to the main street. It had endeared him immediately to the town. Appearing straight out of a storybook with its simulated gas lamps, and flower boxes, it had vintage-style shops owned by real people not corporate giants. He'd been captivated.

The university had sealed the deal, though. When he'd walked the quad to get to the lecture, he'd barely been able to go two steps without finding something to capture his imagination. He almost missed the lecture because he'd been so caught up drawing and taking photos.

Simple as that, he'd decided to stay. Fortunately for him, the custodial position had been available and he'd found a place to live within a week of landing in town. That had been five years ago and he'd never regretted it.

Another glance at his watch said it was now 1.20. It was time to throw in the towel. If she thought he hadn't been serious about his threat to haunt all her known spots until he ran into her, she'd been mistaken. He was determined to get to know Ms Bridget Ross and he sensed she wanted to get to know him too. She was blocking him for some reason and he wanted to know why.

With a deep sigh, he reached for his pack to throw on his shoulder. He would go in and see if Mona had a use for any of the food he'd packed.

'That's a real deep frown you're sportin', sugar.' Bridget's caramel-coated voice broke into his thoughts. 'Aren't you happy to see me?'

His head snapped up and a grin broke out across his face.

'I didn't think you were coming,' he replied.

She looked amazing. He didn't know how she did it, but she made even the conservative button-down sleeveless shirt and cropped pants she wore look like the sexiest clothing on the planet. The deep green of the shirt set off her eyes and hair and the simple khaki capris hugged her full hips and displayed her delicate ankles in a way that made them erotic to him. Her sandals were strappy and showed off perfectly pedicured toes. She looked delicious.

'I almost didn't,' she replied seriously, then she put her hands on her hips and gave him an exasperated look before saying, 'but I couldn't take a chance you were serious about haunting my every move. So, I'm here. But listen up, buddy boy, you better not be some kind of crazed stalker. I'm trained in martial arts and I will kick your ass. Just because I'm small, doesn't mean I can't be effective.'

'Whoa, whoa.' Connor held up his hands and laughed. He honestly didn't care if she could kick his ass three ways to Sunday; he was just glad she was there. 'It's all good. I swear. I'm not a stalker. I just figured you need a little push to get you to go out with me.'

'OK, but let's get one thing straight. No means no with me, got it? I don't want to be manipulated again. Are we clear?' Her eyes spit emerald fire at him. She was honestly pissed.

Instantly, Connor was contrite. 'Bridget, look, I apologise.' He stepped forward and saw something he didn't like at all flicker in her gaze, 'Look, I was teasing. I'll admit I would have tried to run into you again, but only because I really want to get to know you and I'm incredibly attracted to you. But I swear I'm not a psychopath. If you really don't want to go out with me, then I promise I'll leave you alone. Just say the word.'

She considered him for long moment, eying him with scepticism. He could hear his heart in his ears as he waited. This woman got under his skin.

Finally, she sighed and said, 'OK. I'll go out with you, but you're definitely leaving your social security number and driver's licence info with Mona after that stunt.'

'Of course.' He smiled, feeling relief surge through his veins. 'I'm a man of my word.'

Picking up the basket he'd packed for them, Connor indicated for Bridget to lead the way inside the coffee shop.

She was an idiot.

She'd come to give him a piece of her mind, not to go on the picnic with him. But he'd been so sincere.

And he'd been willing to give her the out. Truthfully, she'd believed he was joking all along, but one couldn't be too sure. Her own past had taught her that trust was something earned, not given. He hadn't earned it yet regardless of how nice he seemed.

'I'm an idiot, aren't I?' she said to Mona as she sipped the apple cinnamon tea latte she'd ordered. Connor had excused himself to the restroom and she'd taken the opportunity to vent with her friend.

'For what?' Mona asked distractedly as she filled cream and sugar dispensers.

'For going out with this kid,' Bridget replied as she dropped some discarded sugar packets back into the bowl. 'I mean, he's got to be almost ten years younger than me. He practically extorts a date out of me, and then he goes all Boy Scout on me and I cave in.'

Mona stopped what she was doing and looked at Bridget full on. Her brown eyes seemed to pierce Bridget's green ones.

'Bridget, let's be real, OK. You're avoiding this "kid" – who looks like a full-grown man to me – because of your history and not for any other reason. I've seen him regularly since your date.' She smirked at Bridget's raised eyebrow over that remark and explained, 'We chat when he comes in.' She waved her hand dismissively and moved on. 'He seems like a good guy to me and, if my observation skills are worth anything, he's got a serious jones for you. So, he might be a bit over-eager, but you're only an idiot if you continue to lock yourself in a glasshouse.'

'What bee is up your petunia?' Bridget exclaimed, a little shocked at Mona's out-of-character tirade.

'Nothing,' she grumbled, though the way she was

53

working over the counter with the cleaning rag you'd have thought it owed her money. Stopping, she turned once again to Bridget. 'It's just that you've got a guy you're clearly attracted to actually attracted to you in return and you're going to pass up the opportunity to see where it goes. *That* is what makes you an idiot, not going on this date.'

Knowing where this was coming from with Mona, Bridget relaxed and took her friend in a hug. She whispered, 'I'm sorry, darlin'. Was he in here today again?'

Mona looked unhappy as she stepped back and nodded. 'Yes, I wish he'd go somewhere else.'

Bridget's reply was interrupted as Connor rejoined the women. Taking in the sad look on Mona's face, he said, 'Hey, is everything OK?'

Mona pulled a smile and said, 'Yeah, just dumb stuff. Nothing to worry about.'

'You want come with us?' he asked. 'I think Bridget might even appreciate the company.'

Bridget flushed at his words. She was clearly coming off a bit paranoid and he was being a very good sport.

Mona waved them off. 'Thanks, but no. I've got a lot of work to do today. It's bill paying day, yum!' She pulled a sarcastic face before squeezing Connor's arm and saying, 'Thanks, though.'

She gave Bridget another hug and whispered, 'See. Don't be stupid. Go out with him.'

To Connor she said, 'I know where you drink coffee, ya hear? Take care of my friend.'

He laughed and promised her he'd take very good care of her as he gave Bridget a long, considering look with those ash-grey eyes. Bridget felt her body go languid at the undercurrent of those words.

To her, he said, 'Ready?'

No, not in the least. Nevertheless, she nodded and led the way out of the shop.

This spot was lovely. Connor had brought them to an old manor house that was currently vacant. Seemingly abandoned, the grounds had gone wild with flowers, trees, and shrubbery. The house itself rose up like a faded treasure from the foliage surrounding it.

It was done in the Art Deco style from the turn of the 20th century and it also used a lot of the inherent topography in its design. The stream that ran through the grounds had been incorporated into the gardens. Stone outcroppings were used as visual elements in the back garden where they were currently resting on a blanket under a gorgeous willow tree eating the sumptuous spread Connor had brought.

It was light fare, perfect for the warm late spring weather. A simple pasta salad, French bread rolls, seasonal fruit, and light sparkling wine. She couldn't complain about his taste, that was for sure. She sipped her wine as she listened to Connor talk about his passion for this place in particular.

'I love how the colours are so wild and varied. It's almost like walking through a Van Gogh or a Seurat painting. Pointillism in the flesh, so to speak,' he said as he munched on a roll and washed it down with sips of wine. 'It's like being in a place out of time, you know?'

She chuckled. 'I bet you read fantasy books growing up too, didn't you?'

'Absolutely.' He grinned at her. 'I read the whole Prydain series; all the Deryni books too. I love anything to do with wizards and elves. I mean, the world can be so hard to live in. Why not lose yourself for a little bit in quests for good to vanquish evil? Or in worlds where things are simple and make sense?'

'I agree.' Bridget smiled. She'd done the same thing herself growing up. 'My favourite book of all time is *Dragondoom* by Dennis McKiernan. It has everything: a love story, dragons, dwarves, a strong female character, and a quest.'

'I haven't read that one, but I will now.'

His grey eyes bored into hers as he spoke and she had to catch her breath. He'd been catching her like that the whole time they'd been here. He hadn't made a single move on her, but every time he looked directly at her it was as if he was stroking her body, and not like sleazy Dean Whittier. This was like a touch of silk whispering over her skin and giving her goosebumps while making her want to luxuriate in it.

'You should. I recommend it.' Looking away from him, Bridget picked at the blanket while trying to collect herself. Not an easy task when her nipples were hard and her core wet just from him looking at her. Searching for a new topic since clearly books were too sexy – she almost snorted – she asked, 'Did your love of fantasy influence your artwork?'

'Yup. Definitely.' He dug into his backpack as he continued, 'My favourite artist is Maxfield Parrish. He creates these amazing idealised, almost fantastical landscapes that are so full of colour and feeling, but so many are really an homage to the love of his life.'

Bridget smiled. 'So, you're a romantic, are you?'

He blushed a little and shrugged. 'I don't know about that, but I think two people who love each other is a beautiful thing. I remember my parents were always touching and kissing. I knew they loved each other as much as they loved me. My grandparents were the same way.'

Her heart clenched a little, knowing he was alone in the world now. Her own parents were still together and, despite not being the most demonstrative people in the world, it had been a loving home. She'd never doubted her worth or her place in their world.

'I agree. Love is a beautiful thing when –' Her words trailed off at the sight of the device Connor had pulled out of his pack. 'What's that?'

'This –' he held up the small, electronic device, which was about the same size as an iPad but clearly not one '– is my CleanSlate.'

He fiddled with it a bit and then handed her the device. On the screen was a beautiful landscape with mountains rising up to break through clouds drenched in hues of silver, purple, and rose, with fantastical birds flying around the summit. The realism of those mountains juxtaposed against clouds and birds that would never exist on this planet created an image both surreal and startling in its beauty.

Connor was silent and still as she gazed upon the piece.

'Did you do this?' she asked, looking up at him.

He didn't answer. He just nodded.

'It's lovely. The clouds are gorgeous and those birds are so lifelike even though they clearly exist in some other dimension.'

The grin that broke out across his face was

infectious. She found herself grinning back at him.

'I love to mix realistic and fantasy elements in my art. The CleanSlate is awesome because I can work in any medium on it. It's designed to allow me to do oil, watercolour, pencil, whatever I want. I have unlimited canvases with it.'

'Do you do any actual painting?' Her curiosity was growing.

'Yeah, but art supplies can cost you an arm and a leg. Beside, this is so much easier to carry around and I like the digital medium best. It gives me a lot of flexibility and creative licence.'

The passion he had for his art was apparent in his face and voice.

'Do you have others I can see?' she asked, nodding down at the CleanSlate.

'Sure, just hit that button and it'll scroll through.' He pointed to a small button near her right thumb.

She did as instructed and was amazed at the breadth of his work. He had landscapes, still lifes, and portraits. Each was intricate and lovingly detailed. Many of the portraits featured people doing some mundane activity, but with some fantastical twist that changed everything. She scrolled through his work, her admiration growing for his talent with each one. The last picture, however, caused her to almost drop the device.

'Oh shit!' Connor snatched it from her hands and flushed a deep shade of red. 'I'm sorry, Bridget. I forgot that was on there.'

Her own face was red and she was sure she looked shocked. Raising her eyes to look at him, she said, 'Can I please have that back?' She held out her hand.

His flush deepened, but he handed it back to her. She gazed at the screen in frank appreciation mixed with wonder. He'd drawn *her*. The painting was exquisite. She reclined on a couch that could have graced the parlour of Queen Victoria, but it rested on a cloud. Deep blue sky was her backdrop. She was clothed in what could have been some sort of toga. Layers of silky ivory fabric draped her body. She was fully covered in the painting, but the hints of cleavage where one shoulder strap fell down, leaving an expanse of creamy skin exposed, and the slit up the leg showing an expanse of thigh created an eroticism that was unmistakable. Her face was in profile, but her expression was one of hunger and desire. She looked like a woman waiting for her lover.

'It's –' Her words failed her and she swallowed hard.

He took the CleanSlate from her, gently this time, turned it off, and put it back in his pack before turning to face her.

'Bridget. Look, I'm not going to apologise for drawing you. It's what I do. I draw, but I should have prepared you before you saw that.' He raked a hand through his close-cropped hair and looked at her like a man about to walk the plank. 'Say something, anything, please … put me out of my misery.'

'It's beautiful.' She wouldn't meet his eyes, still overwhelmed at the carnality so evident in his vision of her. 'I've never been painted before. I'm just surprised at how erotic it seemed.'

'Why are you surprised? You *are* erotic, Bridget.'

'Hardly!' she whipped her head up to look at him, speaking louder than she'd intended, but his statement had shocked her. The last adjective she'd ever apply to herself was erotic.

He must have seen the shock on her face, because he smiled at her. It was almost tender.

'I have no idea why you don't see yourself as sexy, but you are. From your brain all the way down to your perfectly-painted toes. Everything about you is erotic as hell. You get me hard in the same breath that you intrigue me with some thought you just spoke.'

She turned her eyes away and flushed even deeper at the mention of him getting hard over her. She was no prude, but she wasn't used to men so casually discussing sexual things with her.

He didn't say anything else, but he did shift until he was sitting more closely beside her. She could feel the heat from his skin through the jeans he wore. The cotton of his T-shirt did nothing to mask it either. A soft breeze washed over them and she could smell the light, woodsy scent of the soap he used. Her entire body was instantly attuned to his.

She saw his hand move but was still surprised when he gently tipped her chin up to look at him. She didn't know what she'd been expecting, but the depth of the desire she saw in his face was not it. She responded almost violently. Her nipples sprang to life, hardening and tingling against the simple cotton of her bra. She went liquid at her core and her heart rate kicked up a notch.

'I want to kiss you, Bridget. Hell, let's be real, I want to do a whole hell of a lot more than that, but I want to start with kissing you.'

His eyes had deepened to an almost gunmetal grey with lust. She was mesmerised by his obvious desire for her, by the touch of his fingers on her chin, by the scent of his body so close to hers. She didn't bother reaching for words, she just nodded.

He leaned in and brushed his lips across hers. They were warm, and soft. As he deepened the kiss, licking into her mouth, she could feel the slight rasp of stubble from where he'd shaved earlier that day. His tongue leisurely explored her mouth. No crevice went without tending, but he didn't force his attention on her.

His hand ran gently up her body, stopping briefly to cup her breast. He lingered but a moment, as if testing the weight and shape, before moving up her body. She luxuriated in the feel of him. The soft invasion of his tongue in her mouth was both foreign and familiar, throwing her even further off kilter.

She moaned and leaned into him, bringing one hand to rest on his thigh, which flexed under her fingers. Her blood was thrumming through her veins and she felt her body tuning to him. Any lingering embarrassment over the portrait was forgotten as she gave herself up to his kiss.

She could kiss him for ever.

Connor brought his hand to the side of her neck and exerted gentle pressure to lean her backwards. At the same time, he turned and subtly shifted his body to cover hers.

She didn't think. She simply reacted. Her knee connected with his balls and he exploded back from her, curling into the foetal position with a sharp cry.

'Connor!' She scrambled to her hands and knees as realisation sank in. 'Oh God! I'm sorry. I'm sorry!'

Hot tears began to run down her face and she

chanted her apology over and over. He wasn't looking at her. His eyes were clamped closed and he rocked back and forth, the pain evident on his face.

It was time to face facts. There was no use pretending any more. She should never have come.

Chapter Seven

He was going to puke. Lying there, huddled in a ball, Connor was going to lose his lunch. How in the hell did he go from kissing a beautiful, sexy woman to holding his nuts and praying for relief? The ache was spreading out from his groin and settling in his stomach, causing him the most excruciating pain mixed with the most severe nausea he'd ever experienced.

He panted through the pain.

She was saying something, but he couldn't make it out. He honestly didn't care at that particular moment. He would care. He would demand an explanation, but right then, he just wanted the contents of his stomach to stay where they were.

Long moments passed where the nausea slowly receded, the pain became a dull ache, and his hearing cleared so that he heard more than the rushing of his own blood.

'Stop,' he groaned, 's'OK.'

He was slurring his words. It wasn't OK, but she was crying and that was tearing his gut up again. He didn't want her to cry.

'Stop, please.' At least he sounded more human that time.

'Are you OK?' she asked. Her voice wobbled and she sniffled before reaching for a napkin and blowing her nose.

'No –' he wasn't going to lie '– but I will be.'

Slowly, painfully, he pushed himself up to a sitting position, moving to lean his back against the tree trunk to remove any pressure from his balls.

'I am so sorry, Connor.' She looked pitiful. Her green eyes were drenched and there were tear trails down her porcelain skin.

'What the hell happened?' It was still hard to speak normally considering his balls were throbbing, but he needed to know what just happened.

'It wasn't you. You didn't do anything wrong. It's just that –' She broke off and, looking away, began tearing apart the napkin she was holding. 'It's just that there are some things I just can't do.'

'You can't kiss me?'

'No, it's not that.' She balled up the wreckage of the napkin. 'It was the way you held my neck and tried to lay me down.'

'So you can't have your neck touched or lie down to kiss me?'

'Right, well, I just can't have you on top of me like that.'

'So I can touch your neck, but not lie on top of you?' His head was starting to hurt as much as his balls. She wasn't making sense.

'No, what I mean is –' Her brow creased and new tears threatened. 'It's just that –'

Connor was losing his patience. He liked her, but this was the second time she'd gone physical on him. He wasn't trying to get involved with a crazy person.

'OK.' He groaned a little as he sat forward and his bruised nuts rubbed against the cotton of his boxers. 'Tell you what. Let's call it a day. I don't know why you lose it with me the way you do, but clearly this was not meant to be.'

'I was raped, Connor.'

He'd begun to rise, only to fall back when her words registered.

As if in slow motion, he turned to face her. She wasn't looking at him. Her tension was obvious in the balled fists resting in her lap and the corded muscles standing out along her neck.

Hypocritically, his own tension drained. It was like having the answer to a riddle you didn't even know you had to solve. It explained why she'd reacted so violently to being startled. And it certainly explained her fighting him when he'd taken a posture that effectively trapped her.

Gently, he lifted one of her hands and smoothed out her fingers so he could take her hand in his.

'Can you tell me about it?' he asked. When she hesitated, he said, 'Please.'

She didn't know if she could tell him. She didn't want to see his face change. To see the pity and have him begin to treat her differently. They all treated her differently after they knew.

'Bridget, if you don't feel comfortable telling me right now, that's fine. I understand. We don't know each other very well yet.'

There he went again with his compassion and willingness to let her take the lead. Squeezing his hand, she shook her head, which he mistook as an indicator that she didn't want to talk and began to pull his hand away.

Squeezing it tighter, she took a deep breath and began, 'I was in college.' Letting go of his hand, she smoothed her capris and looked off into the distance as she continued. 'I was returning some notes to a friend when a guy I'd been kind of flirting with invited me into his dorm room. I went in and the rest, as they say, is history. He raped me.'

There was more to the story. Infinitely more. But she just couldn't go there. She'd never told anyone the full story. It was bad enough she had to live with it; she wasn't going to allow anyone else to judge her for it.

Bridget jumped when Connor took her hand and brought it to his mouth, kissing the back of her hand.

'I am so, so sorry that happened to you,' he murmured against her skin.

She squeezed his hand reassuringly. 'It was a long time ago.'

'What happened to him?'

A wave of bitterness flooded Bridget.

'Nothing. Absolutely nothing.' She pulled her hand from Connor's and began to pluck at the blanket again. 'I never told anyone.'

'Why not?'

'The same reason why so many women don't say anything. I was ashamed. And I wasn't willing to be vilified on the stand. So I just moved on.'

Shame coloured the bitterness, but she pushed it away. What was done was done.

Connor didn't try to take her hand back, but he did move closer and put a gentle arm around her shoulder.

She stiffened. Here it came. This was the part where he stopped looking at her like a woman and began to treat her like a victim.

The last thing she should be treated as was a victim, but how could she convey that to him without telling him everything? How could she get him to understand without losing his respect?

Every single time she'd told a man she dated about the rape it was like this. She went from being a sexy, desirable woman whom they could barely keep their hands off to a victim. Someone they treated like spun glass. Instead of embracing her and kissing the breath out of her, they kissed her like she'd shatter if they pressed too hard.

She may have been raped, but she was still a woman and she hated the way men treated her once they knew. She hated more, though, that there were some very real things she needed them to be aware of. It could be hard to have passionate, animal sex when she tensed every time they touched her neck, or they had to remember not to lie on top of her.

Each time, she eventually gave up. She'd lie quietly, doing her best to not react to anything they inadvertently did. They'd fuck her just as gently and she'd pretend to get off. Inevitably, the relationship would sour, distance would grow, and she'd amicably end their dalliance. All of her serious boyfriends were now happily married and she was going on her fifth year without any kind of meaningful relationship in her life besides her two best girlfriends.

She'd long ago given up on finding a man who could tread that fine line with her between truly uninhibited sex the way she fantasised and being mindful of her past. Connor brought out the deeply sexual woman in her. That much was obvious, but she highly doubted he'd be any different than the others now.

Back stiff as a rod, she waited for the inevitable.

Chapter Eight

Fury pumped through Connor's veins. His hands itched to tear apart the bastard who'd hurt her. He hated men who preyed on woman. There were so many chicks who would fuck you willingly that it was completely uncalled for to take it from anyone. The evidence of the scars left behind was obvious.

Bridget was a gorgeous, dynamic woman who now sat as if she were about to be executed. That she had a scar like this to deal with enraged him as much for the shame he saw in her eyes as for the psychological damage that slimy bastard had clearly left behind.

Right now, she sat stiff as a board beside him and he was at a complete loss. Should he hug her? Should he leave her be? Take her hand? Kiss her? Scream out his frustration.

'Bridget.' He left his arm where it was.

'Hmm?' She still plucked at the damn blanket.

'Look at me, will you?'

She looked at him and there was a wariness in her green eyes that hadn't been there before. Dropping his arm, he moved back to lean against the tree trunk and couldn't miss the disappointment and disgust that flashed across her face.

Frankly, it pissed him off. He may be sympathetic,

but he'd also been kneed in the nuts and was now floundering in completely untried territory.

'What was that look for?'

'What look?'

'The one you just gave me.' He was beginning to sound belligerent and he didn't like that. This woman got under his skin in the worst way.

'I don't know what you're talking about.' She was looking everywhere but at him.

'Yes, you do. You just looked at me like I was a bug and I want to know why. If we're going to move forward, then I need you to talk to me.'

'Move forward? What do you mean?' Her head jerked up and the look of surprise on her face was almost comical.

'What do you mean "what do I mean"?' He blew out a rough sigh and held up a hand when she started to speak. 'Let's back this up a second before we begin to sound any more like two-year-olds.' He smiled at her and she smiled back – a little too tentatively for his liking.

'OK, what I'm saying is that you just shared with me something that had to be horrific and terrifying for you and that, frankly, has obviously left some lasting damage behind.'

She drew breath to speak and he held up his hand to stop her.

'Let me finish,' he said. She relaxed back, cocking her head to one side and looking very kittenish in her anticipation of what he'd say next. 'I am unbelievably sorry that you experienced anything like that. But I am equally insulted that you would think that would change my feelings about you. I also don't like the look you just gave me, as if I'd confirmed some suspicion you had.'

She flushed, confirming his notion that she'd been thinking exactly that.

'If I'm being completely honest, I can barely comprehend what it must be like for you to have lived through that. I find myself flailing here because I want to handle this the right way, and frankly, beyond letting you know that I think you are remarkable and tough and strong. I really don't know what to say, yet those words feel hollow compared to the scars you must carry.'

He took her hand again. 'I want very much to get to know you, and what you've just shared with me doesn't change that one bit.'

She gave him a tremulous smile and squeezed his hand, but her words did nothing to set his mind at ease. 'Look. Don't feel obligated. It's OK. I don't want you to be burdened with this. One of us dealing with it is enough. And, to be honest, I can't deal with another man treating me like a victim.'

'Why would I treat you like a victim?' He refused to let go of her hand when she tugged on it while looking at him like he'd lost his mind.

'Duh, sugar –' damn, he loved that drawl '– I was raped.'

'That doesn't make you a victim.'

If her eyes got any bigger they'd pop out of her head. That lip, though, pulled between her teeth like it was, he just wanted to bite it.

'What does it make me then?'

'It makes you a woman who was victimised, but it doesn't make *you* a victim. That's a mindset. You don't strike me as a woman who makes excuses for herself and lets others walk all over her. Hell, my nuts can attest to that fact.'

She flushed deeper and looked away from him, but he tipped her face up to his. 'So now, if you please, why'd you give me that look?'

Green eyes bored into his own for several seconds. It was as if she was trying to read what he was thinking. She must have given up, though, because she took a deep breath and answered.

'I don't want the same thing to happen that always does.'

'Which is?' he prompted.

'Men always begin to treat me like I'm fragile. That if they touch me with any vigour, I'll freak out or break. But at the same time, I can get overwhelmed and shut down. I'm tired of the contradiction. I can't handle that any more. I'd rather just leave it be right now.'

She looked up at him with those emerald eyes awash with anger and pain and his heart squeezed. She didn't have to fear that from him. He was more worried that he wouldn't be able to restrain himself enough. He'd never been one for gentle, slow sex. He liked his sex rough, hard, and with a healthy dash of kinky.

'Bridget, after everything you said, I'm a hell of a lot more worried about pushing you too far too soon.' He took her hand and brought it to his lips, nipping lightly at her fingertips and enjoying the way her eyes watched what he did. 'I don't want to come off like an insensitive ass in light of everything you shared, but from the moment I got you out here by yourself, all

I've wanted to do was get inside you. I'm not those other guys. I only know that I want to get to know you better, but it would be a complete lie to say I didn't want to be intimate with you too.'

Wary eyes shot to his but she smiled as she said, 'I don't think that makes you insensitive. I want to get to know you too.' Her voice dropped to a near whisper as she said, 'Intimately and all.'

He could pretend he was a better guy than he was. He could be all chivalrous and restrain himself, but the truth was he wanted her and she needed to know that she was desirable no matter what had happened to her in the past. It tarnished nothing. If anything, her strength in coping only made her more desirable.

Leaning down, he tugged her closer and brushed her lips with his. They were soft and yielding. He licked the seam and groaned as she opened for him. He'd wanted this from the moment he saw her that day on the trail.

He explored her mouth, all the while fighting the urge to grab her tight and roll her under him. He wanted to feel her along him, feel those breasts smashed against his chest as he ground his cock into her. That would not be the way to proceed here. Not treating her like a victim didn't mean tap dancing on her scars.

Clamping down on his less productive urges, he pulled back and growled, 'In my lap, Bridget. Now.'

Her eyebrows shot up at the demand, but she put up no resistance as he gripped her hips and brought her astride him. He kneaded the soft flesh of her ass through the cotton of her capri pants and resumed kissing her.

She kissed him back with an abandon that made him ache to strip her naked and take her. Her hips were nicely padded. He'd never have to worry about getting poked by errant hipbones as he pounded into her. The thought of being inside her had his cock hardening and he groaned as she pressed her hips into his groin.

'That's right, Bridget,' he growled and pulled her hips in tighter. 'Rub against me. Let go.'

After a moment's hesitation, she complied and moaned; a deep, low sound that made it that much harder not to let loose and go wild on her. He enjoyed the flex of her buttocks under his hands and the way she deepened the kiss obviously as excited as he was.

Letting go of her, he began to undo the buttons of her top. Gradually unwrapping her to reveal ... the absolute ugliest bra on the face of the planet. It was a cage of cotton. Not at all the delicate lace creation he'd been hoping, no, *expecting*, to see on a woman as sexy as Bridget.

He eyed the contraption and was relieved to see a front clasp. At least he could open it and push it aside, rather than being forced to look at it any longer. With nimble fingers, he did just that, giving an appreciative groan as all that luscious skin spilled out.

Her breasts were full and large with rosy, pink nipples that jutted out from her body. He had to taste them. He sucked one into his mouth and ate up the sound of her moans. She was practically churning in his lap, rotating her hips and pressing hard against the length of his erection.

He licked and sucked, laved and nipped at her nipples, being sure to give each equal attention. She was rubbing herself hard against him and he was loath to do anything to break her rhythm, but he wanted to see her. Leaning back against the tree trunk, he ate up the sight of her.

Tendrils of her fiery hair were spilling out of her ponytail, framing her face. Her eyes were closed and her head back as she ground against him. Her breasts filled his hands as he massaged them, tweaking and rolling her nipples.

She moaned and made tiny mewling sounds and he encouraged her, whispering words of desire and lust even as he struggled to keep his own release at bay.

'Come for me, sweetness,' he demanded before sucking her nipple back into his mouth.

She wanted to come for him. Bad. Her body was running away from her. She was losing control. The sensations were coursing through her body. She was on fire from head to toe and the ache in her womb was painful.

She relished it. Revelled in the ache and burn.

She wanted to grab him and demand he fuck her. She wanted to pinch her nipples until they hurt. Wanted to feel the sting as he spanked her nipples until even the air made them scream.

She wanted him to throw her down, bind her, and have his way with her while she was completely helpless. She wanted more, harder, rougher. Now.

With an anguished cry, Bridget pulled away from Connor, breaking all contact.

'Bridget?' His confusion was apparent. 'What happened? Did I do something wrong?'

It would be so easy to lay this at his doorstep. To

act as if he'd done something wrong. But it would also be a lie and he didn't deserve that.

Shaking her head, she said, 'No, Connor. You didn't do anything wrong.'

Taking a deep breath, Bridget willed herself to relax. To retreat into that space she always found in these moments.

That didn't work.

She felt erratic. Brittle.

It was as if one touch from Connor would send her careening off an edge she'd spent the last 20 years ensuring she never even came close to.

He was dangerous to her carefully cultivated self-control.

'I don't know if I can do this, Connor.'

Connor was at a complete loss. One moment, she's languid and hot, practically purring like a kitten. The next, she's distant and unreachable.

She sat inches from him, but she might as well have been a mile away. She'd righted her clothes and now was once again looking anywhere but at him and trying, *again*, to run. He wasn't having it.

She was under his skin like a tick and, especially now that he had some inkling of her past, he was not interested in letting her get away. This wouldn't be the simplest relationship he'd ever embarked on, but Bridget Ross was the sexiest, smartest woman he'd ever met and he was willing to bet all she needed was patience and honesty. He could give her that. She had to let him, though.

'Why do you always try to run away from me?'

That clearly was not the response she'd been

expecting.

'What?'

'From the first, you literally ran away on the jogging trail. You tried to cancel this picnic and now you want to run some more.' He looked her dead in those bright green eyes he was coming to adore and said, 'I didn't peg you for a coward.'

She could have done a great beached fish imitation with the way her mouth opened and closed repeatedly.

'How dare you call me a coward!' she finally snapped.

'You're acting like one.' He refused to back down.

'Why? Because I think I might not want to date you?' She scowled hard. He liked her better like this.

'No, because you absolutely want to date me and you keep trying to make excuses to get out of it.'

'I don't need a reason to not date you.' She wouldn't look at him.

'Exactly, so if you really didn't want to, you wouldn't be making excuses. You'd just stop. But you are making excuses so I know you want to.'

She was incredulous. Literally staring at him with her mouth open. He wanted to laugh. He wasn't at all sure his logic made sense, but it was damn fun arguing with her. He liked her fiery. He didn't like her shut off.

Finally, she laughed and said, 'You make not one bit of sense, you know that, right?'

Taking her hand, he replied, 'What makes sense is you and me giving this a go. Let's take it slow, OK? I promise to not rush you and you promise to give me a fair shot. All right?'

For several long moments she stared at him. He

could see her weighing the options, looking for an out, but when she spoke she said what he wanted to hear. 'OK. We'll give it a shot.'

Grinning, Connor leaned over and planted a hard kiss on her lips.

'Good.' Reaching for his CleanSlate, Connor said, 'How about I draw you? Will you let me?'

She nodded, but then looked chagrined. 'Connor. You didn't –' She waved a hand in the direction of his groin. 'I could –'

'All I want is to draw you.'

It wasn't completely true. He'd gladly make love to her. But they weren't there yet. He was definitely going to have to take things slow with her. She needed to trust him. Especially if she was ever going to tell him the full story.

Chapter Nine

'How would you like me to pose?' Bridget eyed the tree trunk and wondered what she was getting herself into. The idea of sitting completely still for an extended length of time didn't appeal to her.

'I don't want you to pose *per se*. I'd like you to get comfortable and just relax. Leaning against the tree would be nice, but whatever will be comfortable for you so long as your face is fully exposed.'

Bridget took a deep breath to expel the last remnants of the emotional overload she'd just gone through and switched positions with Connor so that she now leaned against the willow tree.

Watching him work was almost surreal. Deft fingers wielded the stylus on his screen. His concentration seemed complete. He didn't speak, only looked intently at her from time to time. At first, it was quite embarrassing to sit quietly under his scrutiny. He seemed to be seeing beyond the surface; unravelling her layers and deconstructing her, only to reassemble the pieces in his mind's eye. She fancied that he was seeing not Bridget the woman, but lines, shapes, angles, and shadows as he set them indelibly in ink.

Slowly, she relaxed and let her mind wander.

Unsurprisingly, her thoughts turned to Skyler. The note she'd brought in confirming her appointment had been completely ambiguous. She was scheduled in at a private practice just outside of town. So, Bridget still had no idea what was really going on with her. She only knew that the once bright, vivid girl was withdrawn and seemed shattered.

Objectively, that had been happening slowly for a while now. The semester started with Skyler being gregarious and funny. Quick with a joke and always the first to support her fellow students. Bridget couldn't really pinpoint where it had all changed, but slowly Skyler had become more quiet, less involved. Bridget often caught her staring off into space with a worried frown.

As the girl's professor, there were boundaries she couldn't cross, but she always made herself available to her students. Skyler had been a regular at Bridget's study groups originally, but now her attendance was sporadic at best. She looked pale and the shadows both under and in her eyes grew more pronounced every day.

Bridget had a very bad feeling about whatever was going on with her. The scene in the bathroom could have been anything, really, but her intuition said that Skyler was pregnant. Not that you could tell at this point; she was as tall and lithe as ever, but where before she'd seemed to stand tall, now she appeared shrunken. It was as if her spirit was folding in on herself and that was something that Bridget couldn't stand to see.

She knew that feeling. She knew what it was to question your very being. To second-guess everything you ever did that led up to a pivotal moment in time. Every time she thought back to the weeks leading up to her rape, she wished she could go back in time and kick her own ass.

She'd tell that child, for child she truly was in so many ways, to listen when someone warned her in good faith. To realise that sex and dating was not something you played with. Just because someone presented a pretty picture that didn't mean there was anything beautiful underneath the surface.

'What's the scowl for?'

Connor's soft voice drew her out of her brooding thoughts.

'I'm thinking about a student of mine.' She took a deep breath and blew it out. 'She's a young girl. A freshman. I think she's in some kind of trouble, but I'm not sure and she's not talking.'

'You asked her or you just mean she hasn't come to you?'

'No, I asked her directly. I think she might be pregnant, but she looked me in my face and told me to mind my business.'

'At the risk of offending you, she's right. It really isn't your business.'

Bright anger rushed through Bridget, though she knew his words were true.

'My business or not, I care about this girl. She's one of my best students and I'm watching her fade away right in front of my eyes.'

Connor was quiet for a while, just watching her.

'What can you do for her?'

As quickly as it had come on, her anger deflated.

'Nothing. That's what makes this so bad. It isn't

my business. She's a legal adult and can do whatever she wants. I just hope she's talking with someone if she isn't talking with me. All I can do is what I'm already doing. I'm keeping my door open.'

Connor smiled at her and she felt her blood warm in response. He had a way with that smile. It was simultaneously tender and mischievous, as if he knew something he was just dying to tell her at the same time as he really wanted to laugh with her.

'What?' She laughed nervously, pushing phantom strands of hair back from her face.

'I was just thinking that I like you, Professor Ross. I think your students are very lucky to have you.'

She smiled back, inclining her head and saying in her best Scarlett O'Hara, 'Why thank you, suh.' She laughed. 'Are you done with that portrait yet? All this sitting here and holding still is quite exhausting.'

'Yes.' His eyes sparkled and he looked like the cat that ate the canary as he said, 'Close your eyes.'

With a giggle, she obliged. A few seconds passed and she felt the heat of Connor's body as he settled next to her. His thigh melded along hers and she felt his hands taking her own and placing his slate into them.

'OK, open your eyes.'

Looking at the slate, she was struck speechless. Whereas the first portrait had been done from memory and its details were a bit off, this one was startling in its realism while being entirely fantastical. The only real objects he'd painted were her and the willow tree. He'd captured her with a contemplative look on her face. She was mostly in profile, her eyes looking off into the distance. The tree framed her, its droopy branches serving as a living curtain and giving her the appearance of a nymph or some kind of wood elf.

He'd not depicted her actual clothes, but rather had drawn her in a 1920s-style dress with lots of layers and ruffles. The mint green of the fabric set off her red hair and her eyes were almost emerald in his drawing, furthering the otherworldly aspect of the painting.

The background was truly startling. An alien landscape rose up behind her. Purple mountains broke through pink clouds off in the distance. The carpet of grass surrounding her was cerulean while the sky was green, in opposition to reality. She seemed at once completely herself and totally foreign, and the effect was disconcerting. One thing that couldn't be denied, however, was that it was masterfully done.

'Connor.' She was awed by his skill. 'It's amazing. I can't believe you did this. And so beautifully.'

He flushed a little and shrugged. 'Thanks. It's easy when you have the perfect subject.'

She'd be fooling herself if she didn't admit that it was nice for him to be in the hot seat for once, but in truth, this was the work of a truly skilled artist.

'You should show your work. I mean, is taking photographs what you really want to do for a living?'

Connor's stomach clenched at her question. Of course he didn't want to be a photographer, he wasn't one. Not that he'd ever made a point of correcting her assumption. Hell, he had his camera with him right now.

The reality was that he was content with his life.

His job was less than illustrious; in fact, he'd had more than one woman dump him once she found out he was a janitor.

The last had stood up in the middle of the diner he'd taken her to and screeched about how she didn't date men who scrubbed toilets for a living and couldn't do better than the local greasy spoon for a date. She'd demanded he take her home and stormed out of the diner.

He still got furious over that particular humiliation. He'd never been back to that diner and it had been one of his favourite spots. Marge, the owner, had always had two eggs fried with bacon and toast waiting for him when he got off work. He liked to eat breakfast at night. Always had.

After Janelle had dressed him down like a dog in front of the regular crowd, he'd never been back. He really didn't want to ruin what was turning out to be a great day with a revelation that would spoil everything. No one wanted to date a janitor.

'No, I don't want to be a photographer.' He side-stepped the subject. 'If I had to choose between the two, I'd always choose drawing and painting over photography.' Warming to his subject – and infinitely relieved to slide away from dangerous territory – he said, 'Photography, for me, is a foundation. I take pictures to capture moments in time. I often come back and use those photos as puzzle pieces in my art. Maybe I want to paint a flower and I'll pull out some nature photos that I took. Or I might capture an image because it pulls me due to the emotion involved in that moment.

'I have a portfolio of photography. I particularly

love architectural photos. That's what drew me to this place. I was doing some research on the architecture of River Rock and the book mentioned this estate. It used to belong to the Rocco family that founded the town. Their line died out when the last son had only daughters who moved away in 1935. Since then the house has passed through a lot of owners and now sits vacant.'

Catching Bridget's eye, he said, 'She's a beauty, though, isn't she?'

'Yes, it's gorgeous.'

'But painting –' He continued his previous line of thought. 'Painting is like being the master of my own universe. I get to determine every single detail of the canvas.'

'That makes sense, but why digital art rather than traditional brush and canvas?'

'Because my universe doesn't always follow traditional rules. Take, for instance, the painting I just did of you. In my mind, you need to be surrounded by jewel colours. Not the baby blue sky or the mediocre green that is grass. Your hair –' he couldn't resist reaching out and stroking the silky locks '– is like restrained fire. Molten copper waiting to flow down your back. Your skin, so pale and cool, like the ice keeping the fire banked.'

She laughed at his whimsy but that was how he saw her. She was fire and heat trapped in a cool exterior. Heat that he wanted to explore a lot more of.

Eyeing the sky, Connor could see clouds rolling in. With a sigh, he stood and held out a hand to Bridget.

'Come on, sweetness.' He smiled at her obvious pleasure at the endearment. 'It's time for us to go.

There's a storm coming.'

She gripped his hand and helped gather up the remnants of their lunch. With everything back in the basket and his pack firmly on his back, they made their way back to their respective cars.

After throwing the basket and pack into the back of his late model Toyota Pathfinder, he walked over to her Mustang and was struck by the disparity in their lifestyles. Her car cost more than his annual salary. His car was only paid off because he'd gotten it for two grand from a guy who was desperate for cash and he'd dipped into his little life fund to do it. For the first time, Connor wondered if he was biting off more than he could chew.

Of course, he'd never been one to shy away from a taking a huge bite out of something he wanted.

'When can I see you again?'

She smiled at him and, with a flirty little grin, said, 'Well, I'm given to understand there are rules to this sort of thing. So I'm supposed to keep you dangling for at least three days, but then I have a study group, and then classes, and then so forth and so on, so why don't we just go with what works for you?'

Her grin was open and laughing he couldn't help but respond with one of his own.

'Fair enough.' He squinched up his face and pretended to think hard. 'Why don't you let me take you out to dinner tomorrow night?'

'Deal.' She stuck out a hand and they shook on it.

'Question. Do I get to pick you up or shall we meet at the restaurant?'

Pained embarrassment flashed across her face and he wanted to kick himself for what was an obvious question at this stage. One sexy encounter, which hadn't gone all that well, didn't amount to establishing trust.

'Never mind, Bridget.' He cut her off before she could speak, and smiled to take away any remaining embarrassment she might feel. 'I'll text you the name of the restaurant once I'm sure I can get reservations. OK?'

She smiled and nodded. Leaning in, he dropped a quick, sweet kiss on her lips, refraining from taking it any further. He'd pushed her enough for one day.

'Do you want to follow me back to town?'

She shook her head and started her car, 'No. I have to stop by my office for a little while. I'll just see you tomorrow.'

'Sounds like a plan.' He made to step back but she grabbed his arm.

'Thank you.' Her green eyes burned with an emotion he couldn't quite name. 'For everything.'

Rather than cheapen the sentiment with inadequate words, he simply nodded, kissed her one last time, and stepped back, watching her until she rounded the curve of the drive and disappeared from sight.

Bridget watched Connor fade from view in her mirror and contemplated the danger she was in. She hadn't lied. He hadn't done anything wrong. The problem was her. She'd come too close to losing herself with him.

Something about that man ate at her self-control. His mouth on her body had been delicious and she'd wanted so much more. Too much. The ache he'd created had burrowed in deep and low and she'd wanted him rougher, wilder. Dammit, she'd almost demanded he bite her.

She couldn't allow herself to go there.

Impotent fury washed through her and she pounded the steering wheel. This wasn't fair! She was a good woman. She went out of her way to be. She'd never asked for this!

Dammit! Why couldn't she make this go away?

As if in answer to her question, the memories rose up suffocating her. Quickly, she pulled to the side of the road and fought the smothering sensation overtaking her. *No. No. No!*

She wasn't having this. Not here. Not now.

Gripping the steering wheel as if her life depended on it, she concentrated on taking deep, full breaths until her head cleared and she could once again focus.

Forcing the memories away, she threw the car into gear, and drove on without another glance backward.

Chapter Ten

'Thanks for a great meeting, everyone!' Jean, the group moderator, grinned and enthusiastically clapped her hands. 'Evan has provided some refreshments for us all. Same time next week, and we'll be reading Sandra Brown's *Where There's Smoke*.'

Bridget, Claire, and Mona grabbed cookies and coffee then headed over to the leather club chairs surrounding a low wooden coffee table in the centre of the bookshop. The rest of the group mingled and browsed through the store, taking their treats with them and grabbing up their selections before heading out into late evening.

Evan, Claire's husband, always made sure to get this area back together for them since they had started making a habit of hanging out well after the book club ended. She and Claire had met and grown close through this club over the last year and they rarely missed a meeting. About six months before, Bridget had finally dragged Mona to one and she'd become a regular, joining both the club meeting and their little duet. The three of them had become extremely close over the months and she counted both of them as her two closest friends.

While she waited, Bridget contemplated the text she'd just received for what had to be the 50th time.

Unable to get reservations. My place for dinner. 8 p.m. The Lofts @ Warehouse 21. #2.

He wanted her to come to his house for dinner. She wasn't sure she was ready to go there with him. Public places were safe. Well, safer at any rate.

'OK, miss, spill,' Claire said as they settled into their chairs. Mona took the opposite seat, gazing at Bridget with clear concern.

Bridget nearly spit out the coffee she was sipping at the complete non sequitur. 'What are you talking about?'

Claire raised an eyebrow before continuing. 'Don't play innocent with me.' She set her water and cookies on the table. 'You've been fidgeting all night. If you'd shifted position one more time I was going to take you in the back and demand an explanation.' She leaned back and, crossing her legs, levelled her hazel eyes on Bridget. 'Jean could barely get your attention when she was asking your take on Christian Grey's character and you didn't join in unless specifically asked. Not. Like. You. M'dear.' Each word was punctuated with a shake of her finger.

Claire was right. She'd been unable to concentrate on the discussion of *50 Shades of Grey*. Her mind had continued to wander to Connor.

She was not herself when it came to him. Bridget was a very controlled woman. She knew who she was and she operated by a set of rules. One of which was that she did not go chasing down men. Another was that she did not have spontaneous sexual encounters with men she barely knew. She'd broken both of those rules with Connor.

When she'd seen him on campus she'd reacted just as strongly as she had on the jogging trail. She'd just taken off after him. She hadn't ever thought about what she was doing. All she knew was that she wanted to get to him. But when she was finally standing in front of him, she'd been at a complete loss. He'd been ogling her breasts, but worst of all she'd wanted him to.

She'd been tempted to preen and arch, run a finger down the collar of her blouse and watch his eyes follow it. She'd been breathless under his perusal, feeling heat every place his eyes touched. She didn't approve of her wanton reactions to him. It was out of character and, frankly, it bothered her deeply.

And him! He hadn't even tried to hide the fact that he was blatantly eyeing her. He'd admitted it and been completely unapologetic. He'd been laughing at her, playing on her sympathies for having caused him damage. Dang it, she wasn't even sure if she *had* caused him damage, but she'd felt compelled to invite him to coffee.

That had been a shock. She didn't invite strangers out. Period. The men she'd dated in her life had all been friends of friends, or people she got to know over time before they began dating. She'd never gone out with a stranger in her life, let alone been so bold as to ask a man out. This may be the 21st century, but Bridget had been raised with old world sensibilities. Her mother had drilled into her head that only loose women with no morals pursued a man.

For herself, Bridget felt it was perfectly OK for a woman to ask a man out and to take the lead if that's what she wanted to do. It just wasn't something she did. In fact, not since high school had she been so taken with a man that she felt the desire to pursue him.

And that picnic. Hell's bells! She still went hot at the memory of what they'd done. What she'd done, more specifically. She'd rutted over him like an animal in heat and had loved every single minute of it. Too dang much. She'd almost lost control.

That, more than anything, scared her. She was in completely unknown territory with this man. What if she was reading him wrong? What if he was just better at manipulating her? What if she was setting herself up because she wanted to see something there that wasn't there? What if –

Snap. Snap. 'Hello.' Claire was leaning forward, her frown even deeper. 'Bridget, you're worrying me. What's going on?'

'Nothing! Seriously.' Taking a steadying breath, Bridget said, 'He wants me to come over for dinner rather than going out. Says he can't get reservations.'

'The boy toy?' Claire asked.

Bridget nodded and flushed at the ribbing about his age and handed her iPhone to Claire, who read the text before handing it back to Bridget.

'You gonna go?' she asked around a bit of cookie.

'I don't know. I'm not sure I want to be alone with him in his apartment. I don't really know him that well.'

'Hon, don't you think you're being just a little bit paranoid?'

'How so?' Indignation welled in Bridget at Claire's suggestion. Claire knew her history.

'If Connor had wanted to hurt you, he had the perfect opportunity to do so when he took you to that manor house. You two were alone out there. It was miles out of town and no one would have been able to help you.'

'True,' Mona said. 'I had all the info on where to find him, but nothing on where you two were going.' Polishing off the last of her cookies, Mona took Bridget's hand. 'I think you need to be honest with yourself here, and stop using Connor as an excuse.'

Bridget pulled her hand away from Mona, snapping, 'What do you mean?'

'I mean,' she said, leaning back and levelling a calm, caramel gaze on Bridget. 'You're scared. But it's not because you think Connor will hurt you.'

'What is it then?' She sounded peevish even to her own ears, but didn't seem able to rein her irritation in.

'You like him. I think you like him in a way you haven't experienced since the attack and now you're running scared.'

'That's so easy for you to say, Mona!' Bridget's voice was rising, but all her fear and anxiety was bubbling up. 'You haven't had to deal with men treating you like you were diseased just because something happened to you that scarred you. Made it impossible to do certain things.'

Her hands shook as she squeezed the bridge of her nose to fight back the shards of pain spearing her brain. 'You don't know what it's like to be broken because every moment you're there trying to be intimate the shadow of your rapist is between you. Making you question your own judgment about not just men but yourself.'

She was shaking at the intensity of her frustration.

'How can I know for one single moment if my instincts about him are right, when I had no idea what Trent was? I let him into my life. I made it possible for him to rape me. And I never saw it coming. So, how can I trust Connor isn't the same?'

Claire and Mona both stared at Bridget as the silence stretched. She'd never said anything to them about her difficulties with men. She'd only told them about the rape at the most superficial levels and they'd drawn their own conclusions about her lack of a boyfriend.

Claire was the first to move, followed almost immediately by Mona. Both women enveloped her in a warm hug. Their combined scents of ginger and cocoa butter suffused Bridget even as the warmth of their embrace dispelled some of the chill that had settled in her at her outburst.

Mona pulled back and, grabbing a napkin, began wiping at the tears running down Bridget's face. She hadn't even been aware she was crying.

'Shhh.' Mona stroked Bridget's hair and Claire held her hand.

'Honey,' Claire said, 'you're taking on something that isn't yours to bear. You couldn't have known that Trent was going to do that to you.'

'It doesn't matter. I'd been warned. I didn't listen. I got raped.'

The urge to confide fully in her friends was strong, but she resisted. She wouldn't risk that.

'If you're not comfortable, then you don't have to go. It's really that simple. But I think you need to look deep inside and determine if you're just running scared.'

That was the second time someone had used that phrase with her and she didn't like it. Bridget didn't consider herself a coward. Avoiding a situation that put you in a dangerous position was not cowardice, it was prudence. Blaming someone else for your own weakness, though –

That thought stopped her up short. She was blaming Connor.

Dang it. She *was* running.

'I'm going. But I'm forwarding this text to both of you so you know where he lives.'

'No worries, babe.' Claire smiled around her last cookie.

'Fine by me,' Mona said.

After sending them the text, she answered Connor and told him she'd be there. Her heart raced, but she was determined to be fair. If she couldn't control herself she'd just stop seeing him.

Decision made, she gathered up her stuff. 'All right, you two. I'm heading home.'

She kissed both women on the cheek and headed out into the afternoon sun, praying she wasn't making a mistake.

*   *   *

Connor's loft was in the old industrial section of town that had been converted into an arty, urban residential area when the garment factories closed down. Now, where once looms and sewing machines had chugged away, up-and-coming professionals lived their lives and pursued the American dream.

Connor's loft was in the same building that Claire had lived in before she married Evan. In a larger town, that coincidence would have been startling. In River Rock, not so much. It was a small town and people tended to trip over one another all the time.

That she'd been in this building countless times was doing absolutely nothing to soothe her nerves. She jangled from head to toe. The implications of coming to Connor's home were not lost on her. She was walking into an unknown situation with a man she didn't know that well.

Her fingers began to tingle and a rushing began in her head. She rested a hand on the wall next to Connor's door and waited out the dizzy spell. The last time she'd walked into a relative stranger's place of residence she'd been raped. Normally, she spent long weeks, sometimes months before she allowed herself this level of isolation with a man.

Why she was here was beyond her at this moment. Her heart said he could be trusted. Her head told her to run the other way as fast as she could. Her head had led her to a lonely life with no one but her dog to keep her company at night and a soul that cried out for connection. Her heart wanted more.

Taking a deep breath, she squared her shoulders and knocked on the door.

And waited.

She knocked again.

And waited some more.

She knocked harder. He had until she counted to ten and then she was out of there.

One, two, three, four –

The door was yanked open to reveal a breathless Connor dressed only in a towel. His hair was wet and dripping. Trails of water ran down a broad chest that wasn't overly sculpted but was nicely muscled. He had a treasure trail of dark hair that her eye followed until it dipped down into the towel. His hips were lean and his legs were tight and hard.

She flushed as she realised she was staring and yanked her eyes upward. Smoky grey eyes twinkled with laughter.

'Come on in.' He stepped back and waved her in. 'I'm running a bit late, as you can tell.'

Bridget stepped into the loft and turned, not quite sure what to do. Lotus, Connor's Ridgeback, trotted over to her and began the traditional canine ritual of sniffing the new arrival. Seemingly satisfied, she bumped Bridget's hand in an "OK-you-can-pet-me-now" demand and Bridget smiled at the cinnamon-coloured dog before kneeling and scratching her ears. Daisy had that same imperious attitude and that bit of familiarity set her at ease.

'Listen, let me throw some clothes on. I think Lotus has you covered –' he ran a hand through his hair '– but go ahead and make yourself at home, OK?' He sauntered off toward his sleeping area and grabbed some clothes that were laid out on the bed before heading into the bathroom.

While he dressed, Bridget took the opportunity to look around. His loft was completely open with no walls. His kitchen was modest with brightly painted cabinets and stainless steel appliances. The smell of marinara and pasta wafted out, causing her stomach to rumble.

A wooden table was set with white stoneware and gleaming cutlery. Wineglasses twinkled in the light of a row of candles set down the centre of the table and a bottle of wine decanted on one side.

The living area was central to the loft, with a cream-coloured leather sofa flanked by two club chairs in some kind of grey fabric. The coffee and end tables were steel and glass and a bright red rug framed the area, setting it apart from the rest of the loft. Lotus' dog bed was sandwiched between the chair and the sofa and she'd gone and flopped down on it as Bridget made her perusal.

A king-sized bed sat off to the side under a bank of huge, frosted windows. The coverlet was black and the sheets were silver. Two metal and glass tables flanked it and a soft, silver rug lay on the floor. A stack of books sat on one table and she was very tempted to go see what titles he was reading.

He had good taste.

But what was truly stunning was the art covering his walls. They had to be his works. Each was vivid in colour. They lined his walls, creating a surrealistic effect. It was almost as if each painting was a window into a different dimension.

They were breathtaking.

Each was startling in its intensity of colour and realism even as it was fantastical. She couldn't imagine why he kept these pictures to himself. He had talent, and she was willing to bet that Mona would display his work.

Her thoughts were interrupted by Connor's return. He was clearly making himself known so as not to startle her. No one walked that loudly. The depth of his consideration tugged at her heart.

'Like what you see?'

'Definitely.' She turned to face him and smiled at

his obvious pleasure in her appreciation. He was simply dressed in a soft, cotton button-down in a pale shade of blue and jeans that looked just as touchable. Pulling herself out of her wayward thoughts, she said, 'You have so much talent, Connor. You really should be showing these.'

Something she couldn't read flashed across his face and he just shook his head. 'Nah, my work is strictly for me.'

'That's not true. What about your photography? You sell that, don't you?'

Connor tensed and wouldn't meet her eyes.

'Connor? What's wrong?'

He stared off toward the kitchen for several moments before muttering, 'Well, it would have been a good dinner.' He shrugged.

'Huh?' He wasn't making any sense.

'Bridget, I need to tell you something.'

Her chest clenched. Nothing good came of those words.

Connor's stomach flipped at the possibility of additional humiliation. Something told him, though, that lying to Bridget was a quick way to guarantee they had no future and he found himself very much wanting to see what the future held with her.

She appealed to him in a way no other woman had. He didn't question it, though he couldn't pinpoint the why of it. It was too early. He only knew she was much more than the voluptuous body and quick wit. She was a puzzle he wanted to piece together. Too bad he wasn't likely to get the opportunity now.

'Here, sit with me.' He poured two glasses of the

Chianti and offered her one. She accepted it, but didn't sip. 'The food will be ready in a few minutes.'

She was quiet, not saying anything, and Lotus took the opportunity to come over and nose Bridget's hand for a scratch. Almost absent-mindedly, Bridget complied. The contented sigh Lotus let out broke the tension as they both laughed at the dog's obvious pleasure.

'What did you want to tell me, Connor?' Her voice was soft. She didn't meet his eyes, but rather looked intently at where she massaged Lotus' ear.

Tension radiated from her body and, in a moment of insight, he realised she thought this was about her.

Resolve flowed through him; he couldn't allow her to think her revelation had changed anything. Better to just get this over with.

'I'm a janitor.'

Her eyes shot to his and confusion clouded their green depths.

'I'm not a professional photographer. I'm a janitor. At Pinewood, ironically.'

'Why did you lie to me?'

He shifted uncomfortably. The semantics of lies versus omission were not going to help here.

'I am a photographer, Bridget. It is a passion and something that I do. That I don't make my living at it really shouldn't matter.'

'I agree. You're the one who made it an issue by lying.' She clearly was not happy.

He flushed, but continued. 'I didn't correct your assumptions about me because I wanted the chance to get to know you. Up to now, I've found that "janitor" doesn't equate to boyfriend material. My last attempt netted me some really ugly public humiliation.'

He leaned forward, placing his elbows on his knees and decided to lay it all on the line. 'The long story short of it all, Bridget, is that I like you very much. I'm extremely attracted to you and I'd like to see where this leads. My experience has been that women don't find janitors appealing, so I found it convenient to leave your assumptions in place rather than expose myself.'

He paused not knowing if he should say more.

'I apologise, Bridget. If you want to cancel dinner, I understand.'

Bridget continued to scratch Lotus behind the ear saying nothing. He refused to break the silence, allowing her the power position in this. Finally, just as his resolve was wavering, she spoke.

'What's for dinner?'

Not at all what he'd expected, and the breath he hadn't realised he'd been holding whooshed out of him.

'Baked ziti, French rolls, and Caesar salad.'

'Bought or cooked by you?' She still wasn't looking at him, but he'd take it.

'Made by me. Gran would have a fit it I tried to pass off takeout on a date.'

'Gran was smart.'

The timer he'd set on the ziti dinged and he started to rise, but halted as Bridget held up a hand.

'I understand where you were coming from with this. It's not easy to be shamed.' Her voice was whisper soft as she spoke. 'But if you lie to me again, it's done. Got it?'

He was so relieved he wanted to laugh, but he had

the feeling she'd think he wasn't taking her seriously so he settled for a grin and a very emphatic, 'I got it.'

'Good, can we eat? I've been so nervous over coming here, I haven't eaten since breakfast.'

That took the wind out of his sails and he took her hand as she stood, 'Bridget, obviously I can't promise to never hurt you. Things happen beyond our control, but I can promise that I will do my best to always be open and understanding.'

She stared intently into his eyes, her own suspiciously damp.

'OK.' With an adorable sniffle, she added, 'You gonna feed me or what, sugar?'

Chapter Eleven

Dinner was phenomenal. The Caesar salad was crisp and tangy, the ziti was baked to perfection, the rolls were crusty and warm, and the wine was bold and fruity. The melody of flavours was comforting, especially given the way her senses were in a riot.

Dessert was warming in the oven. Connor had admitted he didn't know how to bake, so the apple pie was from the local bakery. She didn't mind. So far, the man had far exceeded all her expectations.

The conversation had flowed easily. He had filled her in on the details of how he'd come to be in River Rock and gotten the job at Pinewood and she'd talked about deciding to become a teacher. She didn't tell him about her current troubles with the dean, though. Something she couldn't pinpoint held her tongue.

She was still finding her way with Connor and she was going to take it slow. The revelation about his job had thrown her, but mostly because it was a colossally stupid thing to lie about. But when he'd told her about the reaction of his past girlfriend she'd been unable to hold it against him.

She, of all people, understood shame.

'Are you happy, Connor?' The question came out of nowhere, surprising even her.

'What do you mean?' His brow furrowed.

'I mean are you happy with where you are in life? You have a tremendous talent –' she waved her hand in the direction of his artwork '– yet you aren't doing anything with it.'

'I don't know if I'm happy –' his brow furrowed even deeper '– but I'm not unhappy. My art …' He ran his hand through his hair. Something, she'd begun to realise, he did when he was uncomfortable. 'It's personal. It's not for the world to see. It's for me.'

'Yes, but why?'

He looked nonplussed, 'What do you mean?'

'I mean, why keep it to yourself? It's gorgeous and I think people would respond to it.'

'Thanks, but I have no interest in trying to make a career in the art world. It's full of critics who like nothing better than to tear you down so they can feel good at your expense.'

He sipped his wine and looked off in the distance as he spoke. She got the sense that there was more, but she certainly wasn't going to push him to reveal things. He might turn the tables on her and she had too many things she didn't want to share yet.

The aroma of warm apples filled the apartment and Connor rose to serve dessert. He surprised her by coming back with only one dish.

'Nothing for me?' she quipped. 'Did I anger you?' She was only half joking.

'Nope, you didn't make me mad. And –' he sat next to her on the sofa '– this is for us both.'

'Really?'

His nearness was doing funny things to her pulse. She could smell the scent of his soap as he took the wineglass from her hands and set it on the coffee table. He took up a bite of pie and the ice cream that accompanied it and fed it to her.

The taste of warm apples and silky ice cream exploded across her tongue. He took a bite of his own, and then fed her another bite. It was incredibly sensuous to be fed by him. It was a first, and she had to admit she liked it.

'Why are you doing this?' she asked.

'You shouldn't question a man when he's trying to be romantic.'

'Is that what this is?'

'Absolutely,' he said and smiled. 'Don't you think it's romantic?'

'To be fed by you?' She raised an eyebrow.

'To have me in your mouth the same way you're in mine.'

Warm grey eyes locked with hers and she realised what he meant. A burst of heat shot through her body and she surprised herself by saying, 'Do you want to be in my mouth, Connor?'

Who in the hell had snuck into her body and put this sexy stranger in her place? Bridget almost apologised until she realised that Connor's eyes had darkened with desire and his jeans were now very tight across the groin.

A sense of feminine power ran through her at her effect on him. It was a heady feeling and she wanted more. Taking the bowl from him, she set it on the table. And ... was at a complete loss as to how to proceed. She'd never been in this position before.

The man always took the lead in every relationship she'd ever had. She'd just suffered through it. She had no idea how to be the sexy siren that left a man begging for more.

The bubble of eroticism she'd been in burst as fast as it had come on, leaving her feeling embarrassed. Clenching her hands in her lap, she couldn't meet his eyes.

'Connor, I'm sorry. I should probably go.' She lurched up from the couch and scooped her purse off the table. Before she could get too far, Connor grabbed her hand, stopping her retreat.

'Bridget, what is it?'

She turned to face him and felt instant remorse for the obvious worry on his face.

'I just feel so stupid, Connor.' The honesty of her reply surprised even her. 'I'm not this sexy, vampy type and I don't know how to seduce anyone.'

His eyes widened in surprise before a slow grin spread across his face.

'Is that what you want, Bridget? To seduce me?' His voice had gone low and husky, doing funny things to her insides.

'I don't really know, Connor.' She took a deep breath, feeling the need to fortify herself for her next words. 'I only know that I respond physically to you in a way that frightens me. It makes me feel out of control and I don't like that.'

A small frown marred his face and he seemed to be in deep thought. Without saying anything, he pulled her back toward the couch and sat down.

'Sit, Bridget.' He patted the sofa next to him. 'Let's talk.'

Confusion bubbled inside her. She didn't know where this was going. Tension surged through her.

106

Why, she couldn't have said, but she felt like she was getting ready to run the gauntlet rather than have a conversation. He looked so sincere, though, and she didn't want to hurt his feelings, so she sat.

'Let's talk about the control thing. What are you trying to control?'

'What do you mean? I would think it would be obvious.'

'No, I don't.' His lips quirked. 'You could want to control me or you could be more concerned about controlling yourself. The meaning alters distinctly depending on your answer.'

Bridget squirmed uncomfortably; this was getting into territory she really didn't want to cover. She liked Connor a lot, wanted him in a way she wasn't at all used to, but she wasn't ready to share her deepest shame with him.

'Bridget, I need you to be honest with me if we're going to date each other. How can we move forward if you're not willing to talk with me about things that affect us both?' He picked up her hand again and began to stroke her palm with his thumb. 'I'll go first, OK? I admit that I've never been in a real relationship before. Life was always getting in the way and then I didn't want to be tied down when I finally got out on my own. But I've never been one to play games. I want you, Bridget, bad. I'm worried I won't be able to be gentle with you. I like sex dirty and rough. I've never been a gentle man in bed and I think you need that.'

Bridget's body was definitely on board with what he had to say. Her nipples were tight and her sex was slick with need. But his words frightened her. She'd been walking a tightrope with him already. If she wasn't careful, she'd fall off, and with Connor, she didn't see a net to save her.

'It's me I'm worried about controlling,' she cut in as he was about to continue. 'I –' She couldn't get the words out. Frustrated tears flooded her eyes and she gripped his hand hard. 'I want you and I don't want you to be gentle with me. I want to feel like a normal woman.'

It wasn't nearly everything but it was true.

'So, answer my first question, do you want to seduce me?'

Ash-grey eyes bored into hers and she saw the desire there. He was a sure thing. It made her smile.

'Yes.'

'Good, I like to be seduced as much as the next guy.' He kissed her hand again. 'I don't feel like you've told me everything, though. What about yourself are you so worried about controlling?'

In a moment of clarity, Bridget realised it was now or never. If she didn't tell Connor now, before things went any further, she never would. But telling him might end things for ever. Her head pounded at the risk she was taking. She'd spent years burying the past and building the walls necessary to move forward, but she felt in her heart this man would never be content to be kept at a distance.

'Connor …' She paused, trying to find the courage inside herself to get the words out. Realising it wasn't going to get any easier, she just started speaking. 'I'm not a very experienced woman, despite my age. I've had very few lovers and I already told you the problems with those relationships.'

108

'Because of the rape?' he interjected.

'Yes and no. Obviously, the rape has made me very cautious in dealing with men. In fact, my being here at your place is wildly out of character for me, but there's more. You see, I was a virgin until I was 18. I had very strong beliefs about sex. Not so much about waiting until I was married, but definitely waiting for the right guy, because I felt like sex shouldn't be limited. That inhibitions were a waste of time.

'My first real boyfriend was older than me. He was 25 to my 18. Seven years would be nothing now, but then it was a world of difference. We had a really good time together and I gave him my virginity. In return, he showed me a lot about sex. We did things together. Things I should never have done. Things I was punished for in the worst way when I was raped.'

'Hold on, Bridget.' Confusion clouded his face. 'Do you expect me to believe a woman as smart as you are actually thinks that her rape was punishment for enjoying sex?'

'It wasn't so much enjoying sex, but more for enjoying the depraved things he had exposed me to.'

'Depraved in what way?' Confusion was giving way to tension as his voice hardened.

Bridget felt nausea well inside her as she prepared to expose her darkest secrets to him. 'I let him tie me up. I let him spank me. He even spanked me here –' She pressed her hand to her breasts and shuddered as the memory of exactly how much she'd enjoyed that particular act came back to her. Her traitorous body still responded to the memory and shame flooded her.

'And you think this is depraved why?'

'Because it's not normal.'

'Says who?' Irritation was evident in his voice, but she knew she was right.

'Connor, any doubts I had were taken away when I was raped.'

Taking a deep breath, Connor said, 'I'm going to table my argument for the time being. Will you tell me about the rape? I need to understand why you think you were punished for enjoying a little kinky sex.'

She didn't want to, but she felt she owed him this much. At least then he'd understand where she was coming from.

Closing her eyes, she fought to calm the roiling in her stomach as, for the first time in almost 20 years, she let the memories roll over her without a fight.

Clenching her hands in her lap, she exposed her deepest shame to him.

It had started simply enough. She couldn't remember why now, but she'd been running late to drop off her friend Joe's history notes. He'd needed them for his class the next morning and she'd promised to have them back to him before he left for practice that night. She'd called but had gotten his answering machine and this was in the days before mobile phones.

Bridget had arrived at his dorm and called him again from the lobby with no success. After hesitating for several minutes, she decided to slip them under his door. Pritchard Hall was an all-male dorm and Joe had warned her to not come through it unescorted, but he'd never given her a very good reason. Other girls seemed to have no problem getting in and out and she felt bad about having been late when he needed those notes.

The elevator dinged and opened to reveal a young, unescorted female student. Taking this as a sign, Bridget got on the elevator and punched in the fifth floor. Joe's door was at the end of the hall and she quickly went down and slid the notes under his door. Mission accomplished, she turned to return back the way she'd come.

About midway down the hall a door opened and she almost bumped into Trent Maxwell, resident rich kid, star golfer, and serious hottie. At six feet, he was filled out nicely, with black hair and green eyes that made him look like Brian Bloom, whom she'd had a crush on since he'd starred in *21 Jump Street.*

'Hey, Ginger. How's it hanging?'

He'd smiled at her, flashing his dimple and she'd quivered a bit inside. She wasn't a virgin, but she'd not been "active" either. She'd slept with exactly one man and that had been after several months of dating.

Trent had been pursuing her recently. They'd been at several campus mixers together and she and her friends had gone to the Sigma Chi party where he'd recently pledged. She'd been friendly and danced with him several times. Even let him steal a chaste kiss, but she'd declined his offers of dates. She was very focused on her chemistry studies and knew she didn't have time for a serious boyfriend, or even a non-serious boyfriend. Her chances of landing the internship she hoped for with Professor Yanchenko were middling at best if she didn't ace her classes and she wanted the internship. It was her hope to end up a permanent member of the Professor's research team and do her grad work under Yanchenko as well.

Trent had made it clear he was interested in her. He'd been fairly handsy when they were dancing, but Bridget was used to that. At five feet with 36D breasts and large hips, she was quite voluptuous and men tended to treat her like their personal sex kitten. It was frustrating, but she'd found charm and niceness kept the vast majority of them at bay.

Trent was a bit harder to manage, but that was more because she was extremely attracted to him. She probably shouldn't have let him kiss her, but she'd been tipsy, and there hadn't even been any tongue involved. Just a sweet kiss that she'd romanticised about for hours afterwards even as she'd declined his date offer.

Now, though, he was lounging in his doorway, giving her that sexy, green-eyed gaze that always made her a bit breathless. She smiled at the nickname. He wasn't the first to call her Ginger, but she certainly liked the sound of it better coming from him than she had her older brother.

'Hey yourself.' She smiled at him and noticed how his eyes took a long, leisurely stroll down her body.

She flushed a bit and hated her pale skin for the fact that it showed. She was in a simple, pale gold sun dress with spaghetti straps which meant she had enough skin showing that he would see her reaction to his obvious perusal.

For his part, he looked as fine as always in jeans and sleek black T-shirt. This was in the days before baggy jeans and his fit him nicely. His T-shirt was tucked in, showing off both his nice behind and the expensive leather belt he was wearing.

'I'm glad to see you,' he said. 'You busy? I've

been hoping to run into you.'

'Really?' She gave him a flirtatious smile. 'Why's that?'

'I've been hoping to change your mind about going out with me? *Alien*^{3} came out and I'd like to take you with me to see it.'

She chuckled. 'You might get me to go to the movies with you, I love the movies, but it'd be dutch and not for some horror alien movie. I told you, I'm not interested in dating anyone right now.'

He grinned and she felt a shiver deep in her belly.

'I know. Tell you what, why don't you come in and hang out with me for a while? We can look at what's playing and I can work on changing your mind.'

She glanced at her watch. It was only five o'clock and her study group wasn't scheduled to meet until six.

She shrugged. 'OK, but I have to leave pretty soon. I have a study group.'

'No problem.' He stepped aside and waved her into his room.

It was pretty standard for a college dorm room except there was a computer, which was still rare in that day and time, and he had a single – no roommate. That was even rarer, since most kids couldn't afford the rates that went with singles.

There were no chairs in the room other than his desk chair, which was piled high with clothes and books, so she sat on the bed. He grabbed the local paper off his desk and came and sat next to her. Rifling through it, he found the movie listings and handed them to her.

'If you aren't interest in a sci-fi, there's that Tom

Cruise movie, *A Few Good Men*.'

'I could do that.' She grinned. 'I like a good legal drama.'

'Well, that's good. I'm going to be a lawyer, you know.'

'Yes, you told me.'

He moved and set the newspaper back on the desk before walking over to a little mini-fridge in the corner.

'Want a Coke or something to drink?'

As hot as she was feeling being in such close proximity to him, a soda sounded like a good idea. Maybe it would cool her down.

'Sure, Coke is fine.'

He pulled a couple of plastic cups from a cupboard and added ice and soda to both before handing one to her. She drank deeply, enjoying the bite of the carbonation as it burned down her throat. He smiled at her, a grin of mischief and intent that had her insides warming. He made her feel really sexy and when he sat down again he was touching her.

She thought to put a bit of space between them, but there was really nowhere to go. The pillows on his bed were on her other side and she didn't want to seem rude.

She could smell his cologne, a light, citrus scent, and her skin pebbled a bit in awareness of him. It's really too bad I'm not in the market, she thought, he's so fine.

'Did you hear me?' He was looking at her with those ice green eyes and she was embarrassed that he'd caught her wool-gathering, but it was becoming increasingly difficult to concentrate.

'No, sorry.' She smiled. 'My mind wandered.'

'I asked why you won't go out with me.' He leaned closer and put his hand on her knee, caressing her leg with light strokes.

She pulled her legs a little closer together, but that did nothing to deter him.

'I told you before. I don't have time for dating. My classes are really tough. This is my senior year and I have a lot riding on my grades.'

'So you said, but I still think you could go out on a date or two with me. It doesn't have to be anything serious.' He began to lean into her. 'You know you like me. Especially the way you danced with me and let me kiss you.'

She leaned back, trying to put some more distance between them, but it was like her body didn't want to cooperate. She was beginning to feel lethargic and exhausted. A sense of danger began to squeeze her chest.

When she spoke, her words sounded distant and slurred. It was as if she were no longer fully present inside her body. 'I was tipsy that night or I would never have kissed you. I'm no tease.'

'Yeah, right,' he said, right before he gripped her neck and pushed her down roughly and began kissing her.

His lips ground against hers in painful demand for entry. She opened her mouth to protest and he took that opportunity to shove his tongue in deep.

She tried to fight him off, but her body wasn't listening to her. The room spun and she was lost to blackness.

She surfaced briefly to Trent kneeling between her

legs; he'd opened the bodice of her dress and was playing with her breasts. Tweaking and pulling at her nipples before sucking them into his mouth. Her body responded to the stimulation, filling her with a horrified pleasure. Some distant speck in her mind told her she should be fighting. She willed her arms, her legs, anything to move but nothing connected. Even as she railed internally, the blackness sucked her back in.

When she surfaced again, her hands were tied over her head and something was inside her mouth. She was naked. Trent was standing over her a belt in his hands. He lashed out with the belt, striking the sensitive skin of her breasts and inner thighs with each lash. The initial blows hurt and she wanted to scream through the gag, but they faded into a sting that flooded her body and reminded her of when Doug, her first boyfriend, had tied her up and spanked her. She felt her body responding to this abuse and cried out against this betrayal. Surely she couldn't enjoy this assault? That thought sent her again into darkness.

The next and final time she came to awareness, Trent was inside her. He was grunting and pumping himself roughly inside her while slapping at her breasts. She felt the sensations take her even as her shocked brain screamed out against this final betrayal. Her body clenched and tightened convulsively and Trent became savage in his invasion before finally moaning as he spilled his seed into her core and collapsed on top of her.

She went completely numb. This time, when the blackness took her, she hoped she didn't wake up.

116

Hot tears streamed down her face, soaking into Connor's shirt. Somewhere during her tale, he'd pulled her into his arms. She'd been so caught up in the memories, she hadn't even noticed. His hand was warm where he stroked her back and he was murmuring nonsense words of comfort to her. Embarrassed by her loss of control, Bridget pushed up and swiped at her face.

'I need to clean up.' Without waiting for his acknowledgment, she escaped to the bathroom. She rinsed her burning eyes with cool water, continuing to splash her face until she felt able to face him.

This was the true reckoning. Now, he'd see how she'd allowed herself to give in to depravity and it was brought back on her to show her that she should never have allowed it to happen to begin with.

'You're a big girl, Bridget,' she said to her reflection. 'You can handle whatever he has to say.'

In truth, she wasn't so sure who she was trying to convince. She'd never told anyone the full story of her rape. Sometimes, she wasn't even sure she could call it rape, since she'd responded to him. The bastard had made her come. Remembered horror flooded her, making her light-headed, and she had to steady herself against the sink.

'Pull it together,' she admonished her reflection. 'You've been above reproach since then. You never give into your weakness. Don't start now.'

Feeling like she was about to face the firing squad, she turned the knob and went to confront Connor.

He didn't know what pissed him off more. That the

bastard who'd raped her had obviously used some kind of drug to lower her inhibitions, thereby robbing her of her very real right to anger. Or the fact that a woman as intelligent as Bridget was letting him get away with it.

He comprehended the association she'd drawn, but she was wrong. Plain and simple.

He still hadn't quite formulated how to tell her what he was thinking when she came back from the bathroom. She looked like a drowned kitten. Her hair was damp around the edges and curling, her make-up gone from the obvious washing she'd given her face. She was adorable and it made him all the madder at her for letting herself believe something so incredibly asinine.

She sat as far from him as the couch would allow and that pissed him off too. Did she think he was going to attack her or rail at her or something? No, that wasn't it. She thought he was going to judge her. His anger lessened but didn't completely die out at that realisation.

'Let me get this straight.' His tone was sharper than he'd have liked and she flinched in response. 'You think that because you enjoyed being tied up and spanked, you were punished for it because your rapist tied you up and whipped you and your body responded to the stimulation. And – I'm guessing here – you think that because those acts were committed in an act of violation there is a correlation with your relationship with your first boyfriend.'

She didn't answer, only nodded. He blew out an exasperated sigh. People really did over-complicate their lives. Especially when it came to sex.

'That's bullshit. You're being incredibly stupid to buy into the idea.'

Shock replaced trepidation in her face and she flushed angrily.

'How can you say that?'

'Because context is everything. That's why. Think about justifiable homicide. If you were to walk up to a stranger, point a gun at them and shoot, assuming you were in no danger of losing your own life, you'd be committing murder. Take that same stranger, turn the tables so now he's assaulting you and you shoot him, every court in the land will say it was justifiable because it was self-defence. One thing remains the same though, the stranger is now dead. It's context that matters. One is justified, the other is not.

'In your case, there is nothing wrong with a bit of kink to spice up sex. And, when two people do it together – *consenting* to it – it can be a great way to explore sensuality and sex together. When one person doesn't consent, all bets are off.'

She drew a breath to speak but he was determined to finish and held up a hand. Reluctantly, she relaxed.

'Bridg, I'd love to tie you up and believe me, my dick gets hard at the notion of spanking your pretty little ass and then fucking you nice and rough. You see, pain and pleasure, they go hand in hand.'

She began to protest. Again, he held up a hand to stop her.

'Hear me out before you protest.'

She sighed, but relaxed back and waited.

'When pain is used strategically, endorphins are released and it actually heightens pleasure. It sounds like your first guy – what was his name anyway?'

'Doug,' she supplied.

'OK, Doug, he understood this. Now, Trent, the dickhead, just wanted to hurt you. That you'd already had a pleasurable experience that involved pain and bondage is why you responded the way you did. Plus he obviously gave you a date rape drug to lower your inhibitions.'

'They didn't find any evidence of one when I went to the hospital.' She didn't look at him.

'Doesn't matter. Both roofies and GHB metabolise too quickly. Physical evidence is rarely found.' At her sharp glance he shrugged and said, 'What? I watched a *Dateline* episode about it once.'

'How can you be so certain that it isn't depraved?'

'Because I don't believe we are set up to fail as human beings. Simple as that. I want to do the things to you that you say wanting to have done is a depraved act. I don't think I'm depraved at all. I think I like to push the boundaries of sensual exploration and that – for me, anyway – involves pain. The key is to find someone with reciprocal desires. I've never forced anyone who didn't want to experience it to go through it. I'm very capable of living without it, but strategic pain gives pleasure a dimension and depth unlike any I've experienced.

'What your rapist did to you was perverted and depraved because he took an act that is intimate and sensual and turned into a violation of your will, body and psyche. That he did it in a way that lowered your inhibitions, and robbed you of a very real need to rage and be angry at his violation, is even worse.

'You've internalised this, Bridget. You're carrying all this on your shoulders when he was wrong. Not you. You need to put blame where it lies, on your rapist, not on you sharing a desire that hundreds of other people in this world share – including me.'

She was silent for a long time. He could see the wheels turning in her head and he wanted to argue more, try to force her to see things differently, but he knew he couldn't do that. She would have to come to the understanding on her own.

Finally, she turned to him, saying, 'You've given me a lot to think about.'

Her face was unreadable and she wasn't making him feel altogether comfortable, but it was better than outright rejection.

'That's all I can ask for.' He gathered up the dishes from the apple pie and put them into the sink. She followed him, bringing her wineglass and setting it on the counter.

He wanted her to stay with him tonight. He didn't want her to leave, and allow distance to grow. This was important. They were on opposite sides of an argument right now and he didn't want to give her the opportunity to twist this into an excuse to stop seeing him.

Taking the plunge, he said, 'Stay here with me, Bridget. I don't want you to go.'

'I'm not so sure that's a good idea.' She bit her bottom lip, something he'd begun to realise meant indecision for her.

'Look, I feel as if we just had a really hard conversation and I don't want you to leave. I won't try anything; I'd just really like to sleep with you in my arms. I'd like to wake up with you.'

'I can't.' She looked unhappy. 'I have to take care

of Daisy. I can't leave her by herself overnight.'

'Let's go get her.'

'Seriously?' The incredulous look on her face made him grin even as his chest lightened. He really did want her to stay.

'Yes, seriously. She and Lotus took to each other and I want you here with me.'

She tilted her head to one side in that sexy, curious kitten way she had and he couldn't help himself. He stepped forward, cupped her face in his palms, and kissed her.

It was a kiss filled with promises and declarations that were entirely too soon to make with any sanity, but that he felt in his heart nonetheless. Sometimes you just knew, and Connor was certain that no matter what happened between them, this woman would be a part of him for ever.

Chapter Twelve

Bridget awoke to the feel of Connor wrapped around her. She felt warm and safe and that was odd for her. She'd spent nights with the men she'd dated before, but they'd never felt safe. Not like this anyway. There was a tremendous comfort in having shared her darkest secret with Connor.

She wasn't at all sure she agreed with him, but he'd definitely given her a different perspective. They hadn't talked about it any more after he'd asked her to stay. Their conversation had been more mundane, full of the confessions and admissions that any two normal people would share in an attempt to fill in the gaps of understanding about a new person you were interested in.

They'd driven over to her house for her to grab some clothes and toiletries as well as collect Daisy. The two dogs had bonded immediately and had fallen asleep curled around each other on Lotus's bed.

Sleeping with Connor hadn't been half as awkward as she'd feared. They'd been up chatting and talking late into the night before exhaustion set in. As she'd changed into her pyjamas, she'd been worried about being uncomfortable or unable to sleep, but as soon as she'd climbed into bed with him, he'd kissed her gently on the forehead, snuggled in behind her spoon-like and been instantly asleep. She'd followed soon after.

She'd slept deeply and dreamlessly. She couldn't remember the last time that had happened.

In the light of a new day, her mind still reeled from the things Connor had said to her. She'd never considered things from that perspective. She'd always assumed that having her rape turned against her like that was punishment for enjoying the things she and Doug had done together.

She'd been raised in a loving household, but sex was not something that was discussed. Her mother had never had "the talk" with her. She'd handed Bridget some pamphlets and told her to come to her with any questions. Everything Bridget had learned about sex had come from the romance novels she'd devoured in her teen years.

Her parents had not been demonstrative people. She'd never seen them be affectionate with each other. Her brother had once joked that they had to be the product of immaculate conceptions because he couldn't imagine their meticulous mother allowing herself to get down and dirty. Bridget had agreed wholeheartedly. Her father's answer to the sex talk was to say that if she ever allowed herself to get knocked up outside of marriage, he'd disown her.

In spite of their taciturn ways, she'd always known she was loved. They'd made sacrifices for her and her brother. Ensured they always had what they needed. That they didn't get the words of love were something both she and Roy had learned to live with.

When Doug had suggested tying her up, it had

seemed erotic and forbidden. The feeling of being helpless and at his will had been sexy and she'd loved every minute of it. When he'd added spanking to the repertoire it had made her feel wanton and just a bit dirty. The orgasms he'd given her had been off the chart.

She'd never questioned it until she was raped. That Trent had done the same things to her in such a vile way had caused her to see what she and Doug had done in a different light. One that had caused her such deep-seated shame that it affected every relationship she'd had since then. Hell, it had changed her entire sense of herself too.

She sighed deeply, feeling overcome by confusion. Had she given Trent too much power? She'd never truly been angry at him; she'd simply assumed she'd deserved it – a lesson to teach her the error of her ways.

Shit, had she been wrong all this time?

Turning over, she gazed at Connor. His face was even younger in sleep. The stubble on his cheeks gave him a rakish look and his arm was thrown back behind his head. Could he be right?

As if her thoughts had summoned him, Connor opened his eyes and looked directly into hers. They were warm grey in the morning light and a slow grin spread across his face.

'Morning, gorgeous.' His voice was husky with sleep.

'Good morning.' She smiled back.

He reached a hand up and cupped her cheek. At his touch, her insides went liquid. She watched his eyes darken with desire and her breath caught.

'Bridget.'

'Hmm?' She didn't want to move, not even to speak.

'I want to make love to you.' He stroked his thumb across her cheek. 'Now.'

She couldn't even draw breath to answer, she just nodded.

'Kiss me.'

It was a command she gladly obeyed.

Connor fought to control the urge to flip her over and fuck her wildly. He wanted her to lead this first time between them. No matter how much he wanted to make this rough and dirty, he needed her to trust him before they could go there.

Connor had spent a long time thinking about what she'd told him last night, and she was wrong. He was determined to show her that it was about consent. That when both people consented, there was nothing wrong with anything she'd experienced. It was time to replace her memories of the rape with better ones.

Those better memories were starting right now. Hell, for him too. Her lips were warm and soft and feather-light. Too light; he wanted more.

'Harder, gorgeous.'

She smiled and deepened the kiss, stroking her tongue into his mouth. He welcomed her invasion and let her explore at her whim. Her hands were rubbing his chest and he desperately wanted her to reach for his cock, but he would let her set the pace.

He couldn't resist burrowing his hands in her curls. They were silken fire draped around his hands. She was growing more urgent, her kiss stronger and deeper. His body was tight everywhere; he wanted his hands on her, his mouth on her, his cock in her.

It was hell trying to hold back.

She broke the kiss. Panting, she looked at him but made no move to go further.

'What is it?' he asked.

'I feel silly.' She flushed.

'Why?' He stroked her lips with his finger. He wanted them wrapped around his cock.

'Because I've never done this. Doug always took charge and then, after I was raped, I always just laid back and let the man take the lead.'

He wasn't at all surprised by her words, but that was about to change.

'That doesn't surprise me, Bridg, but it's time you learned. So, you're in charge. Do whatever you want or tell me what you want me to do.'

*　　　*　　　*

She felt like an idiot. She was almost 40, for heaven's sake, and she'd never been the aggressor in sex. She was intimidated, but she wanted this, wanted him.

Rising up, she sat cross-legged facing him and considered the issue. Not the sexiest thing in the world, but she needed a moment despite the fact that her fingers itched to touch him.

Well, if she was going to be in charge, she might as well follow her instincts.

Reaching out, she stroked the skin of his belly and smiled as his muscles flexed and danced under her touch. His body was gorgeous. Nicely fit and muscled in all the right places. A trail of coarse hair led the way to his groin, disappearing under the waistband of the boxers that were barely containing what promised to be a lovely erection.

The thought of where that erection was going to end up had her womb clenching in anticipation. She'd forgotten what it was like to truly want a man. To need him as much as you needed to breathe. Trent had robbed her of more than she realised.

She traced Connor's pecs before running a finger over the flat disc of his nipple. On impulse, she squeezed it, and was rewarded with a low groan. She wanted more of those sounds from him.

Leaning over, she kissed his nipple before licking it lightly and Connor moaned again. It spurred her on to kiss and suck, lick and gently bite his nipples. She absorbed the sounds of his groans and revelled in his harsh breathing. He was definitely enjoying this.

The sounds of his pleasure were doing crazy things to her body. She was wet and her nipples were hard. She felt achy, hollow and needy, but she wasn't ready to end this. She wanted more from Connor first.

She trailed light kisses down his body, nuzzling his belly button and his hips.

Sitting up, she demanded, 'Take off your boxers.'

He wasted no time. He stripped off his shorts and tossed them aside. Lean and long, his body was delicious to look at. His penis was full and thick and weeping.

She felt a heady sense of power at her ability to arouse him this way. Putting all doubts from her mind, she decided to go where instinct took her. Reaching out, she stroked his cock. Closing her eyes, she let herself take in the sensation of silky skin and heat under her palm. His cock jerked as if in admonition and she gripped him lightly.

She stroked him just as lightly and his cock jumped. She wasn't sure what to do here; she could barely remember what Doug had liked her to do and she hadn't actually touched a man since then.

'Harder,' Connor moaned and flexed his hips, pushing into her hand.

A bit embarrassed but unwilling to end this, she demanded, 'Show me.'

He engulfed her hand in his and tightened their grip while drawing her hand up his shaft, only to squeeze the head and repeat the motion. Once she had the hang of it, he let go.

She stroked his cock, absorbing the feel of him under her skin and the sight of him as she pleased him. His hips rolled and flexed as he fucked into her hand. His eyes were closed and he was panting slightly, groaning every time she squeezed him.

A bead of moisture welled up on the tip and on impulse she leaned over and licked it off. The salty tang exploded across her tongue even as he gripped the sheets and arched.

'Do you want me to come like this, baby?' He growled out the words.

Smoky, grey eyes met hers and she tingled at the lust and heat she saw there. None of her previous lovers had looked at her like that. But then, she couldn't remember actually touching any of them like this either.

In that moment, she knew she'd been very selfish since the rape. However understandable it may have been, she hadn't thought about their pleasure at all.

'Stay with me, Bridget.' Connor's rough command snapped out of her thoughts.

'No, I don't want you to come like this,' she said, though she couldn't resist another taste.

She licked wetly along the head of his cock and was rewarded with more groans and cursing from Connor. Moving her hand, she slowly took him into her mouth and began to gently suckle.

He felt like silky steel along her tongue and he smelled of salt and man. She felt connected to him in a way she hadn't felt with any other man. A seed of fear burrowed into her mind. How could she be sure?

Even as doubt threatened to overwhelm her, Connor burrowed his fingers in her hair and muttered, 'Fuck, Bridg. That feels so good.'

He joined her rhythm; began to thrust shallowly into her mouth. She maintained a light, coaxing pressure along his length, rubbing her tongue along him and squeezing the head with her lips.

'Bridg.' He gripped her head lightly. 'Stop, baby. Stop. I'm going to come if you keep that up.'

She briefly debated taking him over the edge. There was power in the knowledge that she could make a man lose himself. To swallow down his essence and take him into her body that way. But she wanted more, she wanted him inside her. She wanted to feel him between her legs and his hands on her body.

With a long, tight draw, she pulled off him and gloried in his harsh groan. She was definitely liking this. There was no need to think deeper than that.

'Condom?' she asked as she rolled off the bed.

'Side drawer.' He nodded toward the night table closest to him.

She grabbed a condom from the drawer and tossed it on the bed. For the briefest moment, she hesitated. Emotions flickered across her face that he didn't like. Just as he was about to speak, her face cleared and she quickly removed her pyjamas.

His body clenched in response to the sight she presented. Her breasts were full and swollen with desire. A light flush painted her pale skin and her underwear – hell, did this woman believe in lingerie? They were white cotton ... briefs?

Thankfully, she stripped those off too, revealing a neatly trimmed thatch of coppery curls. He was going to have to work on this part of her self-image. She clearly had a problem with seeing herself as sexual or being sexual. She'd surprised him so far. He hadn't expected her to go so far when he'd challenged her. He'd just wanted her to feel in control of the situation.

Her mouth on his cock had been heaven. Soft and wet, it had been a struggle to not grab her head and thrust deeply into her mouth.

Damn, she tried his control! The blood was rushing to his dick and his entire body was on fire with the need to get inside her and claim her.

Fuck, Connor. Relax, he told himself.

He couldn't afford to screw up this first time. There would be time to play and push her in the future. This was not the time.

She crawled over him, straddling his hips. She was slick and wet and he couldn't help himself. He stroked her slit with a finger and sucked the moisture from the tip. She was tangy and sweet. He wanted to bury his tongue inside her.

She moaned; a soft, low sound that was music to his ears. The condom was on the bed. He wanted to grab it and move this along, but she had to do this. So, gathering what self-control he had left, he waited.

Thankfully, she had mercy on him.

She snatched up the condom and rolled it on him a little clumsily, but she got it done.

Rising up, she fisted his erection and settled herself over him, pressing him deep inside. It was like being sucked into an exquisite, velvet vice. She rocked and rolled her hips until he was fully seated and then she stilled.

Her knees were locked on his hips and she panted, her breasts rising and falling. She bit her lip, seeming to be thinking hard. Not at all where he wanted her. He wanted her in the moment. Not thinking, only feeling.

He flexed his hips and pushed deeper inside her, causing them both to moan. He fisted his sheets and flexed his hips again, grinding their bodies together.

Bridget's eyes closed and he saw a frown flit across her face before she said, 'Touch me, Connor.'

Hell, yeah.

He reached for her breasts, cupping and fondling them. Her nipples were hard nubs, tight and beaded. He pinched and squeezed them; she moaned, arching forward into his hand.

She began to move along his cock. Rising up and dropping down hard, taking him deep. Pulsing and throbbing inside her, he wanted to come so badly, but he was determined that she come first.

Licking his thumbs, he rubbed the moisture into her nipples and she gasped.

132

'That's so good, baby. I like that.'

He was trying to watch what he said too, but he wanted to encourage her. He wasn't sure the more explicit things he wanted to say would go over well. Either way it worked; she was becoming wilder as she rode him.

She ground down on him and pushed her breasts into his hands. She wasn't saying anything but her eyes were squeezed closed and she was whimpering.

He reared up and sucked one of her nipples into his mouth. At the same time, he gripped her hips and thrust deeply inside her. She moaned long and hard. He sucked harder and thrust deeper. She became more urgent.

She churned and bucked on top of him and he gritted his teeth to stave off his own climax. This was what he wanted. He didn't want her thinking. But he could feel her resistance. That wasn't acceptable.

Matching her rhythm, he thrust deep and hard. She was too erratic for him to continue sucking those luscious breasts, so he switched to fingering her clit. He wanted her to come apart.

Her clitoris was swollen and protruding, and he alternated between rubbing and squeezing the hard bud. She bit her lip and ground down into him. She was holding back, he could feel it. He wanted her screaming his name, wanted her wild.

'You're fucking gorgeous,' he groaned.

Her head was thrown back and her curls tumbled around her head. Her breasts were swollen and her nipples were red and pouty from his ministrations. She was clenching around his cock and he wasn't sure he could hold out.

133

Suddenly, she grew wild; bucking hard, grinding her clit against him. Short, huffing gasps turned into one long moan as her body began to convulse. She cried out wordlessly and clenched hard around him.

He couldn't hold out any more. Gripping her hips, he pounded into her and let himself explode. His cock jerked with each hot jet and he wished there were no barriers between them. He wanted to mark her.

She wouldn't be getting away from him. He was going to see to that.

Bridget collapsed over Connor and tried to control her breathing. Without question, that was the best orgasm she'd ever had. She'd had a moment there where she'd almost lost it. Almost given in and begged Connor to make her burn when he'd begun to play with her nipples.

He may have given her food for thought, but she wasn't sure she agreed with him yet and she wasn't taking any chances. Either way, what they'd just shared had been amazing.

She rolled off him, concerned she would become too heavy, and snuggled in next to him.

Kissing her forehead, he said, 'Give me a sec. Let me take care of this.'

She watched him stroll naked to the bathroom. He really did have a fine ass. She smiled, knowing that she'd found someone with whom she might be able to have a real relationship. Something she'd more or less given up on. Time would tell the real story, but she wasn't willing to walk away without seeing where this went first.

Connor climbed back into bed and pulled her

close, but whatever he'd been about to say was lost to Lotus jumping up on the bed.

She licked their faces thoroughly, leaving them both squealing. Bridget was pleased to see that Daisy had better manners and was still on the floor, though she was equally as ready for them to get up.

'Ah well, sugar. Doggie duty calls,' she said as she got out of bed and hunted up her clothes.

'Lotus, Daddy was trying to get some more action.' He ruffled her head. 'I'm going to have to teach you about timing.'

Bridget laughed at him and said, 'Come on, lazy. Let's walk the dogs.'

'All right, but I meant what I said.' He pulled on a pair of sweats as he talked. 'I'm not close to done with you.'

A small shiver ran down her spine. She felt like there was more to what he said than the words he spoke.

'Is that right?' She quirked an eyebrow in his direction.

'Yes, that's exactly right.' He looked her dead in the eye as he spoke.

Suddenly she felt off kilter again.

He must have sensed something, for he dropped the shirt he'd been about to put on and gently pulled her into his arms.

'Bridget, I want you to trust me so that you can finally let what happened go. That's all I really meant. I want to show you what sex can be between two consenting adults and I want to show you what we can be together.' He kissed her gently. 'If you'll let me, that is.'

135

'OK,' she murmured into his shoulder despite the butterflies that had multiplied exponentially in her stomach. Squeezing Connor, she repeated, 'OK.'

She hoped like heck she knew what she was doing.

Chapter Thirteen

Dale Whittier liked the finer things in life. As he stirred a spoonful of organic cane sugar into his freshly-brewed, dark roast Colombian coffee, he contemplated how he'd come to be at Pinewood. Serving as Dean at some tiny little university in the middle-of-nowhere Vermont had not been on his agenda. He'd been a rising star at Stanford University. Firmly on his way to achieving his personal goal – president of the university.

But then that little bitch had fucked everything up when she'd reported him. The ensuing scandal had squelched his plans. She'd been a student at the university, for God's sake. How on earth could he have been expected to know she was still underage? Besides, she'd thrown herself at him, not the other way around.

He had had no need to go seeking jailbait. She'd been in his senior level chemistry class and was obviously infatuated, flirting with him at every opportunity. Always pretending to be shy and yet making sure her buttons were always undone just enough that he got a face full of tits every time she leaned over her desk.

She'd come to every single study session and

office hours too. And she'd always brought cookies and other treats. If he said he liked chocolate chip cookies, she made sure to bring them the very next time.

She did everything except beg him to fuck her. Who was he not to oblige? If she wanted to ride his cock so bad, he'd let her. Then the bitch had reported him. Cocksucking little cunt. He'd been allowed to "quietly resign" for his ethical violation.

He'd done the bitch a favour and what had he gotten for it? A one-way ticket to Vermont and this tiny university that was below him. The only saving grace being that now, rather than Professor, he was Dean of the School of Sciences and once again back on the fast track to president.

And he certainly didn't lack for pussy. With his combination of money and looks, women practically threw themselves at him. Gold-digging little whores that they were. They all just wanted his money. They served a purpose, though. A grin split his face as he thought of that purpose. He did love to fuck. He couldn't get enough. And he took what he wanted. There was nothing better than a woman submitting to his will.

Oh, he didn't force himself on them, he was no rapist, but he loved that look of utter helplessness; the self-recrimination that flooded their eyes as he took them. Little Skyler had been the best so far. He especially loved a virgin.

Initiating them was its own intoxication. Their tight little pussies, untried and waiting for him to mark them. Every man who came after would be for ever held in comparison to him whether they wanted it or not. Every man who came after him would benefit from his training. He served his fellow man even as he served himself.

Skyler could suck a mean cock now. She could swallow him down and lick his nuts in one breath and what she could do with her pussy was off the charts. She could milk the come out of him in no time flat.

Her tears had been sublime. She'd tried to break things off with him, claiming an attack of conscience, but he wasn't done with her yet. Her scholarship was under his control and he'd made sure she knew that. Sure, she could switch majors, lose her scholarship. That's all she had to do to end their affair, but she lived and breathed chemistry. Her dream, as she'd so sweetly shared with him that first "chance" meeting over coffee, was to work for the FBI as a forensic chemist and do drug analysis. CSI-type stuff.

You didn't do that without a chemistry degree. With her family being so financially strapped, she needed her scholarship. She couldn't just pick up and transfer. Dale grinned at how neatly he'd trapped her.

Pulling back the cuff on his silk sweater, he checked the time. Ross was late. She was so passive aggressive with him. She honestly believed she wasn't going to fuck him. He snorted and took another sip of his coffee. They all gave him what he wanted in the end.

With Bridget, the chase had been fun. Her little gasps and shivers when he "accidentally" touched her were especially sweet. Unlike most, she was playing hard to get. It had been cute at first, but it was wearing thin.

She needed to get with the programme. Skyler was

outliving her usefulness and she'd already proven to be irresponsible. The little cunt had gotten pregnant after swearing she was on the pill.

He wasn't going to be saddled with a brat; she'd better keep that appointment or there would be hell to pay. His physician was discreet, at least, he didn't have to worry about this getting around campus, but the fun of fucking her was gone now. He couldn't relax and let go knowing there was a brat in there, and she'd proven she could no longer be trusted.

Yes, he was almost done with her. It was time for bigger fish and Bridget was definitely bigger in all the right places. Big tits that would wrap nicely around his dick and an ass that was begging to be fucked. He bet she was a crier too. She'd weep pretty tears the entire time and he'd taste them as he came. His body hardened at the thought.

As if summoned by his thoughts, Bridget walked through the door.

His heart thundered in his chest at the sight of her, just as it did every time he saw her.

Bridget's stomach lurched at the realisation that Dean Whittier was alone in the conference room. She'd deliberately come five minutes late just to ensure she wasn't the first to arrive. She glanced at the clock on the panelled wall; it was definitely 8.05 a.m.

Whittier sat there looking elegantly predatorial. He was immaculately dressed in a sweater and slacks, sipping coffee as if he hadn't a care in the world, except for the fact that he looked like a lion who'd just scented a gazelle.

'Bridget.' He inclined his head her way. 'You're

looking lovely as always.'

'Where is everyone?' She stopped short of actually entering the room and stood framed in the doorway.

'The rest of the staff will be here at 8.30, I wanted to speak with you privately first.' He set his coffee on the table and indicated for her to sit with a sweep of his hand.

Reluctantly, Bridget took the seat at the far end of the table, putting as much distance between them as possible.

Dean Whittier stood and moved to close the door. Her heart rate jacked up a notch at being alone and behind closed doors with him.

'Coffee?' he asked, moving over to the sideboard and picking up the carafe.

'No, thank you.'

He ignored her and poured her a cup. He even added cream and sugar, leaving her bewildered at his knowledge of how she took her coffee, and set the mug in front of her. Rather than return to the seat she'd found him in, he sat catty-corner to her.

'Ross, as you know your tenure evaluation is coming up at the end of the semester.'

He leaned forward and looked her in the eye. She trembled at the look of smugness she saw there. There was nothing warm in those eyes. They were the blue of ice and she shivered as they bore into her. Gripping the coffee cup, she vainly tried to absorb some of its warmth into her body.

'I think it's time that you and I got on the same page.'

He stroked a long, elegant finger along her arm, raising goosebumps and causing her stomach to clench again as she pulled her hand back, shoving it between her legs. Anger flashed across his face, but he quickly schooled his expression.

'What page would that be, Dean?'

He smiled and stood, coming to stand behind her. The way he moved reminded her of a reptile, cold and slithering. She tensed and her skin prickled at the feel of him behind her.

'My dear Bridget.' He leaned over her, resting his hands on the back of her chair but brushing her skin in the process. She could smell his cologne; it was a spicy scent that on anyone else would have been intoxicating. Instead, it made her nauseous. 'You know what I want. Playing hard to get with me is cute, but it's wearing thin. I control your tenure review. If you want my signature on that page, you're going to give me what I want. Do you understand? Because if you don't I will make sure not only do you lose your job here, no one will hire you when I'm done with you.'

'You bastard!' Bridget hissed and lurched up, pushing the chair back as she did so. Whittier fell back, catching himself on the wall. Panic flooded her and she began to tremble violently from head to toe. 'What do you think you're doing? Threatening me with my job. This is harassment.'

Her heart raced and dizziness threatened to overwhelm her, but she refused to give in. She went on the offensive instead.

'Besides, what do you have over me? Huh? The last time I checked I performed my duties as a professor here more than competently. My student evaluation average is one of the highest on campus and I've published more in the time I've been here than anyone else in the department. So, you'll have to enlighten me as to what you're referring to as it relates to my tenure evaluation.'

Rage suffused his face as he straightened and pushed away from the wall, smoothing his clothes before speaking in a cold voice. 'Listen to me, Ross. Who are you going to run to? President Harvey? That doddering old fool does exactly what I tell him to do. He wants my family's money in this university and he knows that harming me is harming his budget. So, good luck with that one.'

He was right. Harvey had acquiesced to Whittier so much it was a running joke that he needed a straw to suck up as hard as he did.

Either way, she wasn't going to stay here and be preyed upon. Those days were over. She rushed to the door, wrenched it open, and almost ran headlong into Martha McBrand.

'Oh!' Martha cried out as she stepped back.

Bridget quickly pulled herself together and gently brought the door fully open, leaving it that way. As her colleagues began to file into the room, Bridget once again settled into the chair closest to the door and felt growing despair as Whittier's threats sank in.

*   *   *

'Stop, Daisy!'

Bridget admonished the dog who was currently carpet surfing on the area rug in Bridget's living room. Normally, she found it amusing when the dog flopped on her back and began rubbing around as if she had the worst itch in the world. Tonight, however, there was no solace to be found. Not even the mint

143

chocolate chip ice cream was helping and it was her go-to comfort food.

Bridget had come home hoping to find some comfort in her personal space. She'd taken great care in decorating her home. Her living room was eclectic yet modern with comfortable furniture that was soft and enveloping while still having clean lines. She'd decorated in warm tones of pale browns, gold and orange, with touches of flair in the art and knick-knacks. It reflected the woman she considered herself to be – warm, welcoming, and classy. She'd always found sanctuary in her home.

Tonight, she just felt alone.

She'd considered calling Connor, asking him to come over, but decided against it. She wasn't ready to let him that close. Despite what they'd shared, she wanted to take this *very* slow with him. He left her unsettled and she didn't like that.

On the one hand, they were good together. He made her laugh. But he challenged her in ways that made her want to run the other direction. His ideas about sex were intriguing, but they also meant she'd wasted almost 20 years of her life.

Uggh! Let it go, she told herself. You've got more pressing problems.

Dale Whittier could very well ruin her career.

She'd thought about calling Claire and Mona, but she already knew what they'd say. They'd tell her to report it. To not let him get the best of her. And, while Bridget agreed in principle, it wasn't that simple.

This was her career at stake.

She could report the harassment, but even if her complaint was successful, she'd find herself labelled a troublemaker and have a hard time finding work elsewhere.

If she got her tenure successfully, she'd be almost untouchable. It was one of the reasons she'd selected Pinewood to begin with. With so few universities maintaining a tenure programme these days, a teacher was constantly auditioning for their job. They'd be lucky to get more than a one-year contract, but the responsibilities were still the same despite the lack of payoff in return for the professor.

When she'd been in that position, she'd still had to advise. Still had to participate in university activities. Still had to be accountable for the curriculum, passing rates, and student evaluations. She'd still had to publish and be relevant but had no assurance that the 50 to 60 hours a week she put in would result in her contract being renewed or her salary not being cut when it came time to renegotiate.

She'd suffered through a few of those types of contracts when she first began teaching and quickly determined she'd wanted a tenured position. When the position had become available at Pinewood she'd done her damnedest to land it and she deeply resented the dean for putting her back up against the wall this way.

She probably wouldn't have taken the position if he'd been in charge when she interviewed. She wasn't one to put herself into the line of fire if it could be avoided and she'd known the day she met Whittier that he was going to be trouble. His eyes had lingered too long. His tone had been suggestive and he'd made her feel like a piece of meat under inspection for consumption.

Dean Winslow, Whittier's predecessor, had been a kind man with a compassionate face that lit up when he spoke of the research he did in addition to leading the department. Her interview had taken place over coffee in the teachers' lounge because he'd said he wanted all the candidates to get a feel for what it was really like in the department rather than a sterile interview in his office. They'd gone much longer than the 45 minutes he'd allotted for the interview as they'd discussed their passion for teaching and how satisfying it was to see the light bulb go off in a student's eyes when they finally grasped complex chemical concepts.

She'd instantly liked him and they'd become close that first year. Winslow had become a mentor to her. Unfortunately, his heart had begun to fail and he'd decided to retire. He still served on the board of directors, but he spent most of his time in his garden now or with his children and grandchildren.

President Harvey had hired Dean Whittier. It had not been a popular decision. The search committee had recommended another candidate: a woman with a stellar record and a charismatic personality. Whittier had seemed coldly arrogant throughout the entire interview process. Bridget had been on the search committee and universally they'd agreed that Sheila had been the better candidate. The president had overridden their recommendation, giving the position to Whittier. A month later, the university was getting a brand new fitness facility. You didn't have to be Einstein for that math to add up.

Either way, she was stuck with him now, and he was leaving her little choice. She had to find a way to expose him and his harassment without getting herself fired. She already knew how the victim in a situation like this could be turned into the villain. She'd seen enough women made out to be the criminal despite being horribly violated. She'd never been willing to be one of them.

It had been bad enough that she'd come away from her experience at Trent's hands feeling as if she'd deserved what happened to her. She hadn't been willing to put herself through the public humiliation of having it confirmed. Then, as if the rape wasn't lesson enough, the baby had been the final crack in her confidence.

Trent hadn't used a condom. He'd impregnated her that day. This was before the use of the "morning-after pill" was widely available. When she'd found out she was pregnant, there had been no consideration for her. She'd decided to have an abortion. She wasn't going to bear the child of violence. She wouldn't even consider it.

She'd located a nearby clinic and arranged to have the abortion. During the procedure, she'd seized in reaction to the anaesthesia they'd given her. Her uterus was perforated. The resulting damage meant she'd be more likely to win the lottery than to ever carry a baby to term.

The loss of her dream of being a mother had done her in. For the first time, she'd felt helpless, powerless. That was when the idea that she was being punished for her experimentation with Doug had come to her. Those seeds had taken root and she'd been unable to shake them. That, more than the rape itself, had changed her life in ways she still suffered from today. In the aftermath, the greatest damage that had been done to her was that she'd begun to question her own judgment. Where Trent hadn't been able to hurt her body, his act of violence had succeeded in damaging her psyche.

She felt the same way now. Helpless. Powerless. Whittier was backing her into a corner and she wanted to fight. She just didn't know how. She'd never been a quitter and she wasn't quitting now. But how did she expose him for the scum he was and not lose her job? She would not be vilified when she was in the right.

There had to be a way. There had to be.

With no answer forthcoming, Bridget took her dishes and placed them in the dishwasher, setting the timer to run well after she was asleep.

A long, hot bath did nothing to spur inspiration. With a troubled heart, she drifted off to sleep.

Chapter Fourteen

Skyler sat in her Jeep in front of the River Rock Medical Building. She had no idea how long she'd been there. She only knew her hands were aching from clutching the steering wheel. She was definitely late for her appointment, but, no matter what she told herself, she was unable to summon the will to leave her car.

Clearing her mind of all thought, she reached for the keys still dangling in the ignition and started the car. With no clear destination in mind, she began to drive.

After what seemed like for ever but was only about 15 minutes, she found herself in the parking lot for Pratt Hall, Pinewood's chemistry building. The irony was not lost on her that she'd come to where it had all begun for her.

She'd seen him for the first time walking these very halls. His attention toward her had been so flattering. She'd seen him as a charismatic genius. When they'd run into each other at the coffee shop, she'd been completely swept away by his caring consideration for her. The way he treated her as an equal.

She'd given him her virginity.

Nausea flooded her at that thought. She'd given the most intimate gift she had to give to a monster. A monster who didn't deserve to continue. Skyler had always been a gentle soul. She'd always been the peacemaker in her group. Right now, though, she'd gladly murder the dean and not think twice about it.

He'd made her believe she was special to him, but now she saw what he was really about. She'd never been anything other than a piece of ass for him to exploit and now he was using her scholarship to control her. Her parents couldn't afford to send her to college. The only thing that had allowed her to go was that she'd won this scholarship and it had clear rules.

No other university had offered her enough aid to cover the full cost of tuition, and her father's cab driver salary simply didn't cut it. Not when there was still her little sister at home. Her mother worked in a day care centre. It was a loving, but very poor home. The scholarship to Pinewood had seemed a gift from God.

Now, it was her prison. She would not let Dale Whittier keep her from her dreams. She simply wouldn't. The question was what to do? How to show the true monster he was and not lose her scholarship?

With those questions bouncing around her brain, Skyler left her Jeep and went in search of the person who'd promised help.

'Professor Ross?'

Bridget startled at Skyler's voice in the quiet of her office. She'd been working late, grading mid-term exams, trying to wrap them up so that her weekend would be free. She was having dinner with Connor tomorrow night and she didn't want them lingering around over the weekend, tempting her to work.

'Skyler.' She smiled in welcome even as she waved her into a chair. 'What can I do for you? I'm afraid I haven't quite finished grading exams so I don't have your score yet.'

Skyler closed and locked the door behind her before taking the seat offered. There was a look of intensity on her face that had Bridget feeling edgy. Something wasn't right; Bridget always kept her door open, but she wasn't sure what was going on right now and she'd wait and see.

'Is everything OK, Skyler?' Bridget stacked the exams she'd been grading and put them in a file folder before setting them inside her desk drawer.

'No, Professor. Things aren't OK, and I just don't know what to do. I don't even think you can help me, but I just can't keep this to myself any longer. I –' She cut herself off as tears welled in her eyes. 'I'm pregnant, Professor.'

Sympathy bloomed inside Bridget. Being pregnant at such a young age was never easy.

'Does the father know?' Bridget pulled a box of tissues out of her desk and came around to offer Skyler one before indicating she should come with her over to the small sofa in her office.

Skyler snorted inelegantly and nodded. Once they had settled in more comfortably, she continued, 'Yeah, he knows. He doesn't want it. He's demanding I get an abortion.'

'Is that what you want?'

Tears streamed down Skyler's face as she wadded the tissue in her hands. 'I don't really know. I haven't stopped to think about it. He's been threatening me and I was just going along with it. But I couldn't do it. I was supposed to be there now. I just sat in my car. I couldn't get out. It was like him winning if I did that.'

'How is he threatening you, darlin'?' Trepidation raged through Bridget as suspicion took root.

'He's using my scholarship as leverage. He's threatening to take it away from me.'

Skyler barely got the words out as sobs began wracking her body. Bridget pulled the larger girl into a hug and simply held her as she cried. She wept the tears of the helpless, the sobs of the powerless. Huge, gulping cries that leave a person weary to the bone.

When she finally quieted, Bridget took a tissue and gently wiped her face.

'Feel better, sugar?'

'No.' Skyler gave a mirthless laugh. 'But I don't feel like I'm going to shake apart any more.'

'That's a start.' She let Skyler go as the girl sat up and scrubbed at her face.

'Who is it, Skyler? Who has this kind of hold over you?' Bridget held her breath as she waited.

Skyler slowly turned to look at Bridget. Her brown eyes were assessing and cool. 'You already know, don't you?'

Bridget shook her head in denial. 'I suspect. I don't know.'

'Dean Whittier.' Skyler's tone was flat and hard. 'I began sleeping with him at the beginning of the term. It was stupid and cliché. I was flattered by the attention of an older man. He took advantage of my stupidity and used me. God,' she wailed, 'the things he made me do. After a while, I had second thoughts. He'd become cold and mean. He seemed to always be so critical of me. I tried to break it off.'

She reached for another tissue as fresh tears began running down her cheeks.

'He told me "I decide when this ends, not you". He said he'd fail me out of my physical chemistry class unless I continued to screw him, and my scholarship has a GPA requirement. I'm barely keeping Bs in some of my core classes, so I can't afford a failing grade in anything.'

She flung herself back on the sofa and squeezed her eyes.

'Have you thought about reporting him?' Anger clenched Bridget's chest at the obvious despair Skyler was in. She hadn't thought Whittier could drop any lower in her estimation. She'd been wrong.

'Yeah, right,' Skyler scoffed. 'Who'd believe me over the dean?'

'I do.' Bridget's voice was soft.

Skyler's head snapped in Bridget's direction.

'Why do you believe me, Professor? You're not even questioning whether I'm telling the truth. Why is that?'

'Are you telling me the truth?'

'Yes, but that's not the point.' Her chocolate eyes bored into Bridget's green ones.

Bridget made a split-second decision and said, 'He's been harassing me as well. He's already proven that he isn't above threats and manipulation to get what he wants. So yes, Skyler. I believe you.'

Skyler launched herself at Bridget, wrapping her in a constricting hug.

'Skyler, sugar, I can't breathe,' she gasped even as she laughed.

Skyler released her and sat back, tears once again flowing.

Bridget took her hand and squeezed, 'We'll figure something out where Dean Whittier is concerned. I promise. But let's put that aside for the moment and get back to the more pressing issue of your baby.'

The words sank into Skyler's brain like water into a sponge. Up until this moment, her pregnancy had been more of an abstract construct in her mind. First, it was a tool she'd hoped to use to get Dale to leave her alone. Then it was about refusing to let him control her.

She'd never once thought of it as a baby. It was the pregnancy. The foetus. But it *was* a baby; more importantly, it was *her* baby. She had always wanted children. It was definitely in her life plan. She had just thought she'd be safely graduated and married before a baby entered the picture.

She had no excuse for what had happened. She'd forgotten to take her pills. She'd let herself be distracted and had been irresponsible. It was simple as that. Birth control only worked reliably when you followed instructions and she hadn't.

Now, though, confronted by the fact that her entire life was about to change, she had to make a decision.

'Skyler?'

The professor had been so kind to her. She'd come to her not knowing what to expect; certainly not compassion and understanding. She'd expected to be disbelieved. Just knowing she wasn't alone was so comforting.

'I'm keeping my baby.'

'Have you thought this through, Skyler? A baby will change your life for ever. What about school?'

Skyler had those questions too and it would be a complete lie to act as if she had the answers, but she knew what she wanted. As the thought filled her mind, so did a conflicting sense of both peace and trepidation.

'I don't have the answers to those questions, Professor. But I know that I'm keeping my baby.'

'You don't have to do this, Skyler. You know that, right?'

Skyler nodded at Professor Ross. 'I know. But I want to do this.'

The professor didn't speak; she just took Skyler in her arms and held her tight.

Chapter Fifteen

Bridget poured a steaming cup of coffee and picked up a chocolate chip cookie before heading over to sit with Claire and Mona. Once again, she hadn't heard a single word of the book club discussion and Jean had given her an earful, to be sure. She almost hadn't come, but she'd known that would only create more questions. As it was, she could see Claire and Mona chomping at the bit to lay into her as well.

With a fortifying bite of cookie, she went to face the inquisition.

Claire didn't hesitate. 'Well. What's going on? Is it Connor?'

'No, it's not Connor.' She sighed. 'Well, not in the way you mean anyway.' She couldn't contain a grin.

Mona leaned forward, interest blazing in her eyes. 'Ooh, I think Bridget's got some scoop to tell.' Setting her cookie and coffee down, she said, 'Spill. Bridg. Let's have it.' She grinned. 'Tell us something good.'

'Better yet –' Claire sipped her decaf '– tell us something sexy?'

Bridget flushed, but couldn't help herself. 'Sexy was off the charts, darlin'. That man is unbelievable.'

They burst out in happy laughter with Bridget.

'Well, he must have been good to keep you so

distracted. Come on, girl. What good is having friends if you can't count on getting the dirt?' Mona said.

'Exactly,' Claire chimed in.

Bridget chuckled but quickly filled them in on her night with Connor. They'd spent several evenings together during the week and had made love again. It was just as wonderful as the first time, though she still couldn't bring herself to truly let it all go with him. She still refused to give in to her urge to go beyond the "norm" and he hadn't pushed her, but she felt a barrier between them.

Tomorrow, he was taking her out to Luna Bella. He'd gotten testy when she'd suggested they didn't need to go to such an expensive restaurant, telling her he wanted to treat her. She'd agreed rather than argue the point. She didn't want him to feel he had to go out of his way to impress her. She was already impressed.

'Why would going to Luna Bella matter?' Mona asked.

'He doesn't make a lot of money. And I don't want him splurging on me when it isn't necessary,' Bridget said.

'What does he do?' Claire asked.

'Starving artist, right?' Mona chimed in. 'I see him drawing all the time at the café.'

'Janitor, actually,' Bridget said. 'At Pinewood, no less.'

Both women looked stunned at the revelation, but quickly recovered.

'Yeah, that wouldn't bring in a lot of money, but Bridg, you gotta let a man be a man. If he wants to splurge on you, let him,' Claire said before finishing off her cookie.

'Yeah, honey,' Mona said, 'Connor's not stupid. If he wants to take you out, I'm sure he can afford it.'

This was why Bridget loved her friends. They didn't even blink at what Connor did for a living.

'That doesn't seem like enough to keep you as preoccupied as you were though. Is there more?' Claire nibbled at her last cookie.

'Yes, but not with him. It's one of my students. And frankly, me.'

Both women waited patiently for her to continue.

'Well, one of my students, Skyler –'

'She comes into the café all the time.' Mona interjected. Her brow furrowed in concern.

'Yup, that's her. She's pregnant, and it's by my boss, no less.'

That particular bomb was met by mute stares.

Bridget just nodded.

'Yup, that was my reaction. But what's making it worse is he's harassing me too.'

Both women exploded at that, talking over each other, their indignation apparent.

'Calm down, calm down.' She held up restraining hands as her friends continued to rail.

'I think they have the right of it.' Evan's deep voice startled Bridget. She hadn't heard him come up.

'What do you mean?' she said.

'I mean, I'm two seconds away from shoving my foot up this guy's ass, that's what. What are you doing about this? Have you reported him?'

'No, and I'm not going to either.'

The group exploded again and Bridget practically had to shout to be heard.

'Listen, all of you, or I'm leaving.'

They quieted down, but not one face was a happy one.

'I'm going to deal with this, trust me on that. But I can't expose Skyler and I'm not about to risk my own career. The president of the university is so deep in Whittier's pocket, I've got no one to tell anyway.'

Again, she held up a hand when they all started to speak at once.

'Listen, I'm not going to let him get away with this. And I damn sure am not giving in, but reporting him won't work.'

Evan, who now sat on the arm of Claire's chair, gave her a hard look and said, 'Don't do anything stupid, Bridget. You come to me if you need help, understand?'

'Oh, don't go all big brother on me, Evan. I'll be careful.'

'I will do as I please, Bridget, and count yourself lucky that's all you're getting from me.' He stroked Claire's hair and Bridget flushed a little, given her knowledge of their particular relationship. 'Does Connor know?'

She flushed even more. 'No, and I'd like to keep it that way.' At Evan's raised eyebrow she added, 'I don't want him worrying.'

'Uh-huh.' She could tell he didn't believe her, but she really didn't want to talk about her resistance to sharing certain things with Connor. It was still too early in their relationship and she had a right to take things slow.

'OK, Bridg.' Evan's dark eyes never wavered from her. 'I hope you know what you're doing. I wouldn't want you to fuck up a good thing.'

The double entendre was not lost on her.

'What can we do?' Claire asked Evan and Mona after Bridget had gone home.

'Nothing, sweetness.' Evan said. He'd grabbed a cup of coffee and was sitting with her and Mona. 'We have to let Bridget handle this as she sees fit.'

'I think there's more going on than she's saying,' Mona said, worry creasing her brow.

'I agree,' Evan said. 'I've known Bridget a long time and she doesn't let people in easily. Where her boss is concerned, I'm sure she'll work it out. It's this thing with Connor that's bothering me.'

'Why, baby?' Claire asked. She knew her husband was very protective where Bridget was concerned. She was like a little sister to him.

'Bridget doesn't let men get close. I heard her first comments about him. She's never said anything like that about anyone else she's dated, but yet she hasn't told him she's being harassed.'

'I'm not following,' Mona said, looking back and forth between the two.

'She has a man who she is really feeling, but she's keeping him at a distance,' Claire provided. 'So she's setting herself up for failure despite having the opportunity for a real relationship. *Finally.*'

'Exactly.' Evan nodded in agreement.

'Yeah, I see what you mean. Connor's great,' Mona said. 'He comes into the café regularly now and we chat. He's definitely into her.'

'I'm worried that Bridget is going to screw up because she holds herself too aloof and refuses to trust the people who've proven themselves worthy of being trusted.' He held up his hand as the women jumped to her defence, 'I know about her history and I'm not judging, but everyone has to let down their guard and trust sometime.'

Claire's heart squeezed when his eyes met hers. They would know. They'd both had to take a leap of faith and trust in each other to come together.

'If she doesn't tell Connor and he finds out, it might blow up in her face.'

'You really think so?' Mona asked.

'Yes, I do,' he replied. 'No man worth his salt wants something like that kept from him.'

'Bridget can take care of herself,' Mona protested.

'Of course she can,' Evan said, 'but as the man in her life, Connor has a right to know when she's being threatened by another man even if he stands back and lets her handle it. Right now, Bridget has introduced a secret into their relationship and secrets are poison.'

Claire knew he was right, but she also knew that nothing would move Bridget before she was ready.

'Shit,' Mona said.

'Exactly,' Claire and Evan said simultaneously.

Connor tossed his CleanSlate aside in exasperation. Normally, he was able to work his frustrations out through drawing, but tonight the subject of his drawing was his frustration.

Bridget's image stared out at him from the screen. It wasn't the drawing that was bothering him. It was the woman.

This past week had been an exercise in self-control. Not just in bed either. Being with her was like being just out of reach of a beautiful diamond. There was a distinct wall between them.

Whenever he tried to talk with her about her job, she always steered the conversation toward her students. She never spoke about her colleagues or her boss. He'd told her all about Sam and his co-workers. That's what people did. They talked about their day, about their lives. But Bridget doled out information in dribs and drabs and rarely volunteered anything that wasn't safe.

It made him feel like he was only getting what she wanted him to see rather than the whole picture and that didn't sit well with him at all. He wasn't one for secrets.

Add in the fact that she was still very controlled during sex and he was growing frustrated. It wasn't that she needed to let him tie her up and whip her – though his body tightened at the idea of her bound and helpless. No, sex was about vulnerability and connection, and she always felt just out of reach.

When they'd made love the second time, she'd been obviously uncomfortable any time he tried to push her even a little. It was enough to make a man want to forget the whole thing altogether.

He was a firm believer that how something started was how it ended and he didn't want to go any further with this wall between them. He understood that trust was earned, but part of earning that trust was taking risks and he felt like he was the only one doing that.

Sighing in frustration, Connor grabbed a Guinness out of the fridge. Sipping the brew, he almost tripped over Lotus, who'd followed close behind him. She nudged one of the drawers and, good master that he was, he fished her bone out for her. She grinned and wagged her tail, happily snatching it from him and flopping down on her bed to chew.

'At least one of us is happy,' he said to her before taking a long draw on his beer.

She looked up at him, a huge doggy grin on her face.

He laughed. Who could hold on to frustration in the face of that look? Picking up the CleanSlate again, he looked at his most recent portrait of Bridget. She was all he'd been drawing lately.

As if summoned by his thoughts, his phone rang and her picture popped up. Frustrated or not, he couldn't help but smile. He was falling for her. He knew it. He wasn't fighting it. But he felt alone in it.

Grabbing up his phone, he connected the call. 'Hey, gorgeous.'

Her sultry laugh through the phone had him wishing she was there where he could take her to bed.

'Hey yourself.' She sounded tired.

'Everything OK?'

'Yeah, tired. I'm about to go to bed, but I wanted to call you and give you my address.'

Connor sat bolt upright. This was so unexpected.

'Your address?' He was shocked. When he'd agreed to take things slow, he hadn't realised she'd make molasses look lightning-fast.

'Yes, sugar.' He could hear her smile. 'My address. Meet me here tomorrow night. OK?'

'Definitely.' He took down her address.

They chatted a bit more before signing off. Maybe things were turning around.

Chapter Sixteen

'Why are we here?' Bridget whispered, trying to draw Claire's attention, but not that of the other customers in the store.

Claire didn't appear to hear her. She was flipping through a rounder of bras as if they'd offended her in some fashion. The clink of hangers was enough to make Bridget flinch.

Something was off. Very off. Her friend, usually so open and charming, was so – she struggled to find the right word – so … tense. Like a rubber band pulled tight.

'Claire?' Bridget tried again.

Silence.

She didn't know what had spurred this impromptu shopping trip and she was beginning to feel uneasy.

When Claire had called, Bridget had been all too happy to skip her usual Saturday morning chores. A quick run with Daisy had satisfied the little pocket pit bull terrier and she'd left her happily snoozing while she went to meet her best friend.

She'd expected gossip and fun. Some light-hearted teasing about her upcoming date with Connor. She was getting eggshells and silence.

She'd hoped they'd hang out, window shop,

maybe go buy some maternity clothes for Claire now that she was starting to show. Instead they were at Intimate Moments.

Owned by Victor Matthews, a designer who'd made it big in New York only to walk away and come back to his home town, it was River Rock's answer to both Victoria's Secret and EdenFantasys.

In addition to exquisite lace and satin creations, many of which were personally designed by Victor, there was the "spice shop", where latex and neoprene joined satin corsets and other fetish gear. Those items were by request only, though.

In short, if you didn't know to ask, you didn't get to buy.

Claire knew to ask. In fact, Bridget had bought her first and only toy from Victor courtesy of Claire.

It had been one of Bridget's most embarrassing experiences. It didn't matter that Victor and Evan were friends and Evan gave him a thumbs-up as a great guy. It didn't matter that she was quite sure Claire had bought much racier stuff from Victor. Bridget had been tomato red from head to toe the whole time she and Claire had been browsing.

Victor had put her at ease with a kind word and some light teasing. She'd liked him at once. Despite his height – he had to be well over six feet tall – he was quite unimposing. Slight of build, though clearly well-muscled, tall and yet stooped in a way that made him seem shorter – he was a contradiction in terms. Right down to his clothing and appearance. He had to spend more time getting ready than Bridget did.

His raven-black locks were always immaculate, as were his clothes. There was never an errant crease or hair out of place.

As stereotypical as it was, Bridget thought he was gay. She'd never seen or even heard a rumour of him dating a woman. Evan was mum on the subject, saying it was Victor's business and to ask him if she was that curious.

She'd never been that rude. He was a gentle soul and she'd never insult him with such a prying question. She did wonder, though.

After that first trip, they'd become quite friendly. He never made her feel stupid for purchasing simple cotton rather than all the feminine frippery that seemed to be expected of women these days. He always tempted her with promises of custom designs if she'd try something different, but he acquiesced with grace and made her feel just as sexy in cotton as she was sure he did the other patrons of his shop.

When she and Claire had arrived, he'd given them bear hugs before excusing himself. He'd promised to be back for the show, leaving Bridget thoroughly confused when he'd said, 'And about time too.'

But Claire wasn't answering any questions. She'd just bolted to the back of store and begun assaulting the bras on the clearance rack.

Well, enough was enough. It was time for some answers.

She slipped the nightgown she'd been considering back on the rack and headed over to Claire.

With her hands on her hips, Bridget said, 'You gonna tell me what all this is about, darlin', or shall I leave you to continue abusing the merchandise?' She waved a hand at the rack in front of Claire. 'Frankly, I don't need any of this stuff and you don't seem to actually be shopping. Come on, sugar. Let's go get you some maternity clothes. It'll be fun.'

It was as if she melted. Claire went from strung tighter than a wire on a cinch to boneless and crying in Bridget's arms. Stunned, Bridget simply held her friend and let her cry. They were wordless sobs that nonetheless shouted with the intensity of her agony. Tears flowed down Bridget's cheeks in sympathy for the unknown pain her friend was experiencing.

Whatever it was, it ran deep.

After what seemed like an eternity, Claire's sobs turned to whimpers and finally sniffles and only then did Bridget realise that Victor had joined them and was holding them both.

She looked up at him with a raised eyebrow and he gave a silent shake of his head. Apparently, he had no more idea than she did what was going on.

'Claire, baby?' She wiped the tears from Claire's cheeks. 'Let's go sit down, sugar.'

Claire nodded, swiping at her cheeks. 'I'm sorry, guys.'

'No apologies, sweetheart.' Victor took her hand and led the way to the back, stopping to lock the door to the shop and turn the sign to "closed" on the way. 'Let's just get you some water and then you can tell us what's going on.'

Victor guided them back to his "showroom" – a small, elegantly appointed space in the back of the store. Sporting a huge, three-way mirror in front of an elevated platform, several comfortable chairs in cream leather, along with a plush sofa in brown suede and a wet bar, it reminded Bridget of a very classy runway. The idea, he'd explained to Bridget the first time she'd been invited back, was that people could use the space privately when they were interested in getting a second opinion on their selections. He also used it for fitting the custom pieces he designed for clients. At least according to Victor, it was a very popular feature of his store.

They flanked Claire on the sofa as if to protect her from some unknown threat. Victor held one hand; Bridget the other. Neither spoke. They simply waited.

Claire quietly wept, staring off into the distance with tears streaking her cheeks. She seemed fragile and small. Not at all the dynamic woman she had grown into over the last year.

'I lost the baby.'

A chill skittered down Bridget's spine at her words. So simple a sentence and yet such devastating repercussions.

'What happened?' Bridget choked out the words through her own tears.

Pulling her hands back, Claire swiped at her cheeks before clenching them into fists in her lap.

'They don't know.' Her words reverberated with bitterness. 'They said sometimes these things "just happen".' She stabbed the air as she formed the air quotes.

'Darlin, should you be in bed or something?' Bridget made to stand, but Claire put a restraining hand on her shoulder.

'No.' The crack in her voice could have shelled nuts. 'I couldn't spend another minute in bed, bleeding and questioning why. I had to get out.' Her voice wobbled on the last part.

While Bridget could understand the notion, she was still concerned for her friend's health. She looked to Victor for support, but he merely shrugged, clearly at a loss. The grief and shock on his face a testament to his care for Claire.

'Claire –' Bridget squeezed her hand '– I'm not sure that shopping is the way to deal with this.'

Claire snorted. 'I'm not stupid, Bridg. Evan and I talked all night. I'm sure we'll talk more. I'll cry more. I'll even rage at some point. No –' she shook her head '– this isn't retail therapy. We're here for you.'

'For me?' Bridget was taken aback. 'I don't understand.'

'Yes. You need to get rid of those things you call underwear and embrace your inner sexy. Especially now you and Connor are sleeping together. And –' she raised an eyebrow at Bridget '– don't give me that look. I'm not off my rocker because of the baby; I've wanted to do this for a very long time.' Her voice was watery, but she was less brittle. Bridget, however, was beginning to fall apart.

'You never said anything,' Bridget snapped.

'I love you, Bridg. I don't want to hurt your feelings, but this seems to go deeper than underwear and I want you to be happy.'

'But Connor is fine. He hasn't said anything.'

'Nor is he going to, Bridg.' She smirked. 'Do you really think he's going to say, "Bridget, as badly as I want into those panties, they are hideous and deflate my dick when I look at them"?'

Victor almost choked trying to hold back a laugh and Bridget shot him a warning look.

Claire continued, 'No, honey. He's just going to get you out of them as soon as possible.'

'There's nothing wrong with what I wear.' She barely got the words out as anger, completely out of proportion to the situation, overtook her. 'Victor, tell her,' she demanded.

He blanched at being drawn into their argument, but nevertheless leaned forward, a chagrined look on his face, and said, 'Claire's right. You are a beautiful, sexy woman and you hide behind all that boring, ugly cotton.'

Shock ran through Bridget at his betrayal. She'd always thought he understood. She began to argue, but he held up a hand to stop her. She bit her lip in frustration.

'I tell you what.' He stood up and smoothed his slacks. 'Try on what I've got put aside for you and if you still don't want it, so be it. If you love it, then you get a slew of sexy lingerie to drive that man wild. OK?'

He held out a hand to her. She stared at it as she struggled inside. She knew she was overreacting, but she didn't want to do it. Period. And she didn't appreciate them putting her back up against the wall like this.

This shouldn't even be an issue. It was none of their damned business in the first place! But what if Connor really was holding back? It's not as if she'd exactly been flexible. And he really had been going out of his way to accommodate her in so many things. Stirrings of guilt began in her gut.

'Please, Bridg.' Claire's face softened and she grabbed Bridget's hand. 'I'm honestly not trying to hurt you. But I don't like seeing what is obviously a scar from what happened. Besides, what harm is there in wearing something to turn Connor on? He'll appreciate it.'

Bridget remained rooted in the chair, paralysed with uncertainty.

'Bridget, look at me.' Claire's voice was soft, imploring. Bridget turned to face her and teared up at the concern in her face. 'You helped me more than you could ever know with Evan. I needed a friend as much as I needed him. Let me be the same kind of friend to you now. You may not like what I'm asking, but please, just try.'

Victor had never moved, his hand still offered. Before she could second-guess herself, she took it.

It was like looking in a fun house mirror. Her, but not her. Even before the rape, Bridget had never worn anything like this. It was as risqué as they came while still providing complete coverage. Emerald green silk and mesh covered her breasts. It was as much a camisole as a bra, with strategic support for her ample cleavage. The design gave the impression of being transparent, when in reality it was not. A shadow of nipple was apparent, but you couldn't actually see anything.

The panties – also the same deceptive material – were some kind of hybrid between boy shorts and a thong. She'd long ago quit following trends in ladies' underwear and had no idea what the term for them would be, but they were surprisingly comfortable given the fact that they were clearly up her rear end.

There was more where these came from. Victor

had handed her a pile of things to try. There had to be at least 20 sets, in a rainbow of colours.

Examining herself critically, Bridget tried to relax the muscles in her body that were clenched into knots. The problem definitely wasn't the fit. They melded to her body as if they'd been made especially for her.

No, it was that Bridget didn't recognise the pin-up girl in front of her. The woman in the mirror belonged in the ranks of Jean Harlow, Marilyn Monroe, and Marlene Dietrich. All of those classic women in satin and lace adored by the masses and tacked on walls around the country. They'd driven a whole generation of men mad with lust.

The thought made her sick. Literally.

Beads of sweat bloomed along her skin. She gripped the wall and did her best to breathe through the anxiety clawing up her chest.

'Bridget?' Victor's voice reached her through the fog. 'You coming out to show us?'

The Earth would change its orbit before she let them see her this way. No way, no how was she walking out there and putting herself on display.

Pins and needles were spreading across her flesh. She could no longer feel the wall under her palm. She felt lightheaded.

What was wrong with her? Panic choked her. She couldn't get the words out to tell Victor to go away.

The sounds of a key scraping in the lock echoed in the small dressing room and tears streamed down her cheeks at the knowledge that Victor would discover her this way.

Black dots floated in front of her face and the room began to recede. She was going to pass out.

'Bridget!' Victor's deep voice came to her from far away before strong hands gripped her shoulders and she felt herself enveloped in warmth as he sat on the chair in the corner and tucked her into his lap.

She sobbed into his shoulder. She had no idea why she was responding this way. It was just underwear, for heaven's sake. But she felt stripped bare and exposed despite being covered in more material than the average bathing suit.

Victor didn't say anything, just held her as she cried. Eventually, he began stroking her back and murmuring soothing noises.

As she wept, the panic receded. The numbness faded. Even her chest unclenched. Eventually, she was able to draw breath and speak.

'This is ridiculous. Could I be more foolish?' Her words were laced with bitterness.

'Why?' He seemed genuinely confused by her words.

'I'm sitting here blubbering like an idiot over nothing more than being dressed in sexy underwear.'

'Are you sure that's what this is about?' He tipped her chin up and began to wipe the tears from her face.

'What else would it be about?' She felt exhausted now. As if she could sleep in an instant.

'You'd have to tell me, honey, but I will say this. Whatever is going on, it's not about the lingerie.' His brown eyes peered knowingly into hers. 'It's about vulnerability. I know you have something traumatic in your past even if I don't know the specifics. All that grandmotherly cotton you wear, that's armour.'

Bridget felt something break open inside her at his words and once more tears flowed. She let them come. She couldn't have stopped them anyhow. She was just too tired.

She heard movement behind her and Victor saying something to Claire, who must have come to check on them. He obviously waved her off though, because when Bridget finally lifted her head, they were once again alone.

'I'm sorry, Victor,' she murmured as she attempted to right his collar which she'd soaked with her weeping.

'Don't be.' He grinned rakishly. 'I've fantasised about you in my lap dressed only in lingerie I designed for you.'

Her shock must have registered on her face because he laughed. It was a deep, masculine laugh that reached all the way to his eyes.

'Look, Bridget.' He tucked a loose strand of hair behind her ear. 'I know people assume that to be in my line of work, I must be gay, but I design lingerie because I adore women's bodies and find them sexy as hell. Yours in particular is amazing. I designed all of these just for you and have been waiting for you to be willing to try them on. I've even fantasised about being the one to take them off of you.'

She tensed and started to rise, but he stopped her with his next words.

'Don't fear me, Bridget. I'm human and you're a very desirable woman. I may have my fantasies about you, but I won't act on them. Two damaged people make for disastrous relationships.'

Her eyes snapped to his and she saw a depth of pain there she could relate to. She relaxed into his lap.

'Damaged?' She wanted to ask for details. The

pain she saw in his eyes was not the kind that came lightly, but she wasn't up to reciprocating and she'd be opening the door if she did.

'Yes, honey. You're not the only one '

She flinched, but he was right. She was being ridiculously self-centred.

'Ask yourself this … Is he worth a little discomfort and vulnerability? You hide behind your cotton armour and deny your femininity. Is that want you want to do with him?'

With a soft kiss on her forehead, Victor put her from his lap and left her alone.

His words zinged through her brain; shining light on shadows she'd long ago stopped paying attention to. When her mind settled down, Bridget began trying on the rest of the items he'd designed for her.

She took in the stranger in the mirror, wondering if Connor truly was worth exposing herself this way. How could she be certain? Or, better yet, was her self-respect worth it?

On that thought, Bridget put her own clothes back on. Neatly hung up all the items on their respective hangers and stepped out into the showroom. Claire and Victor were huddled together on the sofa in what appeared to be a very intense discussion. They stopped their whispering at her entrance and looked at her expectantly.

Walking over to Victor, she handed the entire lot back to him.

'I'll take them all.'

Turning, she left the room. She never saw the grins they exchanged and they didn't see her fear.

Chapter Seventeen

'I want you, Connor.' Warm hands stroked his chest and soft lips nipped at his ear. 'Now, baby.'

A shiver of anticipation trilled down his spine and his cock lengthened. Bridget's body was pressed against his back. Warm, pliant flesh moulded to his and sent his heart racing.

He'd wanted to hear those words from Bridget. To have her take the lead and drop her guard with him. To do more than allow him to make love to her, but to return the sentiment and let him know he was wanted too. He held his breath, afraid to move, afraid he'd wake up because surely he was dreaming.

He felt her shift and her hands stroked further down his body. His body flexed, rolling involuntarily as if magnetised by her touch. He lay still, letting her take the lead, enjoying her being the aggressor.

She gripped his cock, stroking firmly, as if she could draw his essence from him. She just might. The sensations were intense. His balls drew up tight against his body and he fought the urge to give in and spill himself right then.

Releasing him, she gently pushed against his shoulder until he was lying flat and then straddled him. She wasn't naked as he'd expected. Instead, she wore the sexiest underwear he'd ever seen. Lace and mesh were used strategically to hint at all her delicious places.

Her nipples were distended and fighting their lacy bonds. Her sex was covered in lace as well and his cock twitched as he imagined peeling those scraps of material from her body and feasting on the sweetly-scented flesh underneath.

Thank God she wasn't wearing those cotton cages she usually did. The aberration played at his mind and threatened to take him out of the moment. He fought it. If this was a dream, he'd be damned if he'd wake up now.

Slowly, she stroked along her sides and up her midriff to cup her breasts. With a single finger, she drew circles around her nipples. Her bottom lip was between her teeth and he couldn't figure out which he wanted to suck on more.

He growled low as she pulled first one strap and then the other down her shoulders before giving a little wiggle so all of that succulent flesh spilled out.

She moved to take the bra off and he stopped her with a hard shake of his head, 'Leave it on,' he demanded.

He'd fantasised about her like this. Wanton and sexy. Naked to a point, so that what little was covered only made what was exposed that much sexier. He couldn't believe how lucky he was that she'd finally trusted him this much. Finally, let herself go with him.

She squeezed her nipples and moaned, arching her body and letting her curls hang in a fiery riot down her back. He desperately needed to be inside her, but he didn't want to interrupt. Didn't want to disturb this *moment.*

For long, tortuous moments, he watched as she fondled her breasts, cupping and squeezing, tugging and pinching her nipples. His mouth watered with the need to suck on them.

'Stop teasing me, woman,' he growled, but he couldn't deny he liked it.

She chuckled and said in her smoky lilt, 'What're you gonna do about it, sugar?'

'Don't tempt me.' He could barely get the words out his dick was so hard and aching for her body.

'Or what?' She reached out, squeezing his nipple almost painfully before soothing it with her tongue.

She was definitely going to kill him.

'Or I just might turn the tables on you.' He almost hoped she made him show and prove. He wasn't disappointed.

'I think you need to put your money where your mouth is, darlin'.' She smiled at him in invitation.

He wasted no time flipping her over eliciting a surprised shriek as he pinned her down. Instantly, he tensed, waiting for the reprisal as he realised his mistake, but all she did was grin and wait to see what he'd do next.

Not willing to look a gift horse in the mouth, Connor reached into his side table and grabbed the soft, cotton rope he kept there. He tied her wrists loosely to ensure he didn't cut off her circulation before tying her wrists to the headboard. She could move, but she couldn't touch him.

'Is this OK? Are you in any pain?'

She shook her head, saying, 'I'm fine, Connor. I trust you.'

Those words reverberated through him. Her trust was exactly what he'd been trying so hard to earn. Her eyes were dark with desire and he wanted her so badly, but this was what he'd been waiting for. He wanted her to see what it could be like between them.

He wanted her to see that there was nothing wrong with liking sex a bit kinky. Or bondage, or even a bit of pain to add to the pleasure. The only thing that mattered was that both people had to want it.

'Good, you won't regret it.' His words were gruff, but he didn't stop to think about the emotions that coursed through him at the gift Bridget was giving him. He just knew he didn't want to mess this up.

Moving back, he lavished attention on her breasts, sucking, licking, biting and tugging. He ate up the sounds of her cries, her moans and whimpers.

Even as she screamed his name, he moved further down and tugged off her thong before diving between her legs. He devoured her flesh. He traced her nether lips with his tongue. She writhed beneath him, calling his name and begging him to finish her, but he wasn't nearly done.

Reaching once again for his drawer, he pulled out a particular favourite toy. The flogger was soft, meant to cause only the barest amount of pain. At the sight of it, Bridget's eyes went wide and flew to his.

'Connor?' There was no fear, only inquiry in her voice.

'Trust me?' he asked, his stomach tense at the possibility of her ending this.

Emerald-green eyes bored into his and he felt his heart melt when she said, 'Yes, baby. I trust you.'

'The word is "red" if you want me to stop, OK?'

She nodded and once again bit her lip. This time he leaned over and sucked it into his mouth before moving back.

He ran the flogger along her skin, not striking her at all. He just wanted to get her used to its presence. Goosebumps erupted along her body everywhere he touched.

'Still OK?' he asked.

'Yes.' She was breathing harder, but her face was calm.

He struck her breasts and she cried out. He didn't hit hard; the flogger was velvet. Designed to sting not harm. Streaks of red bloomed on her pale skin.

He stroked her skin, soothing it before reaching between her legs. She was soaked. He traced her clitoris; it was distended and swollen. She arched and moaned. He thrust his fingers into her pussy and she clenched around him.

He struck again. Her other breast this time. Again she cried out. He took up a rhythm, alternating between striking her breasts and fingering her pussy. Always checking to ensure she was OK and ready for more.

She went wild. Writhing and moaning, she cried out for "more" and "harder". It was everything he'd ever thought it could be between them.

He struck again, demanding, 'Come for me baby!'

She did.

Her inner walls rippled around his fingers as she screamed succumbing to her orgasm. She cried his name, whimpered and moaned wordlessly.

He couldn't wait another moment. Tossing the flogger aside, he threw her legs over his shoulders and plunged into her. She was hot and wet and enveloped him fully. He pounded deep grunting and hollering as her pussy sucked at him.

His climax rocked him as he cried her name. Holding deep, his body clenched in pained pleasure at the intensity. He'd never experienced satisfaction like it with any other woman. He never wanted to leave her body.

Releasing her wrists, he collapsed beside her and pulled her close. She whimpered and he stroked her back. He kissed her forehead, hoping beyond hope he hadn't pushed her too far. He had to let her know how he felt. 'Bridget, I lo –'

Hooooooooooooooooooonk!

The blare of the horn on the street outside yanked Connor from the dream. He fell out of his bed in a tangle of sheets. Sheets that were definitely going to need to be washed.

He hadn't had a wet dream since he was in his teens. His heart raced and he leaned back against his bed and took some deep breaths to calm down. That dream had been something else. It had been so real. It was exactly what he wanted their sex life to be.

Uninhibited. Raw.

But they weren't there yet; not even close. They were still tiptoeing around the problem and he had no real idea how to take them where they needed to be.

She had to want it. Want *him* that way, and so far she didn't. At least, not enough to take the risk.

With a sinking heart, Connor threw his sheets in the wash and went to take a shower.

181

Chapter Eighteen

Connor walked to Bridget's townhouse, all the while struggling to find some peace. His mind was full of possibilities and daydreams – erotic fantasies that lingered after that dream of his – and that wasn't his usual way.

But then he wasn't used to walking such a fine line with a woman either. Usually, the women he dated were just as eager as he was to jump into bed and explore the sensual aspects of sex outside of the accepted "norms". And they were just as eager to keep it light.

He was in uncharted territory with Bridget.

Connor was doing his best to be patient. The last thing he wanted was to scare her off, but he was finding it hard to hold back. He wanted no boundaries between them. He wanted to know that she was as committed as he was.

It was early days yet, and he wasn't the kind to fall so hard so fast. Hell, he wasn't even willing to use the "L" word at this point, but he already cared. That he could say for sure. He definitely wanted to see if they could make anything out of the chemistry between them. He wanted more than casual with Bridget. It surprised him, but he'd never been more sure of anything in his life.

He couldn't say the same of Bridget.

If he was a rock, she was like an ocean wave – unable to be pinned down. She flitted on the edges of their relationship; there but not fully present. It was as if there was a piece of the puzzle he just couldn't see and if he could see it, everything would finally make sense.

Her rape was an obvious obstacle. She had internalised that event in a way that had scarred her deeply and he was walking on eggshells around that. He couldn't just tie her up and spank her and say, 'There now do you see?' She had to want to go there with him. Had to give her consent and understand that anything two mature people consented to during sex was worthwhile in the communion and bond that it forged.

He'd heard all the arguments about "deviant and abnormal", etc., yawn, freaking etc. He wasn't a religious guy, but he honestly didn't believe that God set people up to fail. There were entirely too many people who had these urges and who had healthy relationships exploring them for it to be wrong. Consent was the key to everything. So long as you found someone who wanted to do it too, then it was all good in his book.

Bridget hadn't consented to what Trent had done to her. The fact that she'd experienced pleasure at any level had done a real number on her head. It was no different than children who were molested and found themselves unable to reconcile their natural sexual response with the betrayal of their innocence. They internalised and judged themselves just like Bridget was doing.

But that understanding did nothing to illuminate what he could do to get Bridget to face that fact. She had to *want* to understand it.

And therein lay the rub. He wasn't at all sure she wanted to. Oftentimes, it was much safer to stay in a box even if it was an uncomfortable or painful one. That she'd given him her address was a huge step, but it wasn't her physical safety that was at issue. She was smart enough to know it too.

No, it was her emotional safety that she had to be willing both to risk and to take responsibility for. So far, she'd done neither. She shared with him only to a point. She revealed nothing beyond the superficial. And she resisted all his efforts to take their sexual relationship beyond the traditional. The closest they'd come to "dark" was doggie style the last time they'd made love.

Connor was no psychotherapist and he damn sure wasn't in the business of saving people who didn't want to be saved. That was futile.

Bridget was different. She made him want more. Inspired him to reach farther, push harder than he ever had, and he wanted her to do the same. He didn't want to be in this alone.

That was what people who cared for one another did: pushed each other to reach outside themselves and be more. Together they could be synergistic; the sum more than the individual parts.

Connor snorted. Enough existentialism. It was going to be what it was.

Period.

Bridget stared at her reflection and wondered for the millionth time if she was doing the right thing. So far, everything with Connor had been going great. He'd lived up to everything he'd promised. He wasn't rushing her. He wasn't pressuring her in any way. In all things, he'd been a man of his word. So much so, that she'd called him up and volunteered her address.

In truth, she'd begun to feel guilty. He'd put himself out so much for her she'd felt like she had to give him something. He could be trusted. She believed that. And, she felt safe with him.

Well, physically safe at any rate. Emotionally … not so much. Which was why she still had a hard time opening up to him fully. Logically, she understood that if they were going to have a relationship, there should be no secrets, but Dean Whittier's harassment wasn't a secret really. It didn't have anything to do with their relationship. It was more of a private matter that she wanted to handle herself. Connor worked at the university too and she couldn't risk him doing something rash if he went all testosterone-male on her.

No, it was better this way. She would find a way to deal with the dean and leave Connor out of it.

They hadn't discussed her revelations about her rape again either, which suited her just fine. She still hadn't come to grips with everything Connor had said. If she'd been wrong all these years, where did that leave her now? How did she cope with the decisions and choices she'd made based on the premise that the rape was a punishment?

Her heart squeezed at the thought.

It was something she wasn't at all comfortable with, and until she was, she didn't want to discuss it. She and Connor were taking it slow. Very slow. And that was as it should be. They were getting to know each other and so far proving to be very compatible. Even sexually.

Well, she was at least. Connor, on the other hand, she wasn't so sure about. He'd seemed disappointed at one point the last time they'd had sex. He'd been playing with her breasts, frankly driving her out of her mind, and she'd almost lost it and asked him to spank her breasts. She'd reacted immediately and shut that down, taking his hands and moving them away from her nipples. She'd said they were too sensitive. Which was true.

Technically.

She just wasn't ready to put Connor's theory to the test. She'd gone for too long one way and she couldn't afford to be wrong. The consequences were too dire if she was.

She squared her shoulders. There. See. She was right to take this as slow as she was. That didn't mean she couldn't bend a little – for Connor's sake.

But not too much.

Which was exactly why she was in this particular dress. Connor hadn't said anything, and she was comfortable with what she wore, but she figured he'd appreciate the dress she had on. A creation of delicate gold silk, all the support she needed was built in, so no bra. She was uncomfortable as hell, but she wanted tonight to be special. To show Connor she was willing to take a step in the right direction even if it was just a baby step.

A final glance in the mirror said she was ready. Her hair was piled on top of her head in ringlets that framed her face. Light make-up accentuated her features and simple gold jewellery set off the peach undertones in her skin. A quick spritz of perfume and she was good to go.

Just as she set the bottle down on the dresser, the doorbell rang.

'Come on, Daisy,' she said to the pit bull terrier, who'd been lazing on the bed. 'It's time to rock his world.'

They walked the few blocks to Luna Bella, a local Italian restaurant in the trendy art district. The weather was warm. Perfect for strolling.

Connor looked amazing in all black. She'd always felt that men were sexiest when clothed in black from head to toe. She'd seriously considered persuading him to skip dinner when she'd seen him, but had decided against it. She didn't want to risk him thinking it was about her not wanting to spend his money.

It wasn't that she thought he couldn't afford to take her out; it was more that she didn't want him to feel obligated if by chance he really couldn't. She wasn't dating him for dinners at fancy restaurants. She was dating him because he was smart and passionate and because he moved her in ways that no other man had.

She may have only removed a few bricks in her wall, but no other man had even gotten that.

'You're quiet tonight.' Connor took her hand and tucked it into his elbow, bringing their bodies into closer contact.

'I was just thinking about how amazing you look. Black suits you.'

'It's good you feel that way, because I'm not going to be the only man who wants to eat you up in that dress.'

Bridget laughed and smiled up at him, only to shiver at the heat in his eyes. No one but Connor had ever looked at her like that. Like she was the sexiest thing he'd ever seen.

It made her tingle.

Connor turned to face her and whispered in her ear, 'What would you do if I took you into this alley right here, lifted that skirt, and feasted on you?'

Bridget couldn't speak as the erotic image tumbled through her mind. Her body went liquid and her breath hitched as desire coursed through her.

Connor slowly backed her up until they were standing just inside the alley entrance and her heart galloped at the idea that he might try to make good on his words.

She opened her mouth to protest but Connor covered her lips with his. Delving slowly into her mouth, his tongue danced and duelled with hers. It was a kiss full of eroticism and longing. He kissed her as if they had nothing better to do and he had all the time in the world.

One hand cupped her breast and the other her ass. He pulled her close so that his erection rested on her belly. Instinctively she rubbed against him. She was shocked to realise that she was very tempted to do exactly as he suggested. To lean up against the wall, raise her skirt, and press his mouth to her centre. To simply be wanton with him.

Connor took the decision from her. Breaking the kiss, he stepped away from her, smiling ruefully.

'As much as my mouth is watering for a taste of you –' he kissed her gently '– I'll not risk you being caught out here like that. There are too many people.'

As if on cue, a group of students out for the night walked by.

'Thank you.' It was a rasp, but that was all she could manage with her heart still racing.

He took her hand and kissed it before tucking it back into the crook of his elbow and continuing their stroll. Fortunately, they were only a block away from Luna Bella because she definitely needed a cold drink after that scorching.

Chapter Nineteen

Bridget watched as Connor pulled the hostess aside and slipped her what appeared to be a $50 bill. She smiled up at him and, with a quick grin in Bridget's direction, led them to a private booth near the kitchen at the back of the restaurant. The booth was round with high-backed seats that would afford seclusion from the other patrons of the crowded restaurant. A small thrill went through Bridget; whether in fear or anticipation she wasn't sure.

Connor's palm rested on her lower back and she felt the heat of his skin against hers. Simultaneously she regretted and thrilled at wearing such a daring dress for the evening. With her back bare, she felt every inch of his palm and her skin tingled with awareness. Arousal made her breasts heavy and achy and she was very lucky that the designer had made this stunning creation with attention to details like built-in support for ample breasts.

Connor took her wrap and handbag as she slid into the booth and then, rather than sit across from her as she'd expected, he slid in beside her. Registering her surprise, he just winked at her and smiled that crooked grin that melted her every single time.

The hostess began rattling off the specials, pulling

her awareness away from Connor, and she was grateful for the reprieve. She didn't really know how to handle his blatant regard for her or, frankly, her wanton response.

She wondered what Claire would say now. After all of Bridget's dramatics when they'd gone to buy lingerie, now here she was sporting nothing but a scrap of silk passing for a thong under this dress, a *bona fide* garter belt and stockings to boot, and feeling like the sexiest woman on earth. It helped that when Connor looked at her like he could eat her for dessert and still not be satisfied.

The image of Connor feasting on her body caused swirls of desire to fan out from her womb and she clenched. Her nipples tightened, and a flush spread along her skin. This dress may have support for a woman shaped like she did, but it was still silk; it didn't hide her aroused state from him. She could practically feel his eyes on her and her embarrassed flush deepened.

Avoiding his gaze, she ordered a glass of white wine and waited as Connor gave his own order for a Guinness stout. She wished she could run and hide until she calmed down.

'Bridget.'

His voice flowed over her, adding to her awareness of him, and her nipples went even tighter. The silk abraded the sensitive flesh and she had to fight not to squirm. She stared at the highly polished wood of the table top and simply ignored him. After her reaction to him in the alley, she was at a complete loss.

'Bridget. Look at me.' He reached out a finger and gently raised her chin so that their eyes met. His eyes, usually so light and laughing, were smoky and hot. They smouldered like the very ash they resembled.

'It's OK, sweetheart. Stop fighting it.'

Hot tears flooded her eyes and she blinked rapidly to clear them. There was no way she was going to cry in public and embarrass herself further.

'There is nothing OK about putting myself on display like a hussy.'

For the briefest moment, anger flashed across his face, but it was quickly stifled and his voice was gentle when he said, 'Being aroused is natural when you're with someone you're attracted to. When you're attracted to someone, it's also natural to act on it. Because of what happened to you, your signals are crossed now. That act has made you distrust yourself.'

'That's easy for you to say. You're not the one sitting here hot and bothered and on display for everyone to know it.'

'Really.' He drawled the word as he reached for her hand. Sliding closer to her, he placed her palm in his lap and she felt the steel of his erection under his slacks.

She instinctively squeezed and he groaned, but when she went to snatch her hand away, he held onto her, pressing her palm down around his cock. Leaning into her, he whispered, 'Stroke me.'

'Here!' She hissed the word, looking around to ensure no one was watching them.

He nodded again, whispering, 'No one can see us. Touch me, Bridget. Feel how much I want you right now.'

She hesitated, but only for a split second. She liked that he wanted her. Liked that she wasn't alone in her neediness. She was coiled tight and some part of her needed to connect with him and know she wasn't by herself in this.

She stroked him through his pants, enjoying the solid feel of him under her palm. The way he responded was dizzying; his body jumping under the cloth of his pants. His soft groans only spurred her on and she moved even closer, adding friction and pressure to her ministrations.

'That feels amazing, Bridg,' he groaned into her neck. 'I want you to do this again when there's no fabric between us. I want to see your hand, so tiny, wrapped around my cock and watch you jack me off.'

He groaned again as she squeezed, fascinated at the sounds he made, the images he projected into her mind, and the evidence of his desire for her right in front of her eyes. His hips were moving now and his breathing was harsh as she continued to stroke and rub his cock. His smoky eyes held hers and she watched the play of his features as they hardened in desire and need.

'It's your call, sweetheart. I'm at your mercy. Do you want me to come for you?'

She marvelled at his willingness to give her this power. They were in public, for God's sake. She was damn tempted to make him come. To watch him fall apart under her hands the way he made her fall apart and know she'd done it to him.

Instead, she leaned over and, for the first time since they'd met, she initiated a kiss. She brushed her lips over his, taking in the textures and the sweet, minty taste of his lips before delicately tracing them with her tongue. He opened to her readily and their

193

tongues began a lazy dance.

She brought her hands up to his chest, resting her palms on him and marvelling at the fierceness and tempo of his heartbeat. Her own was going a mile a minute. Connor didn't repeat his mistake of the picnic. His hands stayed away from her neck, though he turned to face her as he deepened the kiss. One hand rested on her hip and lightly stroked her in tandem to the rhythmic invasion of his tongue in her mouth.

Before she could protest again about being in public – not that she wanted to protest – Connor brushed his hand up along her midriff and cupped her breast, lightly massaging before squeezing her nipple. She gasped into his mouth and he gentled his touch, cupping her breast and stroking his thumb over the distended tip.

'Connor –' She broke the kiss, trying to marshal her thoughts though she had no real idea of what she wanted to say; she was awash in sensations.

'I want you.' He squeezed her nipple again. 'Bad. I want to fuck you tonight. We made love before and I want that too, but tonight … tonight I want to fuck you. I want you on your knees with my cock in your mouth. I want you on top of me, riding my dick like there's no tomorrow.' His hand left her breast and cupped her chin gently. 'You drive me crazy, Bridget.'

Overwhelmed and damn near panting, Bridget couldn't manage so much as a "damn, that was hot!"

Fortunately, she was saved from having to respond by their server showing up to take their order.

The janitor! She was screwing the fucking janitor!

194

The gall of that bitch. She'd fuck the janitor but she treated him like he was less than dirt under her shoes. Who the fuck did she think she was?

And who the fuck did he think he was? Whittier saw him just about every day. Emptying his trash. That was where he belonged, not reaching for what belonged to Dale. He had no right to put his hands on what was his.

Whittier threw back the scotch he'd previously been savouring and considered what he'd just seen. Luna Bella was not an establishment he usually frequented, but this was where the theatre's board had decided to hold their annual dinner. They'd rented a private room at the restaurant to which they'd all adjourned after the screening of a local filmmaker's documentary on homeless children.

Boring didn't quite cover the depth of distaste he had for both the board and their pretentious little pack of upstart creatives who all thought they were going to be the next Coppola. But he had a standing to uphold in this community. Appearances were important to his end game.

Luna Bella was across the street from the theatre, making it convenient. Personally, he found the food plebeian compared to what he was used to. He preferred Gia – River Rock's finest restaurant. Their chef had a Michelin star as well as a James Beard Award. His steak au poivre melted in your mouth. The best thing on the menu at Luna Bella was the Ossobuco, and that was like comparing a Rolls-Royce to a Lexus. No one would deny that the Lexus was a perfectly acceptable car, but it couldn't compare with the elegance and sheer magnificence of the Rolls.

By the time the food was finished, he'd grown claustrophobic from the hot air the board members were throwing around; each person's ego fighting for space. He'd followed the waitress who'd been tossing inviting glances his way. He'd figured he'd get her number and maybe even a quick one. She'd headed toward the kitchen and he'd followed. Anything to liven this night up.

Instead, he'd seen Bridget and the motherfucking janitor going at each other like rabbits. His hands had been all over her and hers had been between his legs. That bitch acted like she was so fucking pristine and here she was out in public acting like a total whore.

There was no way he was letting her off the hook now. He'd considered it. He hated that she looked at him with fear. Hated that he felt compelled to coerce and manipulate her. She, of all the women he'd dealt with, was the one he wanted to come to him freely. And, of all the women he'd dealt with, she was the one who rejected him out of hand.

No more. No fucking more.

He'd have her. He'd have her regardless of what she wanted.

He thought of her fighting him. Crying. Begging. Pleading. She'd be sublime in her pain.

His dick hardened.

'You know,' a soft voice whispered in his ear, 'I could help you with that.'

Whittier looked into the heavily made-up eyes of the waitress he'd followed before. She was staring at his erection, her eyes hot with lust.

The rest of the party was so engrossed in trying to one up each other that no one was paying any attention to them. He set his glass on the table and ran his hand up her stockinged leg. He cupped her ass under her skirt. Thong and garters. Easy access.

'Yes, you can.' He stood and gestured for her to lead the way.

Later, as he pounded into her from behind in the employee bathroom, he imagined she had red hair and green eyes.

She was going to kill him. Right there in the moment. He would die with the worst damn hard-on and everyone would know that he'd bought it trying to keep his hands off the sexiest woman he'd ever met. He knew he had to keep it together or he was going to wreck everything.

She'd finally trusted him enough to start breaking down her walls and he wasn't going to wreck it by behaving like an animal. He'd damn near jumped her in the restaurant, but fortunately he'd managed to stop himself. He still had to tread carefully with her. The barrier was falling, just a little, but it was a start.

He'd almost blown it in the alley. Literally and figuratively. He'd been ready to come then too. But going down on her in an alley was no way to get her to come to grips with her sexuality. It would read as sleazy even if it wasn't meant that way.

With her innate sexiness, she made it so hard for him to stay focused. All she had to do was speak in that low, silky drawl and his cock was standing at attention, begging for her lips to do something other than speak. He'd been serious, he'd been willing to come in his pants right there for her. Anything to keep her hands on him. He hadn't been able to keep from touching her at the restaurant and now, as they walked the few blocks from Luna Bella to her house, he couldn't keep his eyes off her.

The gold silk dress she wore clung to all the right spots, accentuating her full, soft curves. The stiletto heels added height and made her legs seem endless while giving a sway to her walk that mesmerised him. Tendrils of coppery hair floated around her neck despite the attempt to wrangle the curls on top of her head, and a single strand of pearls circled her neck. She was a fantasy. A pin-up mixed with Hollywood starlet, and if he thought he'd come away with both his balls intact, he'd press her up against the nearest wall, find out exactly what she had on under that silk, and bury his cock deep inside her. But you didn't treat a woman like Bridget with that kind of abandon. Not yet anyway. Her past required deference.

One day, if he handled this right, there'd be no barriers between them and their sexual relationship would be about exploration, not healing. Until then though, she had to be handled gently and with care.

Not that his dick gave a flying damn. He shuddered as it came to life at the thought of being inside Bridget. He didn't know how much longer he could keep his control so rigidly in check. Cold showers weren't cutting it any more. He loved the progress they'd made. Loved that she allowed him to make love to her, but tonight he wanted her in a way that cut through his control like a hot knife through butter.

'You haven't heard a word I've said, have you?' Bridget was smiling up at him. Her emerald eyes sparkled with mirth in the moonlight.

Rather than dissemble, he shook his head and said, 'Nope. I've been distracted.' He was surprised to find they were already at her porch.

'Darlin', that's obvious.' She smiled. The curve of her full lips riveted him. 'What's got you so deep in thought that my exposition on Daisy's latest hijinks isn't keeping your attention?'

Leaning against the railing of her steps, he pulled her to him, enveloping her in a gentle hug.

'You, Bridg. You have me distracted.' Tipping her chin up, he dropped a gentle kiss on her lips. 'I think I better go home, before I do something that I'll regret and you might resent.'

She gripped his lapels and held tight as she whispered against his lips, 'What makes you so sure I'm going to resent what you want to do?'

He pulled her in closer, resting her head on his chest while at the same time pushing his hips against hers so she couldn't miss his obvious arousal. He waited for her to tense and was surprised when she just melted further against him.

Plunging ahead, he said, 'That's why, Bridget. I don't think you're ready yet for how I'm feeling tonight and I'm not sure my control will hold tonight.

'I want you too badly. You feel too good. You look too good. You smell too good. And, dammit, I want inside you more than I want to breathe at the moment. But I'm not feeling gentle, Bridget. I want it rough and hard. And, baby, you need gentle. You need calm and considerate. We're still feeling our way through this and I don't know that I can give that to you tonight.' He took a deep, deep breath and set her away from him. 'So, I better go.'

Damp, green eyes searched his face for long moments before she turned away reaching for her key. What hope he'd had that she'd take him up on his offer crumbled to ashes. He watched her unlock each lock – the mechanisms that symbolised her scars as much as they protected her – and in that moment he wanted to rip to shreds the man who had so indelibly changed her.

The last lock clicked and she opened the door before turning to him, a tentative smile on her lips.

'Connor.' She held her hand out to him.

He took it in his, prepared to give her one last kiss and take his leave.

'I'm not made of glass, Connor. What I need is for you to treat me like a woman. Your woman. I trust you, baby.'

Gripping her hand tightly, Connor said, 'Be sure, Bridget. There's no going back once I start.'

Rather than speak she pulled him closer, raised up on her toes, and kissed him.

He didn't kiss her, he ravaged her mouth. And, for once, she melted into it. He nipped at her lower lip and sucked gently to eradicate the pain. He walked her backward into her foyer and kicked the door shut behind them.

'Locks,' she panted against his mouth and he broke the kiss long enough to slam all the locks tight.

Unwilling to wait, Bridget grabbed him by the jacket and pushed him up against the wall next to her door. She ripped the jacket off and tossed it aside, praying Daisy didn't decide to use it as a bed later.

As if summoned by the thought, the pit bull terrier

came out to greet them and simultaneously they hollered, 'Daisy, bed!' Daisy gave them a doggy huff and left in search of her bed, clearly not happy at being excluded, but the last thing Bridget wanted was an audience.

The interruption did nothing to quell the heat between them. It had been building in the time they'd been seeing each other. Growing hotter with each interlude as Connor slowly drew out her sensuality, reminding her she was a woman, not just a female with the requisite body parts. Now, the heat was too much. She might not want to jump off the ledge altogether, but she definitely wanted more than what they'd done the other times.

All of his teasing and play while they were out had left her with a gnawing need inside her. She wanted it satisfied. A plan he was clearly on board with, considering the way he looked at her. Her awareness of him, already heightened from their interlude at the restaurant, grew exponentially.

She could see the pulse at the base of his neck. It was fast and hard; his chest heaved and he all but panted even as his erection tented the cotton of his boxers. She could smell the woodsy, earthy scent of the soap he used and, as she stroked along his skin, she was convinced the small hairs on his body stood at attention. The chemistry between them made manifest.

In another first, she took the lead. Stroking his body, she watched his muscles ripple and flex, dancing under her fingers like he was the puppet to her master. He let her have her way for long minutes. Allowing her to trace his nipples with her fingers. To squeeze and pluck them before leaning in and licking gently, absorbing the feel of the flat discs under her tongue.

He groaned and leaned into her mouth. His hands he kept planted on the wall and her heart squeezed that, even in this moment, he was thinking of her.

It was time for her to think only of him. Time to give him what he gave her.

She sank to her knees in front of him and smiled as his eyes flickered in surprise. He began to reach for her, to pull her up, but she held up a hand and fended him off.

'Be still, Connor.'

With shaking fingers, she pulled down his boxers. Gripping him in her hand, she licked him and revelled in the moan she got in response. She licked him again and again, treating the silky flesh like an ice cream cone and growing more enthusiastic with each moan, each gasp and groan, until finally he stopped her, saying, 'Enough. I don't want to come in your mouth; I want to come in your pussy.'

His graphic words set her blood on fire and had her body clenching in all the right places. Moisture flooded her sex and her nipples were hard. She wanted more. She wanted everything he had to give.

That thought gave her pause. She couldn't lose herself completely. She might not recover. But she wasn't going to fail him tonight. Tonight they'd take another step.

Standing, she kicked off her heels and faced him. Reaching up, she slid the straps of her dress from her shoulders and let the silk pool at her feet. Clad in only her thong, garter, and stockings she waited, unsure of where to go from there.

'Jesus!' The look in his eyes seemed to scorch her everywhere his eyes trailed over her skin, leaving her feeling physically stroked, and she felt herself sway toward him.

He came for her then, stalking her like a big cat with prey in its sights. Rather than scare her, the leap in her heart and the catch in her breath were all about the need to be possessed by him. Even as she backed up, she wanted him to catch her, and catch her he did.

She could go no further as she felt her ass bump up against the table in the hallway she used for keys and mail. Turning, she thought to tease him by giving him her back; instead, she was brought up short by the sight of them in the mirror that hung over the table. It was so large, she could clearly see them both from the hips up.

He dwarfed her. His bronze skin unbroken in his nakedness. He stepped up behind her, pressing his erection into her ass as he reached around her and cupped her breasts. They were full and swollen with desire, her dusky nipples hard and distended.

His hands were large and still her breasts spilled out of them. His touch was electric as he squeezed her nipples. Zings of pleasure raced through her veins. She closed her eyes …

'Watch!' he demanded and nipped her shoulder.

She gasped and did as ordered. She watched as he cupped and massaged her breasts. She absorbed the sight of him pinching and tugging her nipples even as the pleasure threatened to overwhelm her. She took in the image of the two of them together, building in a crescendo of ecstasy as her sex swelled and pulsed with the need to be filled.

She pushed back against him, pressing her ass into his groin.

'Tell me what you want, sweetheart,' he demanded as he ripped her thong from her and kissed each cheek. Kneeling behind her, he tugged on one ankle and spread her legs.

Rising up behind her, he gripped her hips and growled, 'Look at you. You're so fucking gorgeous. You look like a woman waiting to be good and thoroughly fucked, Bridget. Your pretty breasts with your nipples so hard –' he plucked them as he spoke '– and your pussy, swollen and dripping, just waiting for me to fuck you.'

She flushed with embarrassment even as she felt her clitoris pulse with each graphic word he uttered. He groaned as she pushed against him again. Moving quickly, he snatched up his pants and grabbed a condom out of his wallet. After efficiently rolling it on, he repositioned himself behind her. His cock was rubbing along her slit and she wanted more, but she didn't think she could say the words.

Leaning into her, he whispered, 'Say it, Bridget. Say the words.'

'I want you, Connor.' She pushed against him again.

'Where, baby? Tell me where.' He stroked her slit with his shaft, parting the slick folds and teasing her with the lightest of pressure.

'In me, Connor. Please.' She all but growled at him; the tension in her belly was growing. Her skin felt tight and a light sheen of perspiration broke out along her skin.

'Tell me what I want to hear, Bridget. Tell me to fuck your sweet pussy. I want you to say it. Let your inhibitions go, baby.' His voice was rough, guttural, and she quivered at the urgency she heard in it.

She mewled in frustration. She wanted him inside her in a way she'd never experienced with any man. Especially since her rape. She closed her eyes and opened her mouth, but he stopped her.

'Uh-uh.' He pressed forward, the tip of his cock teasing her entrance. 'Look at me and give me the words. You have to own this, Bridget. Trust me.'

Understanding broke over her in that moment. He was right. She did have to own this act, this moment, these words. It was her body, it was her choice. She had to do more than hint and imply.

Meeting those beloved grey eyes in the mirror, she said, 'Fuck me, Connor. Fuck my pussy. Now.'

He pulled back and gently, oh-so-gently, he began to slide into her. Rocking in short, even strokes until finally he was fully seated. He gave her time to adjust to the light burn and stretch of him inside her.

She watched him in the mirror. The flex of his hips and the play of his stomach muscles was fascinating and seeing him moving inside her while feeling him pulse and ripple along her vaginal walls was almost surreal. She needed more though. She needed him to move. To possess her. To bring her to the completion she could feel hovering just outside her reach.

As if reading her mind, he began to move. His hands gripped her hips and he set up a slow, easy rhythm, pulling out almost completely and plunging back in.

Bridget stopped trying to catalogue her feelings

and simply went where they took her, demanding, 'Harder. I won't break!'

He gave her no resistance and fucked her harder, deeper. Cupping her breasts and tweaking her nipples until her own moans verged on screams. Every time she closed her eyes, he said, 'Watch!'

She marvelled at the sight they made. Her lips were swollen, as were her breasts. Her nipples were hard and berry-red from his play. They jutted proudly from her body even as her full breasts swung and jiggled with each impalement of Connor's cock.

Her hair tumbled down around her face and her eyes were sleepy with sex and lust. She looked like a woman in the throes of passion. Connor had the intent look of a man on a mission. His face was hard with lust and pleasure. He towered over her, making her feel both dominated and yet safer than she'd ever felt. Together they looked sexy and uninhibited.

As the image of them joined in passion seared itself onto her brain, he reached down and stroked her swollen clitoris, sending her into an orgasm the likes of which she'd never experienced. Pleasure pounded through her veins, burning through her, causing her to scream in agonised ecstasy. She felt Connor pound into her before finally holding deep, spilling himself inside her.

Her last thought before losing herself completely to the vortex of ecstasy he'd wrought upon her was that, just maybe, she was no longer broken.

Chapter Twenty

Bridget woke to the tantalizing aromas of breakfast and felt her heart squeeze. She couldn't remember any of her former boyfriends cooking for her.

Boyfriend! That thought drove the last vestiges of sleep right out of her mind. Is that how she was thinking of Connor now? It was definitely further along than she'd been intending so early in their association, but after last night, she couldn't deny her feelings went deeper than mere physical chemistry.

She rolled onto her back and stretched languidly. Her body still tingled and was luxuriously sore in all the right places. Connor had been perfect.

They had been perfect.

It had been so intense and rough, but she'd never crossed the line. She giggled in excitement at the realisation that she could actually have it all. A man with whom she could let down her guard enough to experience more than physical copulation and who didn't ask for more than she was willing to give.

But what was she giving him? She hadn't even told him about Whittier.

Doubt threatened to crush her glow and she shoved it away. She may have deepening feelings for Connor, but they'd made no promises or commitments to each other. She was entitled to her privacy.

Flipping onto her side, Bridget snuggled into the covers and inhaled Connor's scent from the sheets. Just the smell of him excited her. So much of this was new to her. Or at the very least, if it had been like this with Doug, she didn't remember.

Connor was fast becoming a human aphrodisiac. Seeing him, touching him, smelling him all made her want to take him straight to bed. Yes, she still slipped perilously close to the edge with him as well. He made her feel so secure. As if everything was acceptable, and she had to catch herself in those moments. It just wasn't worth the risk in her opinion.

Especially not now, when last night had proven they could have fantastic sex without delving into any of the areas that she was ashamed of.

She bit her lip and smiled as she remembered his reaction to Victor' creation. He'd definitely loved it, just as Claire had predicted. And if she remembered correctly, there was a sweet little purple teddy with matching panties hanging in her closet.

Connor would love that.

With a grin, she scrambled out of bed and went to dress for her man.

Connor grimaced as he scraped the burnt pancake off the griddle and into the trash. His mind wasn't where it should be. Rather than concentrating on cooking breakfast, his thoughts strayed back to last night.

He had no right to be frustrated. No right to be dissatisfied. But, damn it, her walls were still firmly in place. Sure, she was making an effort, but it was like getting a drop of water when you really needed a full cup. Rather than slaking your thirst, that drop only made you crave more.

His thirst had grown exponentially after last night.

They'd been right there. He could feel her desire for more. To go further. Deeper. Then, he'd felt her shut it down. He'd wanted to scream his frustration last night, but how fair would that have been when she'd already given more than she had before?

Every time they were together, it was like making love to her through a barrier of shrink wrap. He could feel her, see her, but not truly connect with her. It frustrated him beyond belief, especially because it was good between them. Real good. He should be content. But he wanted more. He wanted all of her. Not the neatly packaged Bridget she was giving him. He wanted her wild, down and dirty, and screaming his name as she demanded even more.

He took a deep, shuddering breath and willed himself to relax. It was too soon for that, but he was finding it harder and harder to refrain both from acting and from confronting her on it.

When he'd woken in bed next to her, he'd had an overwhelming need to fuck her blind. To do all the things he'd dreamed and fantasised about. His hands had literally itched to spank the creamy skin of her ass. He'd imagined putting clamps on her nipples and making her come while he tugged on them.

When temptation had morphed into desire, he'd gotten out of bed, determined to cook breakfast on the erroneous notion that the mundanity of the chore would dampen his lust while also serving as a nice surprise for Bridget. And it would have worked if he could have kept his mind off his fantasies.

They could be so good together if she would just –

Ah hell, Connor. You need to slow your roll, he told himself. You two are still getting to know each other. Relax.

With a deep sigh, he rolled his head on his neck to dispel the tension growing there and focused on cooking. Pancakes were his personal favourite and his gran's secret ingredient never failed to please.

A competent cook, Connor wrangled breakfast in no time and had just finished pouring coffee and assembling it all on a tray when Bridget entered the kitchen.

'Hey, back to bed,' he said over his shoulder. 'There's a reason it's called breakfast in b –'

He lost all thought as he turned and took in the sight of her. Quickly, lest he drop the tray, he thrust it back on the counter top.

Like last night, gone was the ugly cotton. Frankly, he hoped she'd burned it all. She wore a small, silk teddy in a purple so deep it could have been black. The neckline plunged, displaying a mouthwatering amount of cleavage. A wide satin ribbon wrapped around her ribs and tied tantalizingly between her breasts. Some sort of gauzy fabric in the same deep purple draped around her midriff and showed off her taut belly. Matching panties finished off the ensemble.

He was thunderstruck. His cock had no such issues, however, and rose to the occasion with no problems.

'Mornin', sugar.' She smiled wickedly. 'You're up early.' She giggled.

He had no idea if she was referring to him or his dick and he didn't care. She was standing there in invitation looking sexy as hell and all for him.

'It is now,' he growled as he stalked her. She made as if to run, but he grabbed her hand and pulled her over to the table where he lifted her onto it.

Despite his raging desire to push her limits, he reached deep for self-control and gently untied the bow. As the silk fell away, he licked and sucked on her nipples until she was moaning and arching into his mouth. The little sighs she made were all the encouragement he needed. He removed her panties and delved between her sensitive thighs, feasting on her.

Breakfast, and his darker fantasies, were forgotten as they lost themselves in the pure pleasure of one another.

Chapter Twenty-one

Skyler didn't know how much longer she could go on this way. She'd promised the professor she would not do anything rash, but she felt stained. Nothing she did removed the sense of tarnish crawling across her spirit.

It numbed her.

She peered through the grey light of dawn at Dale. He looked so innocent in sleep. The optical illusion was disorienting. To see him now, sprawled across his bed, one arm thrown carelessly over his head, snoring softly, you'd never suspect the evil depravity lurking behind those pale blue eyes. His brown sugar hair was tousled and he had a slight smile. He was stunning.

She'd gladly kill him as he lay there.

It wouldn't be hard. Snob that he was, all of his expensive kitchen knives were razor-sharp. She could easily grab that large one he was always using to chop vegetables.

It would slide easily between his ribs. She'd read that it only took two-and-a-half inches of blade to kill someone. That would more than do the job.

Or maybe just pick up that heavy iron lamp on the table next to the bed and beat him over the head with it. She bet it would be very satisfying to hear the crunch of that despicable brain crushing under its weight.

She wished she had a gun. She'd enjoy watching him cower as she pointed it at him. She wanted him to understand the nature of being helpless. Powerless. No longer in control of your fate. She wanted to see fear in his eyes and taste it on her tongue before she ended his evil once and for all.

Oh yes, Skyler understood the nature of murder now. It was about control; taking it back in a way that was permanent and undeniable. Killing Dale would ensure he never harmed her or anyone else again.

It would be messy, though. Lots of blood. Too much evidence. Her fingerprints were everywhere. She'd be caught. Her baby would be taken from her.

He wasn't worth that. She sighed as the cloying feeling of desolation settled in her chest. Knowing she wouldn't act didn't stop her from fantasising. It was the only thing getting her through the nights with him.

He continued to use her. Continued to hold her scholarship over her head. She had told him she'd gotten the abortion but that had only bought her two weeks to "heal". He hadn't wanted to touch her when she'd said she was bleeding.

Fortunately, she wasn't showing yet. But she only had about a month before she would be and she didn't trust what he would do to her when he found out.

The professor had promised they'd expose him before then, but so far Skyler didn't see a plan coming together and she didn't know if she could continue to play this role with him.

She cringed at his touch. Something he seemed to

213

enjoy. The bastard. He'd grown rougher too and she feared for the baby if he truly hurt her. Last night had been particularly bad. She was still sore and it was painful to sit.

Oh, to turn the tables on him and give him a taste of his own medicine. She smiled at the thought.

'What are you doing over there?' Dale's voice, rough with sleep, startled her out of her fantasies.

'Just thinking,' she said, gripping the arms of the easy chair she sat in as her belly cramped and twisted.

'About what?' He sat up and turned on the light, blinding her momentarily.

Squinting into the light, she told him, 'You.' She figured honesty was easier than lying.

He grunted and threw back the covers before walking naked into the bathroom. She stayed where she was and contemplated the feasibility of making a run for it as the sounds of the toilet flushing and water running filtered out of the bathroom.

She wanted to run. To throw on her clothes and get the hell out of there, but she knew better.

He stepped back into the room, his dick already semi-hard. A crawling sensation erupted over her skin but she suppressed a shudder.

She bit her lip to fight the tears welling behind her eyes. She couldn't keep doing this.

'Come here, Skyler.' Dale patted the bed before gripping his dick and squeezing. 'Put that smart little mouth of yours to use.'

Nausea rolled over her, but she fought it. Kneeling between his legs, she took his dick in her mouth, being careful to remember everything he'd taught her.

Only the fantasy of his downfall sustained her

though this now familiar violation.

'Professor, I'm going to lose it if we don't figure out something soon.'

Bridget heard the desperation in Skyler's voice and her stomach clenched. She'd been wracking her brain for a solution, but she remained stumped.

The end of the semester was next week and her tenure review would come the following week. They needed a plan. Now.

'What about tape? Do you think you could get him on tape?' She was spit-balling here but she needed to keep Skyler engaged.

Skyler snorted.

'I'm no longer allowed to visit his office. He won't "risk a scene".' Bridget could hear the air quotes as Skyler's tone changed. She sighed and continued in a strained voice. 'And, frankly, he has me naked within minutes when I get to his house. He takes my purse. I don't see how I could manage that.'

Bridget had to forcibly relax her grip on her phone. The rage that flooded her at the cruelty Whittier was committing sickened her.

'Skyler.' She plunged forward, not really thinking, just knowing she had to get her away from the man. 'You're going to come and stay with me. I'll get your work and arrange with your other professors to proctor your finals, but you're not spending one more moment where he can get to you.'

She paused, waiting for a response, but all she heard were sobs.

'Skyler?'

More weeping.

'Sugar, talk to me.' Tears welled in her own eyes.

Skyler just continued to sob for several minutes, eventually subsiding into sniffles.

'Thank you, Professor.' She practically wailed the words.

'Skyler, I promise you we'll solve this.' Bridget forced herself to relax and project confidence despite the doubt twisting her gut.

'I know, Professor.' She didn't sound confident.

'Listen, pack your clothes and whatever you need. OK?' Bridget checked her watch. 'What time do you think you'll be ready?'

They quickly agreed on a time to meet and Bridget gave her the address.

Ending the call, she took several deep breaths and considered praying.

'What was that about?'

Connor's voice rang out in the stillness of his loft, startling her so that she dropped her phone.

She slid to her knees as much to avoid looking at him as to get the phone.

'One of my students is being harassed.' She decided that the truth, even if partial, was better than lying. 'I'm having her stay with me for a while.'

She wasn't telling him everything. He could feel it in his gut. See it in the way that she wouldn't truly meet his eyes.

Stop it, he told himself. You're being paranoid.

Connor pulled the T-shirt he was carrying over his head and took a deep breath to calm down. His frustration was getting harder and harder to contain with Bridget. It was obvious she wasn't telling him everything.

Talking with her was a lot like trying to trap a drop of water. She rolled and moved every time he tried to pin her down. The messed-up thing was that he couldn't pinpoint why he really felt this way. So far everything she'd ever said to him was borne out. She lived up to her word and kept her promises.

It was true that their sex life hadn't progressed the way he'd hoped, but the sex was still really good. He just wanted more, and felt like an ass for not being satisfied. She was beautiful. Sexy. She wanted to please him and he felt certain she *was* trying. It was just that he felt a wall.

Some inexplicable barrier that he could feel, but couldn't see. It was always there. Even now.

'Who's harassing her?' He scrutinised her face. There were fine lines of stress around her eyes and she was practically wringing her hands.

'My boss.' She tossed her phone on the coffee table and sat on the sofa. Daisy came over and sat next to her. Lotus barely twitched on her bed.

Bridget absently rubbed her dog's head as she continued. 'Apparently, he's been at it for a while and now she's pregnant.' He saw tears in her eyes. 'She came to me for help and I'm still trying to figure out how to help her in a fashion that will allow her to keep her scholarship.'

'What does her scholarship have to do with this?'

'He's holding it over her head. He's the dean of my department and he's threatening to fail her.'

'Damn, that bites.' He sat next to her and took her hand. One thing that he enjoyed about her was how much she cared about her students. 'Do you have any ideas?'

'No, not a one,' she said and squeezed his hand. 'I need to find a way to expose him that can't be disputed while not putting Skyler or –' She jumped a little and bit her lip.

'What?' he brought her hand to his lips and kissed the soft skin. Tension tightened his chest. He felt certain she wasn't telling him everything.

Anger surged, bright and hot, but he fought it. Something was not right and it was driving him crazy, but he had no grounds to call her out without making himself look like a completely insecure dick.

'Nothing.' She leaned in and kissed him gently. 'I just had a moment of inspiration. I think I know what I'm going to do.'

'Care to share?'

'Not yet. I need to think it through more.'

She smiled at him and straddled his lap, taking his face between her hands and kissing him thoroughly. She still only rarely initiated any sexual encounter between them and he should be thrilled. In this instant, he felt manipulated.

Too bad his dick had no issue with that. He was hard and ready. Just like he always was when it came to Bridget. He wanted to fling her over his shoulder and give her a good spanking for so obviously holding back.

What was it going to take for her to understand that they couldn't go any further if she didn't truly open up to him? Some days he didn't think he could rein in his frustration. He worried his temper would get the better of him. He was an easy-going guy in general, but she was kryptonite to his self-control.

She reached between them and cupped his bulge, pulling his mind away from his ruminations. Lust flowed through him and he knew he wasn't going to stop just as he knew he wasn't going to pressure her.

He loved her too much.

The knowledge that he loved her should have been a relief; instead, his eyes burned and he felt as if he were even further away from her. Reaching up, he gently gripped her head and deepened the kiss, slowly taking control. He stood, wrapping her legs around his waist, and walked over to the bed where he proceeded to show her as carnally as possible exactly how he felt.

As he buried himself gently inside her, he did his best to pretend he didn't feel his hope slowly draining away.

Chapter Twenty-two

'That should do it.' Nico handed Bridget her bag and
flashed his dimples at her. 'You're finally joining the
rest of us in the 21st century, huh, Professor.'

Bridget grinned back at her former student. 'You
always were a smartass, weren't you.'

'True –' the dimples deepened '– but I was also
your best student.'

'That you were.' She settled her purchases on her
arm, doing her best to quiet the adrenaline rush
pulsing in her veins at the realisation that she was
about to put something in motion that she wouldn't be
able to take back once it was done.

'How are Gina and the baby doing?'

His face, usually so angular and austere, softened
at the mention of his wife and newborn daughter. The
flash of jealousy Bridget felt shamed her. No matter
how hard she tried, she could never fully accept the
knowledge that she'd never be a mother.

'They're great. We're not getting much sleep yet,
but Cara is amazing. And Gina, she was born to be a
mother.'

'Oh Nico.' She gripped his forearm, 'I'm so happy
for you.' She was pleased to see she meant it.

'Thanks, Prof.' He walked with her over to the

door. 'Listen, do you need any help setting everything up?'

Bridget shook her head. 'Nope.' She adjusted the strap of her purse on her shoulder and pushed open the door, saying over her shoulder, 'I'm sure I can figure it all out.'

'OK then.' He nodded at the customers who walked in as Bridget left. 'Feel free to call me if you have any questions.'

'Will do, sugar,' she called out as she waved goodbye. She wouldn't, though. She wasn't going to involve him any more than she already had.

Bridget strolled down Main Street to her Mustang doing her best to be discreet. She didn't want to see anyone she knew, especially Evan, who should be at Bibliophile right now.

Yup, there he was. She ducked into the natural grocery across the street and waited for him to finish whatever he was doing to the display in his front window. As she watched, Claire entered the store. In the instant he noticed his wife, he was transformed. His focus lasered in on her and he took her in his arms and kissed her as if she were the breath in his chest.

When he released her, Claire smiled, but her face lacked its usual sparkle. She looked drawn and pale. Bridget's heart squeezed to see her friend in such obvious pain. Still, the love she and Evan shared was plain to see. She hoped to have that herself one day. Connor's face flashed through her mind. She smiled. There were definite possibilities there. As long as she handled this ugly business first. She wanted to be able to focus on Connor and she couldn't do that with

Whittier breathing down her neck.

She'd almost spilled the beans about it all to Connor that morning, but something had stopped her. On one level, she understood that she really had no good reason to keep this from him. But, on the other hand, she felt as if she needed to keep this to herself.

He kept her so off balance she needed to feel as if she had complete control in one area of her life.

Didn't she?

A horn blared, startling her out of her thoughts. She peered through the grocer's display window to ensure that Claire and Evan were gone. The coast was clear so she hot-footed it over to her car. There were plans to be made. Stashing her packages in the trunk, she headed home to tell Skyler what they were going to do.

'You're sure about this?' Skyler furiously twirled a lock of her ponytail around her fingers.

'As I can be.' Bridget sipped the sweet tea she'd poured for them as they talked. 'Obviously, I've never done this before and there is some risk.'

'Ya think?' Skyler smirked before tossing back her own tea as if it were something much stronger.

Bridget reached across the table and took her hand, giving it a gentle squeeze.

'You don't have to do this. We could report him to the authorities. Or I could be the one to do it.'

Skyler squeezed Bridget's hand hard, but shook her head. 'No, if you do it, it will be too easy to claim you set him up. Me, though, once I tell him I kept the baby, he'll lose it. His reaction will be too over the top for anyone to protect him.'

A tremor ran through Skyler and Bridget wanted to wrap her up and protect her from all this ugliness.

'How are you doing, sugar?' She released Skyler's hand and began clearing the dinner dishes from the table.

'OK, I guess.' She joined Bridget at the sink and began drying the dishes as Bridget washed them. 'I still haven't told anyone yet. I don't want to burden my parents with this when I still don't know what's going to happen with Dale.'

'That's understandable.'

Bridget wanted to say so much more, but what could she really say? Skyler needed her support more than she needed a lecture. Besides, a small worm of censure was wriggling up Bridget's spine at the hypocrisy of advising Skyler on total disclosure when she wasn't telling Connor everything.

'Professor?'

'Hmm?'

Bridget wrung out the sponge and joined Skyler in putting the dishes in the cabinet.

'Thank you for this.' Her voice broke and Bridget took the cup from her hands and set it on the counter before enveloping her in a hug.

'Of course, sugar. You can stay here as long as you like.'

Skyler sniffled and pulled away, shaking her head. 'I couldn't do that. You don't need a single mom and a newborn here.'

'Skyler.' Bridget's voice was firm. 'Sit down for a second.' She pointed at the table.

Skyler raised an eyebrow, but sat nevertheless.

'I'm going to tell you something I've never told

anyone.' That eyebrow shot even higher, but she waited for Bridget to continue. 'I can't have children. Well, I guess the more accurate phrase is it's highly unlikely I'll ever carry a child to term. Complications during an abortion left me with too much scar tissue, and even if I ever manage to conceive, I'll likely not be able to carry it.'

Skyler started to speak, but Bridget waved her off.

'My circumstances were a little different than yours in that I was raped. That's how I conceived.'

Shock and anger replaced the sympathy that had been welling in Skyler's face, but Bridget just squeezed her hand.

'It was a long time ago, don't worry about it.' Taking a deep breath, she continued, 'I had an allergic reaction to the anaesthesia and had a seizure. The end result is … I'll never be a mother. I also had no one to turn to. My parents, while they love me, would not have handled the knowledge of the rape well, let alone the abortion. They'd have demanded I kept it and I wasn't willing to do that.'

She sighed and rubbed the bridge of her nose, 'Look, hon, I'm not trying to burden you with my past, I'm simply trying to give you context to understand that when I say you can stay here as long as you need, I mean it. You contribute as you can, but you have a safe place here – for you and the baby – as long as you need it.'

Skyler stared at Bridget for several moments before bursting into sobs. Hard, gut-wrenching sobs.

'Honey.' Bridget moved over to put an arm around her shoulders. 'Shh,' she murmured soothingly. Soon, Skyler settled enough to splash cold water on her face.

Turning, she said, 'Thank you, Professor.' She grabbed Bridget and hugged her fiercely.

Laughing as she struggled to catch her breath, Bridget hugged her back and said, 'Call me, Bridget, hon. I think we're past Professor.'

Chapter Twenty-three

Connor's skin flamed as he pushed open the door to Intimate Moments. He had to be going over the edge to be doing this but he was rapidly reaching the end of his patience with Bridget. On that thought, he spun on his heel to leave. He was being an ass. It wasn't as if she didn't have valid reasons for the things she did. That he didn't agree with her take on what had happened didn't give him the right to push her too far too quickly. It had only been a couple of months, after all. It's not like they were talking years or anything.

On the other hand, when was the timing ever going to be right? The longer he let her go on without pushing the envelope, the more comfortable she was going to get in her shell with him. It would only make things worse the longer he went without confronting her and trying to take them forward in their sexual relationship.

He spun again and advanced into the store, only to stop short once more.

What if he was wrong? What if she was doing what was best for her and he screwed everything up by being selfish? Was he being selfish? Thinking only with his dick?

He spun again and headed back toward the door.

He needed to think this through.

'Perhaps I can help you, or would you prefer to continue turning in circles?' A large man with a curious smile on his face stepped into the showroom where Connor was. Definitely not who Connor would have expected to work here.

'Do you work here?' Connor's face flamed again. He was seriously out of his element in this store. While he'd had some toys over the years, he'd never walked into a store before. He'd always done the online, brown paper wrapper deal.

'You could say that.' He held out a hand to shake as he walked over to Connor. 'I'm Victor. The owner. And you, brother, look utterly confused.'

Connor chuckled helplessly. That was a definite understatement.

'Yeah, you could say that.' He ran a hand through his hair, took a deep breath, and sighed.

'Female trouble? Do you need a sexy apology?'

'What?' It took a second for his words to register. 'Oh!' He flushed deeper. 'No. Nothing like that. I was, uh, I was thinking about getting some toys for my lady.'

Victor's eyes crinkled as he grinned.

'Have you ever done any in-person shopping for toys before?'

'Nope, strictly online, but I want to be very careful in what I get so I wanted to see everything in person first this time.'

'Makes sense.' Victor turned and waved Connor toward the back of the store. 'My playroom is in the back. Come on in and we'll see what we can do for you.'

A little nonplussed at picking out toys with this guy in tow, Connor just shrugged.

'It's OK, brother. You're not the first guy to do this and I've probably heard and seen it all. Just pretend I'm a sexy female.'

Connor burst out laughing at that. This guy, while definitely a bit on the metrosexual side, was as close to resembling a female as a tiger was to a bear.

Victor smiled, 'Works every time. Come on, let's get you hooked up.'

Connor followed him to the back and entered a room the likes of which he'd never seen before. Unlike the rest of the store, which was done in elegant shades of taupe, silver, and robin's egg blue, this room was much grittier, with shades of rich purple adorning the walls and lots of white, black, and orange to offset it. The vibe was raw and dark.

The walls were lined with shelves holding all manner of toys, lotions, and creams. On one side there were rounders full of latex, vinyl, and neoprene. On the other, corsets and other lacy creations that left nothing to the imagination were available. Whips and ropes and other bondage accessories draped an entire wall and a swing of some kind hung in the corner. Connor wondered if anyone had ever asked for a test run on that thing.

'Yes.' Victor broke into Connor's thoughts.

'Huh?'

'Yes, people ask to try it out.' Victor nodded in the direction of the swing. 'My answer is only with your clothes on and still zipped.'

He laughed at Connor's stunned expression.

'Dude, I don't read minds, but your eyebrow shot

upward and you were staring at the swing. One plus one equalled two is all.'

Connor laughed nervously again. He needed to get a grip on himself. He was being foolish. It's not like he was some green teenager buying his first box of condoms from the local drugstore.

'So, what is it you had in mind? Lingerie? Dildos? Vibes?'

Connor flushed again, but choked out, 'A vibrator for sure. Maybe a flogger. And some restraints, but something really easy and soft.'

'A beginner?'

'No, but a very hesitant former practitioner.' He wasn't really comfortable explaining his situation, but he needed to make sure he got the right products. 'I've heard about those wands. Do you sell those?' He wanted to keep this conversation moving forward.

'Why hesitant?' Victor cocked his head and quirked an eyebrow but didn't answer Connor's question.

'She's got some trauma in her past; she associates it to the bondage and other kinky stuff she did. She's blaming it.' As he spoke, he felt himself loosening up. He hadn't had anyone he could talk to about this.

The expression on Victor's face changed from curiosity to a focused intensity that made Connor almost take a step back.

'What is your name?' His eyes narrowed slightly.

'Connor. Why?' He forced himself to stand where he was, but seriously considered taking a cane out of the stand beside him and arming himself.

'You're Bridget's Connor, aren't you?'

Connor scowled. What the hell was going on here?

'How the hell do you know that?'

Victor smiled, and held up his hands in a gesture of supplication. 'Calm down. There's nothing to worry about. Bridget is a customer and a friend. She was in here with Claire the other day and she recently acquired quite a few pieces from my collection. If she heeded my advice at all, you should have seen some of them, I hope.'

Connor's mind flashed back to the lingerie that Bridget had been wearing recently and he grinned. Her willingness to take that step had played a role in his coming here today. He'd figured if she was willing to put her toe in the water, maybe he could get her to dip in a bit further.

'I'll take that satisfied grin as a yes.' Victor smiled briefly before turning serious. 'If you're planning on using these toys on her, you'll need to be prepared for resistance. She's got some pretty deep baggage.'

'You know about the rape, then?' Connor blurted, but the shock that passed over Victor's face said he hadn't. Connor scowled.

'Look, I knew she'd had some kind of trauma, I just didn't know the specifics. Don't worry. I won't say anything.' Victor closed his eyes briefly before saying, 'Why don't you come sit and talk with me for a minute? Then we'll figure out what to do about toys for Bridget, OK. I don't want to do anything that might make things harder for the both of you.'

Connor felt the knot in his chest uncoil as he followed Victor into an elegantly appointed office and workroom. Dominating the room was a drafting table covered in sketches and one of those stand-up forms that looked like a woman's torso pinned with different fabrics. Various combinations of lingere hung on the walls. In the back corner, there was a tidy desk sporting a laptop and phone along with some very comfortable looking leather chairs. It was an orderly oasis in the storm of creativity.

'You want some coffee or something?' Victor seated himself behind his desk and gestured toward the coffee pot on a small table behind him.

'No, thanks.' Connor settled in a chair and waited as Victor poured a cup.

'You know, I've been trying for years to get her to buy something other than that hideous cotton she wears and it wasn't until you came along that she was even willing to consider it.'

Connor just raised an eyebrow, but he'd be lying if he didn't admit to the warm and fuzzy that knowledge gave him.

'That being said, she damn near broke down just trying that stuff on and it took a hard conversation to get her to even consider actually taking it home.'

'Her scars run deep.'

Victor snorted. 'That's an understatement.' He took a swig of his coffee, winced at the apparent heat, and set the cup down before meeting Connor's eyes. 'What is it you're really trying to do here, and are you serious when it comes to Bridget? Because frankly, my man, if you're not, you'd be better off leaving this little avenue alone. She doesn't need her head fucked with.'

It was Connor's turn to really scrutinise Victor. He had to give the guy respect, though. The concern in his face was clear and there wasn't a trace of jealousy. By objective measures, he was sincerely concerned

231

for Bridget's wellbeing, and that gave him points in Connor's book.

'Dude, I don't know you from a can of paint, so I don't really owe you an explanation. But I care about Bridget, and from what I can see so do you, so I'll give –' Leaning forward, he began to talk with Victor about all of his frustrations and desires for his relationship with Bridget.

He spilled his guts, not bothering to reflect on the fact that he was sharing some of his deepest thoughts with a complete stranger. He needed someone else to talk with about this.

'The thing that's killing me here is that I feel like she's holding back about something beyond her sexual desires. But for the life of me, I can't figure out what it is. We talk all the time, spend tons of time together, and still I feel like there's this wall. I guess I think that if I can keep us moving forward in bed, that the rest will fall into place too.'

'I understand what you're trying to do, but are you prepared for what might happen if she fights you?'

Connor blanched. He really tried not to think about that.

'I've thought about it. I don't want to lose her. She's the best thing to happen to me in for ever, but I feel like we're not really together either. I mean, if we can't meet in the middle here, if I can't know that we're truly together, then it's probably better if we end things now.'

Victor sighed. 'I hear you. I hope this doesn't go that way. Bridget needs to get out of her head. She's letting this hold her back and she seems to have a good thing going with you.'

'I hope so, but I'm definitely feeling my way in the dark here.'

'Well, let's get you some help with what you can feel in the dark.'

Connor laughed, 'Dude, that was awful.'

Victor grinned. 'I know, but hell, I own the shop. I can crack bad jokes if I want to.'

Connor just shook his head and followed Victor into the playroom. A few strategic selections later, he headed back out onto Main Street full of plans for their upcoming evening together.

'Have you thought about our conversation about your rape?'

Bridget went rigid at his words and Connor wanted to kick his own ass. So much for planning how to broach this topic. Instead of his carefully planned words, he'd just blurted out something careless.

With a deep sigh, he set his beer down on the coffee table and took Bridget's hand.

'Listen, I apologise. I didn't intend to blurt that out like I did. I actually had some carefully thought out, sensitive words planned.' He grinned, hoping to lighten the suddenly gloomy mood. 'But obviously, my mouth got ahead of my brain.'

She smiled, but remained wary.

'What is it you really want to talk about?' Bridget leaned back, turning to face him and gripping one of the sofa pillows like a shield.

After his trip to Intimate Moments, Connor had been searching for the right time to broach this topic. While he had promised to give her as much time as she needed, it was becoming pretty clear that she wasn't going to bring it up.

He'd prepared several of his purchases in the hopes of taking their sex life to the next level. Part of him felt like a greedy bastard to do it, but another part felt like it was critical that Bridget shed her notions of shame around her desires if they were ever truly going to be together. He wasn't ashamed of his desires. He didn't want her to be.

Connor raked a hand through his hair. Suddenly, the wisdom of this conversation no longer seemed clear.

'I was curious if you'd put any more thought into the idea that your rape was not, in fact, punishment for enjoying kinky sex.'

'I've thought about it.' She picked at the trim of the pillow rather than look at him.

Frustration took root in his belly, but he clamped down on it.

'And?'

Defiant green eyes met his own, 'I don't see why it matters.' She leaned forward as she spoke, her voice growing urgent, 'I mean, we have great sex. Don't we? It's certainly the best I've ever had. Why do we even have to worry about it?'

Connor felt his jaw drop open. It took a few seconds for his brain to reboot and he scowled.

'You don't see why it matters?'

She nodded and smiled.

'Are you insane?' he hollered.

She flinched and Connor almost smacked himself. He was handling this badly. He drew in a deep breath and counted to ten. It was important that he remember she'd spent two decades convinced she was wrong to

234

enjoy pain during sex or any kind of kink.

'Bridget, do you understand that I want to do much more to you than what we've done?'

She flushed, but didn't respond. If anything, she drew in upon herself. He pressed on, his voice gruff with need.

'I want to spank you and watch your skin turn pink and then I want to fuck you hard so that you feel that burn the whole time I do. I want to tie you up and have you at my mercy while I do whatever I want to you. If that's make you cry right before I make you scream as you come, so be it.'

He could see her breathing hitch and her nipples harden under the cotton of her shirt. His cock stirred in response.

Damn it! That is why this was so important. She wants it too!

'Fuck, Bridg. Don't you see? My dick is hard just talking about it. And, baby, whether you're willing to deal with this or not, you want it too.'

He gave her no time to respond; he reached out and squeezed her nipple hard. She jerked away, flushing red.

'Your nipples are hard, Bridget. Tell me the truth. Is your pussy wet too?'

She closed her eyes and refused to look at him.

'Look at me!' He was damn near yelling at her. Her stubbornness was infuriating him.

Her eyes popped open. They were swimming with tears.

He almost caved. Almost let her off the hook, but this was important to him.

It would be a different story if she honestly didn't

want this. No one had a right to force anyone to go against their beliefs. This wasn't honest, though.

She wanted it too. She was letting an irrational belief stop her from experiencing this and worse, she was internalising shame over it. That's why he could not let this go.

'Answer me.' He took her hand, but remained firm. 'Are you wet, baby? Does the thought of pain mixed in with pleasure excite you?'

Tears, shiny and wet, slid down her cheeks as she nodded.

'Why does that make you cry?' He believed he understood, but she needed to understand she was wrong.

'Because I don't trust myself to know. I doubt myself and I'm scared of making another mistake in judgment. My first one ended up with me getting raped.' Her words were drowned in tears as sobs took hold of her body.

He gathered her into his body, sitting her on his lap like a small child. She cried helpless, wracking sobs as he held her and whispered words of comfort and love.

He loved her. He knew it in his heart. He also knew that it wouldn't be enough if they didn't cross this hurdle together.

Ultimately, it wasn't about the sex. It was about having no emotional barriers between the two of them. If she kept this wall up when she so clearly wanted it, they likely wouldn't survive.

He'd debated back and forth over whether he was pushing something out of selfishness, but he didn't think he was. The kink was just the symptom. This was about trust. This was about sharing something with someone that you gave to no one else. This was about honesty at its deepest level.

She was being dishonest. This was something she wanted. She craved. And she was denying herself out of misplaced guilt and fear. This would only grow and infect the rest of their relationship.

He could let the kink go, never ask her for it again, but it wouldn't change the foundation of dishonesty.

No. He wasn't going to let up.

He wasn't, however, a complete asshole. He wouldn't force the issue any further tonight.

When her sobs finally died down, Connor went and got a damp washcloth from her bathroom. As he gently wiped her cheeks, he said, 'I understand your fear, Bridget. But if you don't trust yourself in this, why don't you consider trusting me until you do?'

She cupped his face and kissed him. Her kiss was urgent, almost panicked.

He knew a refusal when he got one.

Bridget kissed Connor as if that kiss would save her soul. She'd been more than wet at his words; she'd been two seconds away from falling to her knees and begging him to make it all real.

She didn't want to deal with this. She didn't want to take the risk.

She wanted him to drop this subject. She wasn't ready and she didn't want to argue. As she kissed her way down his body and took his cock in her mouth, she was determined to make him forget all about it.

Chapter Twenty-four

'Calm down, sugar.' Bridget chuckled as she took the Mustang smoothly into the turn lane. 'If you fidget any more, you're going to wear a hole in my leather seat.'

He scowled in her direction. He'd been in poor humour all day. She had a feeling it had a lot to do with what *hadn't* happened last night. She'd found the toys in his nightstand this morning. One look at the handcuffs and flogger and she was especially glad she'd managed to take his mind off using them on her.

At least, she'd thought she had, but he'd been edgy and surly all day. It was enough to put her on edge as well. Needless to say, she'd been grateful when she'd gotten the invite from Claire to dinner. Claire had specifically said to bring Connor along. Apparently, it was time to bring him into the fold.

In truth, it warmed her heart that her friends cared enough to do this. She hoped they'd all hit it off. Even though she was confident they would, that niggle of concern was always there until something was said and done.

'I'm just tired,' he said as he looked off into the distance.

'Well, I did wear you out last night.' She laughed

and smiled at him, only to falter a bit at the strained smile he forced in return.

'You certainly put the moves on.' He squeezed her hand but his tone was distant. An icy worm turned circles in her belly.

She'd done everything she could think of last night to show him how good sex was between them without the need to venture into the shadowy areas she preferred to keep in the dark.

She understood his point. She truly did. And she'd be a complete liar to say she didn't want to do exactly what he suggested. But why did they have to? Why was it becoming a point of contention?

No. She wasn't backing down on this. They were good the way they were and there was no need to complicate things with questions that didn't need answering. It was a small sacrifice in the long term.

He would just have to understand.

'Do your friends know what I do?' He sounded like he was choking on the words.

Instantly, she softened. Here she was being completely self-centred, thinking this had to be about her, and he was worried about being embarrassed or judged for his chosen occupation.

'You mean that you're a phenomenal artist, sexy and intelligent, and rock my world in bed?'

She took his hand and damn near crashed the car at the fury in his face.

'Connor!' she gasped, seeing him so angry. 'Yes, I told them what you do. They don't care. I would never disrespect you that way. I'm not ashamed of anything you do.'

He mussed his hair as he raked a hand through it

and blew out a breath.

'I apologise, Bridg.' He kissed the back of her hand. 'It's not even that I really care about what they'll think of me, but if anyone were to disrespect you over it, I think I'd get an assault charge.'

Her heart squeezed at his concern for her. That he'd come to her rescue the way he would was one of the reasons she loved him.

The breath in her chest dissolved at the realisation that she did love him. Not just that, she wanted to be with him. For good. The words leaped to her lips, only to die as she thought of Dean Whittier. She hadn't told Connor and, frankly, didn't plan to. His very willingness to jump to her rescue was exactly why she needed to finish this with the dean. No, only when the road was clear in front of them would she tell him. Until then, she'd have to show him.

She pulled the Mustang into the alley behind Claire and Evan's brownstone. Turning off the engine, she faced Connor and took his face in her hands.

'You have nothing to worry about, sugar. I have the best friends in the world and I have the best man in the world. The two can't help but come together like peanut butter and jelly.'

He laughed at her deliberate corniness and she felt warm inside again at seeing him smile for real.

Leaning over the centre console, she kissed him gently, brushing her lips across his. She wanted to take him into her arms and make all of his pain from being rejected and judged go away. Wrapping her arms around his neck, she deepened the kiss, pouring all of her love and desire into this communion of lips and tongue.

When they finally parted both were breathless.

Connor smiled that crooked smile she loved and murmured, 'Keep that up and I'll be turning this car around, Ms Ross.'

She grinned. 'Mmm, I like that idea. Except I don't think Evan will stand for it.' She nodded over his shoulder to where Evan was standing, arms crossed across his chest and one imperious eyebrow raised.

With a laugh, she wiped the lipstick from Connor's mouth and got out of the car.

'Why are you looking like a fearsome grizzly, Evan?' She reached into the backseat for the wine she and Connor had brought as their contribution to dinner.

'He hasn't passed the test yet and he's out here with his tongue down your throat. I'm supposed to be intimidating and scary, Bridget. Don't you know anything?' His voice was deliberately whiny.

Connor laughed and held out a hand, which Evan shook firmly. 'It's good to know she's got other people looking out for her. She's a handful.'

'You figured that out, did you?'

'Figured it out? She more or less hit me over the head with it the moment we met.'

'Really?' Evan grinned at Bridget. 'I don't think I've heard that story yet.'

'Hey now,' she called at them as they left her to follow, but she wasn't truly upset. That her two favourite men had so obviously hit it off made her happy. This was going to be a good night.

'Bridget says you're an artist, Connor.'

Connor flinched. He never liked discussing his art.

It was just too personal. He almost never showed it to anyone. Of all the women he'd dated, Bridget was only the second to ever see his work. It was too much like putting his soul on display and it made him feel too exposed.

'I dabble, but I'm not a professional artist,' he said, deflecting Claire's question.

The night had gone better than he'd expected. Bridget's friends were a welcoming group. Mona, he'd gotten to know pretty well from her café, but Claire and Evan made an intriguing couple. He got the impression there was more going on to that pairing than met the eye.

It was in the little touches and phrases between the two of them. She'd jokingly called him "sir" at one point and Evan's reaction had been anything but joking. He'd looked like he wanted to throw his wife on the table and have his way with her, audience be damned.

Yeah, he had a feeling those two were definitely kinky.

Which only furthered his frustration where Bridget was concerned. Her best friend was obviously kinky so she'd had exposure to the idea of it not being wrong. He took a deep breath to dispel the frustration that flared at the memory of how Bridget had soundly shut him down the night before.

She'd pulled out all the stops to show him exactly how good sex could be without any true kink. And, had it actually been sincere and not an obvious manipulation, he would have been over the moon. But it hadn't been sincere. She'd been detached and calculating throughout the entire experience.

It would have hurt less for her to just stick him with a knife straight through the chest.

'Connor?'

'Hmmm?' He pulled his thoughts back to the present and focused on Mona.

'Did you hear what I said?'

'No, sorry. My mind wandered.' He smiled.

'I asked if you'd ever thought about showing your work?'

'Oh.' He shook his head. 'No. It's not something I'm really interested in.'

She smiled and nodded. 'OK, but if you change your mind, I'd love to see some of your work. I feature a lot of local artists at the café.'

'Yeah, I've noticed. That mixed media artist you're showing now is really talented.'

'Thank you.' Irving, Mona's date grinned.

'Is it yours?' Connor hadn't taken note of the artist's name.

He nodded. Connor had to admit, the last thing he would have expected this man to be was an artist. He was built like a linebacker, all broad shoulders and muscle. Connor had figured him for an athlete, not an artist.

'Didn't expect that, did you?' Irving laughed a deep, gruff rumble. 'Most people don't. I get a lot of that look.' He gestured at Connor's face.

'My apologies, man.' Connor laughed with him. 'You look like you should be scoring touchdowns.'

'Well, that part helps with the ladies.' He put his big paw of a hand on Mona's shoulder and squeezed. Mona flushed a pretty shade of pink.

'Don't go getting full of yourself.' She poked him

in the ribs, causing him to flinch.

'But it's so fun,' he good-naturedly returned the ribbing.

Thankfully, the conversation turned to Irving's work and Connor's was forgotten, which was just fine with him.

Chapter Twenty-five

'Why are you talking with me about this?' Connor gritted his teeth and bit back the curses that wanted to spill from his mouth. They wouldn't be productive.

'Sugar, I told you I was going to talk with Mona,' Bridget said as she reached across the breakfast table and squeezed his hand. Where normally that smoky Southern drawl would have melted his tension, her tone was an obvious attempt at placation and it only served to aggravate him more.

'Yes, I remember.' He pulled his hand away. She'd brought the subject up after they'd left Claire and Evan's house the previous weekend. Picking up his coffee, he took a long gulp and winced as he burned the roof of his mouth. Setting the cup down, he gritted out, 'I also remember telling you not to do it.'

'You're being silly about this.' Bridget sipped her own coffee and gave a dismissive wave of her hand. 'You have an amazing talent and you should be doing something with it.'

'Says who?' He was being belligerent and childish, but in that moment he didn't care.

She just stared at him with a scowl. He wasn't usually so argumentative. Hell, he prided himself on being an easy-going guy, but she had crossed a line.

Worse, she didn't even realise it.

'Look, there is a very good reason why I don't share my work. I thought you understood that.'

He stood and gathered his breakfast dishes up, placing them in the sink. He'd deal with them later. Right now, he had to get moving or he'd be late for work.

'What reason is that, Connor?' She wasn't letting up. 'You've certainly never told me.'

Gripping the edge of the sink, he did his best to rein in his temper. Why was she being so fucking pushy? This wasn't like her.

'Yes, I did.' He turned to face her. Her brow was crinkled in confusion and her eyes were dark with worry.

It only served to fuel his temper more.

'That first day at the café.' He saw her brows squeeze even tighter. 'Fuck, Bridget! Over coffee! My parents!'

He was yelling now and he didn't like the wary look on her face one bit, but he couldn't seem to find his self-control. He'd expended so much of it on their relationship that in this moment the well was dry.

'Connor, I don't understand,' she entreated. 'Talk to me. Please.'

'I killed them, Bridget!'

Before he even realised what he was doing, Connor snatched the mug he'd set on the counter and threw it. It shattered against the cabinet, raining down in small, green ceramic shards on his kitchen floor. Lotus and Daisy came running, but a sharp "stay" from him kept them from treading through his mess.

His chest was heaving and there was a rushing

sound in his ears. Leaning heavily on the counter, Connor counted backward from 20. When the sound of the ocean receded, he looked at Bridget. She was rooted in place, her knuckles white around the mug she held.

He felt like an ass, but his control was lost.

'They died the night I got the award for my art. I was obsessed with art when I was a child. I was also spoiled and threw tantrums when I didn't get my way.

'That night, we were running late. Dad had run into some traffic on his way home from work. I kicked up such a fucking stink about it he didn't even change his clothes.'

His voice broke and his eyes burned. He could still see the irritation on his father's face. Connor had been relentless, nagging him to hurry so they wouldn't miss a single moment of his big night. His adolescent ego had been so overblown.

'If I hadn't been so damned focused on impressing the world with my talent, they'd still be alive. If I'd just let my dad be, we wouldn't have been in that intersection when that drunk ran the light.'

Swiping at his cheeks, he said, '*That* is why I don't share my work.'

Bridget moved to his side, but he held her off with a hand.

'No.' His voice was thick with grief he felt as if he was choking. 'I don't want comfort.' He reached for the broom and dustpan. 'Tell Mona thanks, but no thanks.'

'You're wrong, baby.' She picked up the trash bin and uncovered it for him so he could dump in the remains of the mug.

'Bridget,' he warned. 'This topic is not open for negotiation.'

'Well, I'm not done talking about it,' she snapped, catching him off guard. 'The only person responsible for killing your parents is the woman who got behind the wheel drunk. You were a child doing what a child does and you have nothing to be ashamed of.'

Rage, white and hot, built in Connor's gut as she spoke. Wasn't this the pot calling the kettle black! Oblivious to his change in mood, she continued without looking at him as she put the trash bin back in its place.

'You've associated something painful and tragic to something perfectly natural for a child and you are letting it keep you from exploring your full potential.'

'Are you even listening to yourself?' His words were more sneer than anything else. 'How dare you come at me this way when you won't even admit the truth to yourself about what you want in bed?'

She reeled back as if he'd slapped her, bumping into the counter and rattling the silverware drawer.

Drawing herself up, she retorted, 'Those things are hardly the same.'

'Don't kid yourself, Bridget.' He ran his hands through his hair, searching for calm and failing to find it. 'What? Hypocrisy only applies when it's me. Is that it?'

The colour drained from her face and he felt slightly sick. Still, the words poured out.

'You hide behind this bullshit you spew about penance and punishment for some "imagined" crime, but the truth is what you want to do in bed is not some deviant sin you need to be punished for

248

enjoying. It is nothing more than sensual exploration that is perfectly fine so long as both parties consent. Your rape was a perversion of that because you didn't fucking consent!'

He slammed his fist on the counter. She flinched.

'You want me to tie you up, Bridg. You want me to cause you pain and then make you come. Yet you deny it and hide behind an artificial wall you created and you don't even see how you're limiting what we have by doing it. You think we can grow like this, but we can't.'

He struggled to calm down but there was no calm to be found. Feeling like the ground was opening up underneath him, he ploughed on.

'You may think it's OK to have walls and barriers between two people. But I don't believe there should be any when two people care about each other. And I damn sure don't believe in artificial boundaries in bed. I believe that as long as both parties consent, and no harm is being done, anything goes.'

He dragged in a deep breath and did his best to calm himself down. He'd been trying to be so patient. This wasn't how he'd wanted to tackle this with her, but his patience had netted him very little so far. They'd plateaued. He wanted so much more with her and she wasn't willing to consider it. He was tired of being shut down.

It was time for her to fish or cut bait.

'Bridget.' He walked over to her and took her hand. Tears welled in her eyes and he felt awful, but damn it if he was going to apologise for the truth. 'Look, I apologise for shouting, but I meant what I said. I think we need to talk about this, but right now is not the time. I don't feel in control of my temper and I don't want to say anything more I might regret.'

He kissed her forehead and rubbed away a tear that streaked down her cheek.

'Let's talk tonight, after work, OK? I'll make dinner.'

She didn't speak, but nodded.

Taking her in his arms, he hugged her tight before releasing her and going to shower.

Bridget squeezed the bridge of her nose, trying to will away the headache that threatened with no success. Her head felt as if it was in a vice. Her temples ached and her eyes burned. It had been a constant thing since her argument with Connor that morning.

Tears welled but she fought them. Crying in front of her class would never do. She glanced around to ensure that none of her students was paying any attention to her. Fortunately, they were all busy with their final exam. Pencils were flying and calculator keys were tapping.

Surreptitiously, she wiped her eyes. Her emotions had been on a tilt-a-whirl all day. It was bad enough they were arguing more and more over small things, but that had been gut-wrenching.

She'd never seen him so furious, especially with her.

Each word had been like a tiny knife in her heart. She'd thought the subject was dropped. He hadn't said a word since their talk, and she'd been happy to let it go.

He apparently had not. This morning had proven that they were far from beyond it, though. She could only hope that dinner would go better. Her stomach clenched at the thought of having to talk about it again.

Maybe, she was wrong. Maybe she should trust him –

'Problem, Ross?' Dean Whittier's voice crawled across her skin, jarring her from her thoughts. She hadn't seen him come in.

'No.' Taking a deep breath, she began to straighten up the papers on her desk.

Things had been different with him as well. She couldn't put her finger on it, but it was almost as if she could feel the malevolence he had toward her. Her skin prickled every time he was near her.

He'd finally stopped all his suggestive comments, but he was popping up in her classroom more often. Something she couldn't do anything about since it was his prerogative to audit her classes, especially with her tenure review coming up.

She'd find him looking at her with a look so hateful, she felt physically attacked.

Today was no different; he appeared to be assessing her the way a lion might a gazelle in the Serengeti. She was definitely the prey here.

'I wanted to inform you that your tenure review has been arranged for two weeks from tomorrow. The panel has been selected and you'll receive a formal notification of all the procedures. Charlene's putting together a packet for you.'

'Thank you.' She refused to be cowed, but looking into those dead, blue eyes make her stomach twist viciously.

His eyes narrowed, his lips twitched mirthlessly,

but all he said was, 'I'd think carefully about what it will take to get that tenure, Ross.'

Her heart sank, but she just stared into his eyes despite the desperate urge to look away.

After several moments, he gave a soft chuckle and turned to leave, murmuring, 'Yes, indeed. Think on that, Ross.'

Dale closed the door to Bridget's classroom behind him and made his way to the men's room. His dick was rock hard and he didn't want to walk down the hall advertising his hard-on.

He couldn't wait to remove that defiant look from her face. She thought he couldn't see her fear, but it was written all over her.

Good. The bitch. Everywhere he turned, there she was with that janitor. She had no right to turn him down and then bed down with dogs.

Whore.

He was going to enjoy putting her in her place.

He leaned one hand against the stall as he took his cock in hand. All he could think about these days was her. It didn't even matter who he was with, in his mind they all had red hair and green eyes.

He stroked his rigid flesh as the image of Bridget formed in his mind. Those ruby lips would wrap nicely around his shaft. She'd suck hard, pulling on him as if to suck the come right out of him.

Lately, he hadn't even been satisfied with his usual conquests. He'd continued to fuck the waitress from Luna Bella. She was up for anything and it suited him to use her. Especially now Skyler had disappeared.

She didn't answer his calls and she wasn't even in

252

class. A check of her records had shown that all of her work was turned in and she'd even taken her finals early.

The little bitch had just disappeared off the face of the planet.

Whatever. She was inconsequential in the end. It hadn't been the same since she'd let herself get knocked up, anyway.

No, the one he wanted was down the hall, but soon enough she'd be exactly where he wanted her.

That tight little ass would be his to plunder and those tits would bounce as he fucked hard into her. She'd whimper and moan and beg for him to stop and he wouldn't. He keep fucking her harder and harder and –

His release caught him off guard, slamming into him. Every muscle went rigid as he pumped into his fist, only the barest edge of his fury draining out with his semen.

Chapter Twenty-six

Connor slammed the door on his locker and grabbed up his backpack. He hoped to catch Bridget in her office. The hurt on her face had haunted him all day long. He owed her an apology and he didn't want to wait until they met for dinner.

She had office hours every day after her last class and they'd be finishing up in about an hour. He figured he'd pick up a coffee from Mona's for her and make it just in time for hours to end. After that, he'd just have to work harder at accepting her position on kink.

When he'd finally managed to put his own desires aside, he'd come to the conclusion that, despite his beliefs, it was Bridget's decision to make.

When he'd asked himself the question of whether he wanted her in his life without kink or not in his life at all, the answer had been simple. He wanted her in his life. Hell, more than that, he never wanted to lose her. She was it for him. He knew it down deep in his gut.

He was going to tell her too. As soon as he saw her.

A glance at his watch had him picking up the pace. He was going to miss her if he didn't get a move on.

Bridget glanced at the clock on her wall and did her best to find patience with her student. Her hours were officially over and Clay was determined to press his point. He was a solid student, but he was a whiner and he wasn't pleased with his lab assignment grades.

She'd already explained to him twice that unless he wanted to repeat the experiment and do an entirely new work-up the grade would stand, but he kept trying to cajole her into giving him a higher mark on the existing lab.

'Morris.' The dean's voice had them both jumping. 'Professor Ross has made herself clear. Either repeat the lab or take the grade. Your choice.'

Clay turned almost purple with embarrassment at being caught out by the dean. Mumbling an apology, he agreed to keep the grade and hustled out of Bridget's office.

Grudgingly, she murmured, 'Thank you, Dean.'

Whittier didn't bother responding as he walked into her office and dropped an envelope on her desk.

'What's this?' Bridget took up the envelope and unpinned the flap, sliding out a single sheet of paper.

'Your tenure review information.' The door lock snicked into place. Bridget's heart raced as realisation dawned on her. He'd just locked them in together.

'What are you doing?' Her voice was shrill as fear flooded her.

She stood up and rounded her desk, going for the lock, only to be stopped by Whittier catching her around the waist with an iron-hard arm. He pulled her against him so that her back was pressed fully against his body. She could feel his erection.

Not that he was hiding it. He pushed her against her desk and rubbed his dick against her ass.

'I told you to think very hard about what you were going to do to get your tenure, didn't I?'

Despite the fact that she was trembling from head to toe, she managed to grit out, 'Let go of me, Dale. This is assault and if you don't let me go, you're going to regret it.'

'What are you going to do to me? Huh? You're nothing but a hypocritical little slut.'

He grabbed her hair and pulled her head back. It felt as if all the individual strands of hair were about to rip right out of her skull. Cold ropes of adrenaline raced through her veins even as fear paralysed her.

The room spun; the rushing in her ears drowned out his words. But nothing could erase the feel of his hands on her body. She heard buttons pop as he ripped open her blouse. The sheer cream silk of the bra she was wearing ripped as he jerked it down, spilling her breasts out into the cold air conditioning.

Her nipples hardened and he pinched one hard. Shards of pains shot through her body and she cried out. He laughed and twisted harder. White-hot pain flooded her veins and chased the fog from her brain. In some detached part of her mind, she noted that she only felt pain, no pleasure. She had no time to digest its meaning, however. She wasn't going to stand here and put up no resistance.

'You think you're going to deny me yet fuck the janitor.' He let go of her hair to grip her bruisingly around the waist. She felt him fumbling with his zipper between their bodies. 'If you want that tenure you need so damn badly, you're going to get with the programme, Ross. You're going to fuck me and when I'm done fucking you, you're going to get on your knees and suck my dick. And,' he grunted as he yanked on his zipper, 'when I'm done coming in your mouth you're going to swallow and thank me for doing it.'

Rage coursed through her. He thought he was going to force himself on her and get away with it. He actually thought he was going to use her job to control her.

No job was worth being a victim. No job was worth her self-respect.

'Get your fucking hands off me!' she screamed even as she grabbed the fountain pen she'd been using to grade papers and plunged it with all her might into Whittier's leg.

He hollered, high and long, and fell back. His legs buckled under him and he hit the floor.

Then all hell broke loose.

Connor felt the door cave in under the force of his shoulder. Thank God the doors were old and the locks even older. The coffee was forgotten and currently lay in a puddle on the floor where he'd dropped it when he'd heard the commotion going on in Bridget's office. The dean was in there, attempting to rape his woman.

There was no way in hell he was going to let that happen.

As the door exploded off its hinges, Connor assessed the situation and saw Bridget, her breasts naked and exposed, and the dean on the floor with what looked like a pen sticking out of his leg.

A small part of his brain was proud of Bridget for fighting back. The other part of him could only think about killing the son of a bitch who thought he'd do something so fucking despicable.

He lunged at Whittier and, straddling his chest, punched him solidly in the jaw. He enjoyed the crunch of skin and teeth under his fist even as he felt the skin on his knuckles give way.

'Connor!' Bridget was calling his name. He barely registered it through the fog of anger suffusing his brain.

Eventually, he came to himself and saw what he was doing. Dean Whittier was struggling under him as he choked him. The man's face was red and his eyes bulging.

Connor wanted very much to kill the bastard but he wasn't worth a prison sentence. The one who deserved to be going to prison was Whittier.

He dropped him unceremoniously and didn't even pretend not to enjoy the sound of his head hitting the tile floor. Whittier moaned but didn't move.

Lurching to his feet, Connor whirled and grabbed Bridget, who'd managed to pull herself together. She was crying and clutching the torn remnants of her blouse together.

'Baby, are you OK?'

She nodded and collapsed into his arms.

'Take me home, Connor.'

'We need to call the police.'

'No!' her voice was sharp. Stepping away from him, she walked over to where Whittier still lay whimpering on the ground. With the pointed toe of her stiletto, she jabbed him in the ribs and he curled into the foetal position. 'No, cops, because the dean here is going to give me my tenure, aren't you? If you don't, I have a witness to what you did and I'll report you to the police so fast your head will spin.' She kneeled down and smacked Whittier hard on the cheek. 'You hear me?'

He groaned and nodded.

'Good.' She started to rise, but stopped, 'One more thing, Dean.' She reached out and gripped a handful of his hair, forcing him to face her. 'If you ever so much as brush against me, I'll do a hell of a lot worse. Got it?' He nodded.

Without blinking an eye, she snatched her pen out of his leg. He screamed and even Connor flinched. Bright blood oozed out of the wound, turning his pants deep scarlet.

Connor stepped over Whittier's body as if he were so much trash and wrapped his jacket around Bridget. 'Let's go.'

He didn't understand everything that was going on here, but that was going to change.

Chapter Twenty-seven

She was sleeping peacefully, but there was no peace for Connor. His brain still reeled from everything she'd told him. Skyler was in the kitchen; he could hear her in there, making tea or something from the sounds.

The knowledge of what that sleazeball Whittier was doing to these two women made him wish he'd killed him when he had the chance. The bastard didn't deserve to draw breath.

He opened the bedroom door and paused to look at Bridget. She looked small and pale against the navy blue sheets. Her red hair spilled across the pillow like coppery ropes and the strain of the night's events was erased in sleep.

He loved her. He wanted her. But she didn't trust him.

More than anything, that was what he'd realised tonight.

He'd seen the knowledge in her face when he'd asked her how long it had all been going on. She'd copped to the fact that it had started coming to a head weeks ago, even though Whittier had been a threat long before they'd started seeing each other.

She'd also told him her plan for exposing the dean.

Her tenure might be secure after tonight, but Skyler was still at risk.

He gnashed his teeth at the danger she was putting herself in to do it. People like Whittier didn't take defeat lightly and he could very well retaliate. She hadn't been willing to hear it, though. She was a mama bear where her student was concerned and he couldn't fault her. He'd probably do the same thing.

The fact remained that he'd been right. She'd been hiding this from him.

Trust.

One little word that had more meaning than anything else.

They didn't have it, and without it, they didn't have anything.

She'd never lied to him, he had to concede, but she hadn't been honest either. That she'd kept this from him showed that she wasn't willing to invest in him the same way he'd invested in her. He'd told her everything: his deepest shame, his greatest hopes.

He had to give her credit for telling him about the rape. That couldn't have been easy, but rather than bringing them together it had become the excuse to keep a distance between them in bed.

She wasn't willing to meet him halfway. She wanted everything from him and wasn't willing to give him anything.

If it were possible for a heart to shatter, his now lay in pieces at his feet.

He'd tucked her into bed and lain with her until she'd fallen asleep. Tonight had been traumatic for her and despite the cost to himself, he was proud of her for standing up for herself.

That their relationship was over could wait for the morning.

Shutting the door quietly behind him, Connor sat on the porch for a long time, watching the stars and wishing things were different.

Bridget hurt. Everywhere. Her back was on fire and felt as if every muscle were in a knot. Her breasts were sore, especially where Whittier had grabbed her nipple so viciously. Even the soft cotton of her sheet abraded the skin. But, surprisingly, she felt rested.

She'd fought back!

She grinned. By the time Connor had burst through the door, she'd already managed to fight him off.

The thought of Connor had her rolling to face him, except his side of her bed was empty. He'd obviously slept there, as the pillow was indented, but he wasn't in bed.

Sitting up, she started to call out, only to jump when his voice came behind her. 'I'm over here.'

Turning, she saw him sitting in the chair across from her bed. He looked like hell. His eyes were lined with strain and he didn't look like he'd slept at all.

Her voice faltered. 'Connor? Are you OK?'

For a very long time, Connor just stared at her. Icy cold tendrils of fear began worming their way up her spine. She didn't know what was going on here, but she didn't like it at all.

Just as she was about to say something, Connor rose from the chair and knelt in front of her. Taking her face in his hands, he kissed her. It wasn't a gentle kiss. It was hard and hot. He plundered her mouth, licking into it and sucking gently on her tongue and lips. She surrendered to his kiss, letting him mark her.

Abruptly, he lurched away from her and threw himself back into the chair.

'Bridget, I can't do this.'

The ice that had receded as he'd kissed her surged through her body, leaving her light-headed.

'Can't do what?' She didn't understand what was happening here. She gripped her sheets in her fists, trying to find something to ground herself.

'I can't be with you when you don't trust me enough to truly let me in.'

'I trust you, Connor.' Her voice was shrill, but she was beginning to panic.

'No, baby. You don't.' He stood and walked over to her window. His voice was quiet, but each word rang out as if he were shouting. 'You've done nothing but keep me at a distance. You aren't even trying to work through your issue with sex and you hid what was going on with Whittier from me.'

'I have a right to my privacy!' She hollered the words without thinking.

He turned slowly to face her and the look in his face sent her heart plummeting.

'Yes, you do. You even have a right not to want to do anything in bed you don't want to do.'

He leaned against the window sill and crossed his arms over his chest. He was gorgeous and sexy and so angry he almost vibrated from it.

'That's why I came to your office. To apologise for pushing you and to tell you that I love you.'

The room tilted wildly as his words registered. He loved her! Joy seared through her at the idea that she'd gotten this all wrong. He loved her. She opened her mouth to tell him how much she loved him too, only to go slack-jawed as the rest of his words finally sank in.

'But I realised something last night. You haven't even tried to meet me in the middle. You want me to come to you, to invest in you, but you haven't once reciprocated. You didn't tell me about Whittier. Not because you were worried about what I'd do – even though that's what you want to believe. You didn't tell me so you could retain that control. The same way you won't even consider what I'm asking for in bed. It's just so you can feel in control.'

'Can you blame me?' she conceded, but it felt like the air in her lungs had turned to cement.

He snorted and shook his head, 'No, Bridget. I can't blame you. God only knows how it must be to have been raped and to deal with what you've dealt with as a result. But I also know that I want more than what you're offering me.'

He stepped over to the bed and took her hand, bringing up to his lips and kissing it gently.

'I want it all, baby. I want my woman to trust me enough to take the same risk on me that I'm taking on her. I want us to explore everything that sex can offer us together and, more than anything, I want to know that my woman trusts me not just to protect her, but to know when she needs to protect herself.'

He leaned over and kissed her forehead. Bridget clutched at his shirt, but he stepped away and walked to the door.

'Connor!' She lurched across the bed, only to get tangled in the sheets and fall.

'I do love you, Bridget. But I want more. Take care

of yourself.'

'Connor, stop!' she hollered out, but the only response she got was the sound of the door closing behind him.

Chapter Twenty-eight

'I should throw this in your face.'

Connor flinched at the censure in Mona's voice and quickly took his coffee from her lest she choose to act on her impulse.

'Mona. Listen –'

'No.' She held up a hand to cut him off, then pointed in the direction of an empty table. 'Sit over there. I've got words for you and you're going to hear me out.'

His stomach twisted. He'd been avoiding the café all week for exactly this reason, but this morning he'd decided he was acting like a baby and had stopped in for the coffee he'd grown addicted to.

It wasn't that he could argue with Mona. He was miserable. He missed Bridget so bad he could barely think straight. He found himself reaching for the phone to share something with her all the time. He couldn't even sleep through the night because he missed the feel of her pressed against him, hogging the covers.

Connor set his coffee on the table and waited. The café was bustling as usual. Couples and groups were busy living their lives, communing with each other.

He yearned for that connection in a way he'd never

done before. Now he'd had it, it was like going through withdrawal to be without it. He'd second guessed his decision countless times but he just couldn't get beyond Bridget's clear refusal to invest in the relationship the same way he had. He didn't want things so far out of balance. He'd rather be alone than end up resenting the woman he loved.

Well, he'd gotten his wish there. Even Lotus was mad at him. The two dogs had bonded quickly and it had broken his heart when he'd noticed her sleeping with a chew toy of Daisy's that had been left behind. He hadn't had the heart to take it from her, even though the sight of it cut deep.

He'd removed all traces of Bridget from his house, packing the few items she'd left into a bag and leaving it in her office at the university. He just couldn't bear to have anything of hers near him. It angered and hurt him too much.

'Come with me.' Mona's voice startled him out of his ruminations and he sloshed his coffee. A glance at her face showed no sympathy. 'Leave it, Nadia can clean the table.'

With a resigned sigh, Connor picked up his mug and went to face the Inquisition.

She didn't even wait until he'd closed the door to her office to round on him.

'What the hell is wrong with you? What are you thinking?' she hollered, only to hold up a hand to stop him when he began to answer. 'Don't bother. You clearly aren't thinking.'

Pacing, she continued her tirade.

'Do you have any idea what you've done? Bridget is miserable. All she does is sit and stare. I can't even get her to come into the shop because this is "where it all began".' She made air quotes. 'You broke her heart and I want to know why. Couldn't you see she loves you? She did things for you she wouldn't do for anyone else. Are you really that much of a dick?'

Each word was like a dagger in his chest. She was vocalising every doubt he'd had. He hated the idea of Bridget unhappy, but what was he supposed to do?

Plopping herself down into her chair, she narrowed her eyes and hissed, 'What do you have to say for yourself?' She crossed her arms over her chest and waited.

Connor, who'd sat in one of the chairs in front of her desk as she'd railed at him, took a long draw on his coffee, letting its heat sting as it flowed into his gut. The pain was very focusing.

'Mona.' He met her accusing brown eyes directly. 'I love her. Deeply.'

From the way her eyebrows damn near joined her hairline, she clearly hadn't been expecting that and this time it was he who held up a hand to stave off a reply.

'But me loving her isn't enough if she isn't willing to put anything on the line. And, as much as you might not want to hear this, she hasn't.' Sitting back, he crossed his own arms over his chest. 'Did you know about the dean?'

She blanched but nodded.

'Yeah, well, I didn't find out until I came across him trying to force her to fuck him.' He gritted his teeth over how much that still stung. 'Don't even get me started on all the other ways she made clear to me she'd only do what was easy for her to do.'

He blew out a frustrated breath.

'I opened myself up to her. I put all my baggage on the table for her. But I can't be with someone who isn't willing to share the ugly with me too. Bridget wants to put our relationship into a neat, controllable box. Well, once you cage something it's only a matter of time before it dies.'

He took another fortifying gulp of his coffee.

'I spent a lot of time thinking about this and, as much as I might want it to be different, it's Bridget's prerogative to not share or invest. But, it's also mine to want more. If we aren't on the same page, we'll only hurt each other. I decided to end things before we got to that point. But if you think I'm not miserable, you're wrong.'

Much to his embarrassment, his voice cracked.

'Damn it!' she fussed. 'Damn it! Damn it! You were supposed to be unreasonable so I could think you were a class-A dickwad and just hate you.'

He snorted. 'Well, I keep wondering if I'm being that already.' He stared into his coffee, wishing the answers would just appear. 'You know what kills me the most?'

She shook her head, murmuring, 'No, what?'

'She's letting the past define and cage her. I know in my heart that we could be amazing together, but she's letting one event shape her whole life. And she's completely wrong in how she sees it.'

'Sounds a little hypocritical to me.'

Connor heard the vertebrae in his neck crack, so taken aback was he by her statement.

'How can you even say that?'

An eyebrow raised and she leaned over her desk.

'Bridget told me about your parents.' She waved a hand to dismiss his objection. 'Get over it. I badgered her to find out why you really wouldn't show your work and she finally caved after you dumped her.'

He flinched at the harshness of her categorisation of his actions.

'Long story short, m'dear, you are doing exactly the same thing with your art. Just as Bridget has a right to define just how far she'll let you into her life.' She clasped her hands together on the desk. 'The question is how can you ask something of Bridget that you yourself aren't even willing to give?'

At a loss for words, Connor just stared at Mona, who stood and came around the desk. Stopping at his side, she squeezed his shoulder.

'My offer stands, Connor. I think you need to look inside and determine if this is really about your parents or if you've just grown comfortable not taking the risk. It's not easy to put your heart on display for the world to judge. I know.'

She left him there, quietly closing the door behind her.

How long he sat there, he didn't know. It was if someone had just opened the door to a closet that had been stuffed full and abandoned. Opening the door results in an avalanche and all you can do is endure the fall until it's finally empty.

Memories tumbled through his brain, taking on new shape and perspective. That long-ago night replayed itself in vivid detail until finally Connor understood. And, in that understanding, he forgave himself.

A single, hot tear trailed down his cheek. He still

missed them. He wished they could be here to see him now. Swiping away the moisture, Connor picked up a notepad and pen from Mona's desk and jotted down what he wanted to say.

Leaving her office, he passed her on the way out and pressed the note into her hand before giving her a quick kiss on the cheek.

'What's that for?' she asked in surprise.

'For kicking my ass.' He smiled at her and, leaving the café, he headed home to plan.

Completely bewildered, Mona watched Connor leave. It ate her alive that those two hadn't made it. She'd never seen Bridget so happy.

'What can you do?' she sighed under her breath.

Unfolding Connor's note, a grin broke out across her face. Maybe, just maybe, there was hope after all.

In a barely legible scrawl, Connor had written, "You pick the date and time. We'll call the show *New Dimensions*." Along with his email address and phone number.

Mona tucked the note into her pocket and headed back to her office. There was planning to do.

Bridget gripped the steering wheel of her rented Taurus and willed her lungs to work. Her chest felt as if it had turned to stone. She forced air into her lungs and, closing her eyes, visualised all her tension as a big, red balloon floating into the sky. Rising. Rising. Rising and finally popping.

Opening her eyes, Bridget felt no change. So much for the visualisation exercises her rape crisis centre advocate had recommended. Clearly, will alone was not enough in this case.

After Connor had left, Bridget had truly felt as if she would die. The grief of losing him had been a crushing weight. She hadn't been able to eat. She hadn't slept. She could hardly function.

Skyler had threatened to have her committed to a psych ward. Ultimately, it had been Skyler's obvious fear that had pulled her out of bed, but she'd still been only going through the motions.

Connor's words echoed in her brain relentlessly. No matter how often she argued with his phantom, she couldn't escape the realisation he'd been right.

She had grown complacent in her self-imposed prison. It provided her the excuse she desired to avoid confronting the shame and confusion she carried as a result of being raped. Especially how she'd responded during her rape.

She desired things she simply didn't know how to process in the aftermath. Finally, she'd found the courage to call her local rape crisis centre and request counselling. Cathy, the advocate she'd begun seeing, had been wonderful. As compassionate as she was, she still called a spade a spade. Her brash, matter-of-fact attitude was exactly what Bridget needed.

She'd only had two sessions so far, but she already felt she had a better perspective on what happened. In particular, her misplaced shame over her reactions while drugged.

Ironically, Dean Whittier's attack had served as a catalyst. The pain he'd inflicted on her had been just that – pain. There'd been nothing sexual about it and she'd responded the way anyone would have under the circumstances.

She'd also been in her right mind, not drugged as she had been with Trent.

Once she'd realised that, she'd been able to start the process of facing herself and recognising her urges for what they were. A desire for sexual and sensual exploration. A need for pain in a sexual context that heightened pleasure.

She couldn't say why she was wired this way. But, in the end, she'd accepted the why didn't really matter. So long as no one was harmed, there was no reason not to explore this aspect of her sexuality. Like Connor had said, consent was key. Both parties needed to agree, and Trent had removed her ability to consent.

Connor had also been right that she hadn't even really tried. She'd been content to let him make all the sacrifices. And, through her resistance, she'd lost him.

Tears stung her eyes, but she blinked them away. Now was not the time for that. She had a purpose and she was going to see it through.

With a deep, fortifying breath, Bridget stepped out of the rental and, for the first time in almost two decades, she gazed upon her alma mater.

Corinthian University was everything Pinewood was not. Where Pinewood was stately and traditional, Corinthian had grown up within the urban sprawl of Chicago. The buildings were glass and steel and the only greenery was the carefully cultivated park area near the campus' administrative building. The dorms were really a ring of converted apartment buildings that lined the outer edges of the small campus. The only real similarity between the two was the students.

Grouped in clusters, they had laptops and iPads and were the picture of youth and potential.

That outer ring of dorms was where Bridget stood facing not just her former school, but the ghost of her past.

She adjusted her grip on her keys, being certain to unlock the pepper spray that now hung from the ring. Seeking closure didn't mean being reckless and she had no idea what she was walking into.

It didn't take long for Bridget to come to Pritchard Hall. Over the years, the building had been upgraded and the exterior had been whitewashed. The cosmetic enhancements did nothing to erase the crime scene aura radiating from it.

For her, it was tainted, and no coat of paint would change that.

Once inside, she was startled to see the number of young women occupying the lobby. From the heavily decorated doors lining the walls, it was clear to see that Pratt Hall had been integrated. Some of Bridget's tension released at the realisation she wasn't facing a legion of hormone-ridden college boys in her quest to reclaim her past.

She stepped onto the elevator, pressing the button for the fifth floor. The elevator beeped as it passed each floor; by the fifth, all of Bridget's nerves had returned. Her palm ached from clutching the pepper spray. Some part of her expected to run into Trent. To be forced to relive the single worst event of her life.

The elevator doors opened. Instead of Trent's gorgeous, lying face, she saw a petite, female student bedecked in all her rebellious glory. Bright purple hair hung past her shoulders and various studs and barbells poked out of her face. Nevertheless, the girl gave Bridget a friendly smile and stepped past her to enter the elevator.

Heart racing, Bridget moved down the hall. With each decorated door, her sense of déjà vu dissipated. She found the one she was looking for. Rather than the plain, wooden door it had been, it now sported a jaunty message board with various notes for Courtney and Trish. The muted strains of pop music floated from behind it.

With a trembling hand, Bridget knocked on the door and willed herself to relax.

'Just a sec!' a soft voice called out moments before the door flew open.

Bridget bit back a lecture on always checking before opening a door.

'Can I help you?' Her high-pitched, babyish voice in no way matched the tall, lean young woman in front of her. Briefly, Bridget wondered if this were Courtney or Trish.

'I hope so.' She forced a smile. 'This is probably a very odd request, but I was hoping you'd let me come in briefly just to see your room.'

The woman scowled and seemed ready to shut the door in her face. Bridget stepped into the doorway to prevent that just in case.

'Please,' she implored, 'I realise this sounds crazy, but I used to be a student at Corinthian and something happened to me here in this room. Something I've come to put to rest.' She met the woman's eyes. 'If you'll let me, that is.'

The young woman peered at Bridget for several moments, clearly weighing her words.

Finally, much to Bridget's relief, she stepped aside and let her enter the room. Again, Bridget had a split second of disorientation as she expected to see Trent's bed and clothes strewn around. Instead, there were two neatly made loft beds with brightly coloured bedding lining the walls. The space under them was being used as workspaces and simple desks were adorned with laptops and all the other accoutrements students these days seemed unable to live without. Artistic posters covered the painted cinderblock walls and a grass-green, shag rug dominated the floor.

Every trace of what had been was gone.

Bridget turned a full circle, allowing the present to overtake the past. With each passing moment, the edges of those memories softened. They would never fully leave her, but perhaps now they could fade.

'What happened?' the girl was leaning against the doorframe, watching Bridget with open curiosity.

She debated telling her, but didn't think it was fair to saddle her with the knowledge when she still had to live here.

'Someone I trusted hurt me.' It was the essence of the story. It would suffice.

The girl didn't say anything, but there was a knowing look in her eyes.

With a final look around, Bridget felt herself relax for the first time since she'd gotten on the plane to come here. Life had moved on and now so could she.

She smiled and thanked the girl, never once looking back as she left the building.

It was time to go home. She had a dean to take down.

Chapter Twenty-nine

'One more time,' Bridget said as she vainly tried to unlock her fingers from around the steering wheel.

If they screwed this up, both she and Skyler would be ruined.

'Professor, I know what I have to do.' Skyler's words were clipped and her jaw tight. Her own hands were clenched into fists in her lap.

Bridget's heart squeezed for her student. Skyler was about to let herself be publicly shamed in order to ensure Whittier was exposed once and for all. Bridget just hoped nothing went wrong. She might have leverage over Whittier, but her instincts said it would be foolish to trust him. She was risking her career, but she'd recover. The one who had the most on the table here was Skyler. They couldn't screw this up.

She let off the brake and inched forward in the line of cars for valet parking. The year-end mixer was always well attended. It was the time where everyone got to meet the up-and-coming talent at the university. It was also the worst kept secret around that more than one star student had been poached from under someone as a result of this party. Nevertheless, no one missed the opportunity to show off the tangible proof of their teaching skills.

During his tenure, Whittier had always chosen to host the mixer at his home. She always suspected it was to show off his wealth.

The two-storey Colonial in River Rock's historic district was massive. For this particular event, Dean Whittier always opened the music room and ensured some celebrity or another was there to play. Last year it had been Yo Yo Ma, the famous cellist. Bridget couldn't remember who was supposed to be playing this year. Her mind had been too preoccupied with planning Whittier's exposure.

'Skyler,' she said, doing her best to rein in her fear. She needed to stay strong for them both. 'Humour me, OK? Let's go through it again.'

Skyler bit her lip and choked off whatever she'd been about to say. Instead, taking a deep breath, she recounted all the steps she needed to take to ensure they exposed Whittier. When she finished, Bridget reciprocated, adding a silent prayer they'd succeed.

If her knees shook any harder she was going to fall. Professor Ross seemed so calm and collected and she was a mess. The dress she was wearing felt too tight and she felt on display. As if everyone in the room could tell exactly what was going on.

It didn't help that being in this house brought back all too many memories of her shame and humiliation at Whittier's hands. She snorted as she remembered the first time Dale had brought her here. She'd been so overwhelmed by the sheer wealth he surrounded himself with.

Funny, how it could be exactly the same and yet appear so different now. The foyer they stood in was the first clue that she hadn't been in Kansas any more. Marble floors and a huge glass table topped with flowers she couldn't identify had greeted her that first time, just like now. A huge crystal chandelier hung from the ceiling, casting a flurry of rainbows on ivory coloured walls and the steps flanking the entryway.

She'd felt like she'd walked right into a movie set. Like Scarlett O'Hara should have been gliding down the steps, ready to enter the ball. Tonight, she just felt like she'd walked back into a prison. Fear choked her and she wanted to vomit at the memory of her last night in this house. She'd never been so close to snapping in her life.

Thank God for Bridget. The professor had truly been the miracle she'd needed. She'd been serious in everything she'd said. Just yesterday, Skyler had come home to find her putting together a crib for the baby. She'd cried then. All the tears that she hadn't been able to shed had flowed unchecked at the sight of the crib.

She was going to have a baby. That was becoming more and more real for her every day. And even though it would never know its father – she would make sure of that – she wasn't going to be alone. She still hadn't told her parents. She knew they loved her, but they were going to be so disappointed when they found out. She honestly didn't know what it would do to their relationship. She also knew she didn't want to leave school. It would do no good for her baby to have a single mom working a menial job. She needed her education.

Right now, though, she just wished all this were over. The risk was so high and she really wasn't looking forward to being put on display the way she was about to be.

'Skyler?' Bridget was touching her arm.

'Hmm?' she pulled herself out of her head and faced the professor, who was walking back to her from the doorway leading to the party.

'I've spotted Whittier. He's at the back with the president and some of his cronies. I don't think we'll get a better opportunity so I'm going to go ahead and get started. Stay out of sight for at least ten minutes to give me some time, OK?' She checked her watch and added, 'I'll text you as soon as I'm done.'

'OK.' She took a deep breath and nodded. 'That shouldn't be hard. I need the bathroom anyway. I think I'm going to puke.'

Bridget narrowed her eyes at her and scanned her face, 'Are you OK? Is it the baby?'

Skyler nodded. 'Morning sickness. Well, evening sickness. I just need to catch my breath and splash some water on my face.'

'OK.' She didn't seem sure. 'We can call this off right now, Skyler.'

Skyler shook her head so hard she felt her hair swing. 'No! We're doing this. I'll be fine.'

Bridget wrapped her in a hug. She smelled flowery and soft, but she had a spine of steel when she needed it. Skyler was more grateful than ever. She never could have done this on her own.

Pulling out of the professor's embrace, she put on her best smile. 'OK. Go on, Inspector Gadget, I'll be fine.'

Bridget chuckled. 'You watch too much cable, you know that?'

Nevertheless, the joke had the effect Skyler hoped for. Bridget turned and left, heading off in the direction that Skyler had detailed for her while Skyler went to empty the contents of her stomach before she embarrassed herself.

As quietly as possible, Bridget closed the door to the dean's study behind her. The room was as impressive as the rest of the house. Spacious and airy, it was a library to fuel her own dreams. Books of all kinds lined the walls in glass-enclosed shelves.

It took a few seconds for that fact to sink in.

Oh hell, no!

She needed open shelves, not glass-covered ones. Frantically, she scanned the room, her panic rising. This didn't work if she couldn't get line of sight for the camera. For several heart-stopping moments, Bridget saw all of her carefully prepared plans falling apart. She wanted to cry; they hadn't come this far for it all to blow up now.

Just as she was about to throw in the towel, she spotted a shelf on the back wall by the large window. Elation filled her.

Yes, that would work. Better, in fact.

She hurried to the back of the room; she was wasting time. Reaching into her purse, she pulled out the ultra-slim video camera she'd purchased from Nico. At the same time, she powered on her portable hotspot to ensure it was ready when she needed it.

The shelf held several awards that the dean had received as well as a clock. She set up the camera, being sure to switch it to motion activated. Pulling out her iPad, she logged into the remote website account she'd set up and accessed the live feed from the camera. A few adjustments to angle, and she was ready to go.

Now, let's just hope Skyler is able to do her part, she thought.

Bridget began putting the hotspot and iPad back in her bag, only to whip around as the door to the library opened. Adrenaline shot through her veins and she went cold from head to toe. She couldn't get caught.

With no time to think, she dove under the desk and thanked her lucky stars she was wearing a pant suit and not a dress. She also thanked the dean for being the conceited, self-important man he was or else he'd have some other desk than this ancient monstrosity that had a cavernous opening where she currently huddled.

'How dare you bring him here!' A shrill, feminine voice that Bridget recognised as belonging to Jean Cartwright, one of the physics professors, rang out in the still of the study.

'He's my star student. Why wouldn't I bring him here?' responded her companion. From his slightly sibilant, soft voice, Bridget identified Jean's husband, Louis.

'Don't be coy with me. I know you fucked him while I was gone. Did you think I wouldn't find out?'

Bridget couldn't speak for Louis, but she sure as hell was shocked at the accusation. She'd never pegged Louis for a cheater. He seemed so devoted to his wife.

'Nothing to say for yourself?'

'Jean, let me explain.' He'd obviously moved closer to the desk since his voice was louder.

'No. I don't want to hear any explanations. I told you not to fuck him, didn't I?'

Jean sounded less outraged than Bridget would have expected at discovering her husband's infidelity.

'Yes.' At least he sounded contrite. But Bridget was definitely confused.

'And why did I tell you not to fuck him?'

Bridget would have thought it would have been self-apparent, but she couldn't exactly call out, 'Duh!'

'Because I wasn't allowed to come while you were gone.'

'Exactly!' She heard Jean walk over to the large, leather chairs that fronted the dean's desk and sat. 'Your cock belongs to me. You get to fuck Robert when I say and only when I say. And you damn sure don't bring him to an office party after defying me. Do you understand?'

Her voice, normally shrill and slightly nasal, had taken on the same cadence Evan's did when he went all dom-ish on Claire. Realisation slapped Bridget in the face. Louis was Jean's sub.

'For that, you don't get to come for the next week. Understand?'

'Yes, ma'am.' He sounded almost breathless.

'You're also going to receive punishment when we get home. Understand?'

'Yes, ma'am.' Now he sounded downright eager.

'Good. Now come here and give me what you gave Robert.'

Bridget cringed at the idea of being present while they had sex.

'That's a good boy,' Jean crooned. The zing of a zipper coming down filled the silence. Louis groaned and Bridget heard sucking and slurping noises. From Louis' moans she could only deduce that Jean had decided to suck his dick.

She really hoped they'd finish soon. She needed to get back to Skyler.

Mastering her frustration, she decided to at least be productive. She pulled out her iPad to check that the camera was working properly and had a good view of the room.

The screen instantly filled with the image of Jean on her knees in front of her husband. Bridget quickly hit the home button, killing the visual. She really didn't want that in her head.

Fortunately, Jean seemed to decide that Louis had been tortured enough. Bridget heard fumbling and some muted whispers. They seemed to have made up, at least. A few seconds later, she heard the door open and close.

Bridget wasted no time in getting out of there and searching out Skyler.

Chapter Thirty

That little bitch actually had the gall to show her face here. It was bad enough he had to tolerate Ross being here. He couldn't very well disinvite his most popular professor, but she could have had the grace not to show up. Instead, she'd not only come, she'd brought Skyler.

Skyler, who'd disappeared without a trace three weeks ago.

Skyler, who refused to answer his calls.

Fucking cunt.

Anger seethed in his gut as Dale watched the two women mingle with the other partygoers. Something was definitely not right. He would have expected smugness from Bridget. Instead, she seemed tense.

He knew every inch of her face and body. He'd spent countless hours observing her. Learning her. She had no idea exactly how intimately acquainted with her he was.

An unschooled observer might not notice it, but her face was pale and her lips, usually so lush and full, were pinched. That was the only clue that she wasn't her usual, gregarious self.

She was elegantly dressed as usual. A simple copper silk blouse and camel-coloured pants ending in chocolate leather boots. She had style. As she moved, her breasts jiggled slightly and his hand itched as the memory of the feel of her tits filled his mind.

She'd felt good underneath him. Pinned to the desk. Whimpering, ready for him to have her. They'd been full and heavy. Her nipples hard and wanting.

His cock twitched and he pulled his thoughts back to the present. She'd pay for humiliating him the way she had. She thought she had him over a barrel with that janitor boyfriend of hers. But she was wrong. He hadn't figured out how to bring this back on her, but he would.

Skyler looked downright sick. She was literally green around the edges, as if she were likely to vomit.

She should be. Showing up in his house like this. She had a lot to answer for and he planned to get his answers now. Not later. She might disappear again.

Excusing himself from the president, who was droning on about the risks of raising tuition to the group of toadies he'd cultivated, Dale navigated the crowd toward the two women.

'He's coming this way,' Skyler hissed to Bridget.

'Stay calm,' she replied. 'This is what we wanted, remember.'

It might have been what needed to happen, but it was the last thing Skyler wanted to happen. She wanted to leave and never see the bastard's face again. She wanted to rip out his lying tongue and make him choke on it.

Not good for the baby, Sky, she reminded herself. Calm down.

She took a deep breath, plastered on a smile, and turned to face the demon of her nightmares.

'Skyler.' The dean's eyebrow twitched and his eyes narrowed. 'I'm surprised to see you here.' He turned his gaze to the professor. 'You too, Ross.'

'Why wouldn't I be here?' Bridget smirked at Dale. 'No one misses the year end meat-market.'

'Am I to believe, then, that Skyler is your chosen protégée?' He sipped from what looked like brandy.

Skyler's chest went tight. She hated dealing with him when he was drinking. He was bad enough sober. Drunk, he was much more vicious. She could only hope that he hadn't been at it for very long.

'You can believe whatever you want, Dean.' Bridget drew herself up to her full height, but didn't come anywhere close to matching the dean in being imposing.

He sneered at her. 'You and I have unfinished business, Ross, but right now, Skyler and I have a conversation we need to have.'

Before she could react, he took Skyler by the arm and began leading her out of the room. But he wasn't taking her towards his study where she needed to get him. He was leading her back towards the foyer. She guessed where he intended to take her and there was no way in hell she was going anywhere near his bedroom.

They'd made it to the foyer before she had the presence of mind to snatch her arm from his grip and veer off toward the study.

'Get back here,' he hissed and reached for her.

She looked over her shoulder but kept on moving. He was going to have to catch her.

287

'Sky –' He started to call after her, but obviously thought better of it, not wanting to draw attention to them.

Another glance over her shoulder showed him setting his drink down and following her. The scowl on his face didn't bode well.

Her heart kicked into overdrive; she felt like she was going to throw up. Knowing she was supposed to get him alone didn't make her want to do this.

She all but ran to the study, throwing open the door and bolting inside. Bridget had said to get over by the desk and she had just made it inside before Dale stormed through the door. She expected him to slam it shut, but he closed it softly. The click of the lock, however, resonated through the room with the force of a thunderclap.

Skyler prayed Bridget's plan worked.

She whirled to face him and her breath dissolved in her chest at the venom in his face. She'd seen him angry, but now he appeared almost murderous. She didn't want him close to her. Turning, she intended to put the desk between them.

She didn't make it.

He grabbed her arm in a bruising grip and yanked her to face him.

'What do you think you're doing, you little slut?' His grip tightened hard enough to make her gasp out loud. Leaning in close, he said, 'What makes you think you get to ignore me? Hmm? Didn't I tell you I wasn't done with you?'

Skyler struggled vainly, trying to pull her arm away from him. Giving up, she lifted her chin and said, 'We're done, Dale. I don't care what you say;

I'm not sleeping with you any more.'

He laughed, a sound so bitter and cold it made goosebumps erupt on her skin.

'Is that what you think? You are quite precious, aren't you?' He smiled but there was no mirth there.

Paradoxically, he stroked her face with a gentle finger, brushing an errant lock of hair out of her eyes. Just as she relaxed, he gripped her chin viciously, grinding her lips into her teeth and forcing a whimper from her.

'You clearly need a lesson in who is in charge here. Your scholarship is under my control, or do I need to remind you that I can make it so you are run out of this school? I expect you to do as I say. That means you answer your fucking phone and you come when I call you. I told you before, you upstart little cunt, I will fuck you when and how I please.' He shook her hard enough to rattle her teeth.

'No,' she cried out and struggled harder, trying in vain to get away from him. 'I won't do it.'

He fisted her hair, pulling her head back and forcing her to look at him. 'You have no choice.' A malicious grin twisted the features she'd once found so endearing.

'I kept the baby,' she cried.

In that moment, she understood the phrase "calm before the storm" The entire room seemed to still. Dale was frozen. The shock on his face would have been comical if not for the fury building in his eyes.

Whack! He slapped her so hard her ears rang. White lighting flashed in her head. Her brain reeled and she fell against the desk as he thrust her away from him.

'I told you to get rid of that!' He was yelling, but his voice seemed to be coming from a long way off.

He raised his hand to strike her again. She reached deep inside and gathered herself. With a fierce cry, she hurled herself at him, pushing with all her might.

He stumbled backward, losing his footing and falling to the floor.

She didn't wait to see what happened next. Moving as fast as she could, Skyler's feet tangled under her and she almost fell into the door. She fumbled frantically with the lock. Throwing the door open, she ran, praying it was salvation she fled to and not her doom.

Bridget's knees went weak as Whittier pulled Skyler away. Her instincts were screaming at her to stop this, not to let it continue. But, they needed to halt him once and for all. It was time for him to stop preying on women.

She took a steadying breath and willed her body to relax. She had no time to waste. Ripping open her bag, she pawed frantically for her iPad. Scanning the crowd, she spotted President Harvey in a group of senior administrators.

Perfect! He wouldn't be able to cover this up just to keep hold of Whittier's money. She wanted to believe he was ethical, but her heart told her not to take the chance.

Deftly, Bridget navigated the crowd. As she moved, she pulled up the feed and almost dropped the tablet at the sight of a furious Whittier advancing on Skyler.

Harvey had his back to her and she tapped him on

the shoulder. He glanced at her, scowled, and turned back to the group immediately.

He was blowing her off!

She glanced at the screen. The dean had grabbed Skyler.

Bridget's heart began to race and her hands shook. There was no time.

She tapped him again and said, 'President Harvey, you need to see this!' She raised her voice to be heard over the crowd.

He looked over his shoulder again. 'Ross, I'm sure it can wait.' He turned back to the group and resumed pontificating on the impending budget cuts.

'Damn it, Brad!' she hollered, her patience gone, 'No one gives a damn! You need to watch this and see what's going on under your friggin' nose!'

Silence fell over the room like a curtain. The president turned to face her, his plump face almost cherry red with indignation.

He opened his mouth – to yell most likely – but the dean's voice rang out from the iPad and all attention focused on the device in Bridget's hand. Within moments, a crowd had clustered around her. President Harvey was to her immediate right and Bill Fogarty, the vice president, flanked her to the left.

Both watched in disgust as Whitter manhandled and threatened Skyler. Bridget's stomach clenched as the tension and violence ratcheted higher. She bit her lip, determined to keep the focus on the dean while they watched as much as she wanted to repudiate Harvey for putting money over integrity when he hired Whittier.

She couldn't hold back a cry of distress when

Whittier hit Skyler. The crowd erupted as well. Bridget whirled and pushed through the throng, determined to get to her student.

She didn't have to go far. Skyler flew into the music room at a dead run. The side of her face was bright red and a small trickle of blood trailed from her lip where Whittier had split it.

The crowd erupted at her appearance. The din was almost overwhelming, but it cut off as if someone had thrown a switch when Whittier appeared in the doorway. Bridget snatched Skyler by the hand and pulled her close, wrapping an arm around her waist.

Whittier scanned the crowd, who all stood staring at him with varying degrees of disgust on their faces.

'What?' he asked, his eyes wary. 'Has something happened?'

President Harvey pushed through the crowd. 'You have some nerve, Dale. Acting as if you didn't just molest and then viciously attack this young woman.'

'I have no idea what you're talking about.' He straightened up to his full height. 'This woman –' he sneered the word '– attacked me when I refused her advances. I was defending myself.'

President Harvey's eyes narrowed and his face pinched as if he'd smelled something foul. 'We saw what you did, you sick bastard.' His voice shook with outrage.

'We have you on tape,' Bridget said, speaking up to be heard over the murmurs of the crowd. She tapped the screen and set the video she'd recorded to replay, holding it up for Whittier to see.

All colour drained from his face, giving him a deathly pallor. He backed up, stumbling and hitting the doorframe.

'You're finished, Whittier.' The president advanced on him. 'As of this moment, you are officially suspended. Given the extensive contributions your family has made to this university, I will give you 24 hours to have a resignation letter on my desk. But, you are done here.'

Pushing past Whittier, he left without a backward look. The rest of the guests followed suit. Not wanting to be alone with the dean, Bridget hustled Skyler out with the throng.

The last sight she had of Whittier was him sinking to the floor in the doorway, looking for all the world as if the earth had just fallen out from beneath him.

She felt not one shred of sympathy.

Chapter Thirty-one

One month later ...

'Leave it. You'll mess it up,' Skyler admonished Bridget as she adjusted her hair for the millionth time.

'I'm a mess, Sky.' Bridget's voice cracked audibly, reflecting the way she felt inside.

'You'll be fine.' She came up beside Bridget and put an arm around her shoulders. 'You look hot. He won't be able to resist you.'

Bridget smiled at her young housemate. Having Skyler with her had turned out to be one of the best decisions she'd ever made. They'd grown close in the weeks since Skyler had come to live with her and it had been a joy to witness her pregnancy. In many ways, when it came to that, she was living vicariously through her former student.

Skyler was solidly into her second trimester and showing. She'd taken to pregnancy well and looked radiantly beautiful. She'd also been a comfort and a distraction from her pain over Connor. That they'd been wading through the fallout from the scandal over the dean at the university had helped to keep her mind off of him as well.

Bridget's tenure had sailed through and Skyler's scholarship was safe. Dean Whittier had resigned as ordered, but a full-scale investigation into all of his oversight decisions had been launched. Several improprieties had already been discovered on tenure decisions for two of Bridget's colleagues and at least one other student had come forward with allegations of harassment.

He was officially ruined. Bridget had searched for compassion, but found that while she didn't hate him, she didn't forgive him either. He'd played too fast and loose with people's lives.

'Bridget?'

'Hmm?' She pulled herself back to the present.

'What are you thinking about? You look fierce.' Curious brown eyes met hers in the mirror.

'I was thinking about Whittier. And –' she turned and hugged Skyler to her '– how happy I am that you're here.'

Skyler grinned and returned the hug before pulling back and turning Bridget to face the mirror once again.

'Are you ready?' she asked.

'I don't know, Sky.' She eyed herself critically. 'I feel so exposed.'

In truth, she felt naked. Victor, at her request, had made this outfit especially for her. She'd expected something chic and elegant, like the items of lingerie he'd designed for her. Instead, he'd given her urban and sexy.

A mix of leather and silk, the dress was sleeveless and backless. The chocolate, leather bodice was quilted and flowed into a bronze silk skirt that hugged her so tightly she was afraid she'd split a seam. Victor had assured her she wouldn't and that it was designed to stretch, but it darn sure wasn't designed for panties or a bra. She was completely naked under it!

Victor had even gone so far as to provide strappy, stiletto sandals and jewellery as well as instructions on how to wear her hair. She didn't even have the option of deviating since he'd be there tonight.

The net result was that Bridget *looked* sexy and powerful yet inside felt nothing but nervous and scared.

She wanted her man back, and she was determined to get him, but she wasn't sure he wanted to be gotten. There'd been not one word from him. No phone calls. No messages. He'd even left what few belongings of hers he'd had in her office after hours one night.

She'd cried for a long time over that discovery.

Then she'd gotten the invite to his show. He'd written on it in scrawling print, "I hope you'll come."

Mona, the traitor, hadn't said a word. She hadn't been a bit sorry about it either when Bridget had confronted her. She'd just shrugged and said, 'He swore me to secrecy, so I guess you'll just have to take that up with him.'

Bridget wasn't going to. She was too happy for him. She hoped it meant that he'd put his past into perspective as she had been working to do.

It was still a work in progress for her, but between her sessions with Cathy and the reading and talking she'd been doing with other kinky folks courtesy of Evan, she'd come to accept that her desires weren't something to be ashamed of.

She'd even had a really sweet offer from a hunky morsel of man at the munch Evan had organised just for her. The gathering of like-minded kinky folks had been a real eye-opener for her. She'd had only one embarrassing moment when Jean and Louis had shown up, but they'd quickly laughed hugged, and moved on.

She hadn't even truly considered the offer she'd received. Exploring kink involved deep trust and the only man she trusted at that level was Connor. Her reluctance must have shown because Evan had pulled her aside asking, 'You OK? Is he pressuring you?'

She'd quickly reassured him that everything was fine before continuing, 'It's just that I don't see how I could do any of this with a stranger.'

He'd smiled indulgently and replied, 'I don't personally recommend it.'

He'd laughed at her clear surprise and continued. 'Look, of course people hook up in this life, but lots of times that takes place at play parties or dungeons where there are other people and monitors to make sure safewords are respected and everything stays safe, sane and consensual.

'Kink doesn't mean throwing out the rules of common sense. If anything, you probably need to be even pickier.'

Relief flooded her at his words. She definitely was not ready to jump in with just anyone. Truly, the only person she would even consider doing any of this with at this stage was Connor.

'Have you thought about calling him?'

Bridget scowled at him. She really didn't like feeling so exposed.

'When it comes to Connor, you wear your heart on your sleeve, babe.'

He wrapped her in a warm hug and she drew comfort from him to fight back the tears that always hovered whenever she thought of Connor.

Pulling back, she swiped away an errant tear.

'I think about it, but so far it hasn't become more than a thought.'

'Well –' he tipped her chin up '– don't wait too long. He seemed like a good guy.'

He was a good guy and she planned to do a hell of a lot more than call him tonight. She was going to claim him once and for all.

Tonight, there would be no more barriers between them.

Taking Skyler's hand, she squeezed it.

'You sure you'll be OK, darlin'?'

Skyler had been struggling with her worries over being a single mom. Just that morning she'd received the papers from Whittier relinquishing all parental rights. She'd been stoic, but it had been obvious that she'd been crying when she had finally emerged from her "nap" several hours later.

'Yeah.' She smiled at Bridget. 'Mom and Lenora are coming over and we're going to head over to Ten Fingers and Toes to get me registered.'

Bridget was so happy that Skyler's family had embraced her during this time. More than that, they'd welcomed Bridget with open arms, making her an honorary family member.

'OK, sugar.' She gathered the velvet wrap Victor has also provided and the small, quilted clutch. Equipped with all her feminine armour, she went to claim her man.

Without question, this was the best night of his life. Connor surveyed the crowd that had turned out to Bean There Done That and felt himself get a little choked up. He might lose his "man card" over it, but he was definitely damp-eyed. In his wildest dream, he hadn't expected this.

Mona had pulled out all the stops once she'd viewed his collection. Especially his centrepiece for the show. She'd closed the shop today, and within hours it had been transformed from casual hangout to urban art gallery.

She'd called local contractor, Wade Stalls, who'd ensured they'd met their deadline. That interaction had been something to see. He'd never seen Mona so flustered.

Connor was feeling flustered himself. So far Bridget had been a no-show. He'd be lying to say he wasn't severely disappointed. But, no matter the outcome, he couldn't regret putting on this show. He'd already sold two canvases and a local art critic had promised a glowing review in the paper.

It was as if he'd come full circle. That the two ends of his life had finally fused together. For the first time in a very long time, Connor felt whole. He had his art back without shame or recrimination. He no longer needed to hide it lest his parents' ghosts rise up to haunt him. He was sharing his art with the world and it felt right.

The only thing that could have made this night better was if Bridget had turned out to share it with him. The time they'd been apart had proven to him that he wasn't going to get over her any time soon. He missed her deeply.

He'd wanted to do this on his own, though. He'd wanted to prove that he'd meet her halfway if she was willing to try. Now, he was kicking himself. He'd waited when he should have acted and it looked like he'd lost her.

'Your neck is going to cramp if you keep that up. This is an art show not a tennis match.' Victor handed Connor a flute of champagne. 'She's not here, but just be patient.'

'How can you be so sure? The show started over an hour ago. You know she's compulsively punctual.'

'Well, everyone has an off day.' He chuckled. 'I'm willing to bet she'll be here.'

Connor sipped his champagne, wishing it were something stronger. He and Vic had grown close after their first meeting. Vic had been another of Bridget's champions who'd wanted to kick his ass in the aftermath of their break-up.

He'd threatened Connor quite eloquently when Connor had gone back to return the unused toys. By the time Connor had finished explaining, Vic was offering to buy him a beer and pretending not to notice his tears. A bond had formed that night over drinks and nachos at Lou's, a local pool hall. They'd hung out regularly ever since.

'You seem awfully sure of yourself.' Connor glanced at Victor and stopped short at the smirk on his friend's face. 'Hold up.' He set his glass down. 'You know something.'

Vic held up a hand to stave off any more questions, 'Don't even try it. I've been sworn to secrecy and I never break my word.'

Connor wanted to shake the smug grin from his

face. This was definitely not funny.

'Besides –' Vic gestured over Connor's shoulder. 'I just won that bet anyway.'

Connor spun and felt his jaw hit his chest at the vision Bridget made.

'You're catching flies, brother.' Vic laughed and clapped him on the shoulder before moving off to embrace Bridget.

She returned the hug and whispered something in his ear. Vic, the bastard, grinned at Connor before taking her hand and kissing it.

He'd kill him for that later. Right now, he needed to get his dick to cooperate. It was joining the party and he definitely did not want to be standing in a crowd at his first art show sporting a hard-on.

Could you really blame a guy when Bridget looked like sex on legs? Every man in the house had noticed her when she walked in. He'd managed to close his mouth, but he was rooted in place. Hell, part of him just wanted to watch her walk.

The way she moved in that dress had his imagination running wild. And that was not where he needed to be. He needed to get his little head out of the equation.

Mona had obviously seen her. As had Claire. Both women came over and hugged her. Whatever words were exchanged resulted in Mona pointing in his direction.

When she finally saw him, her face transformed. She smiled radiantly. It damn near knocked him on his ass. She'd never been so completely unguarded before.

Hope, furious and hot, burned in his heart and he

wrangled it down. This was not the time to get ahead of himself.

She navigated her way over to him. When she was finally within reach, he debated throwing caution to the wind and taking her in his arms, kissing her breathless, and tossing her over his shoulder and making off with her.

He settled for taking her hand and saying, 'You look amazing.'

She flushed prettily, snorted rather inelegantly, and said, 'I feel as if my rear end is on display for the world to see. I should give Victor a piece of my mind.'

'Victor?' Her words weren't computing.

'He designed this for me.'

She did a 360 and his jaw came perilously close to hitting his chest again. There was no way in hell she had underwear on. In that moment, he didn't know whether to kick Vic's ass or buy him a beer to say thank you.

'Well, you look amazing.'

She smiled again and his heart clenched. She was definitely still under his skin.

A waiter walked by and she accepted a flute of champagne. Turning back to Connor, she waved a hand, taking in the room.

'I'm so happy for you, Connor. I hope this doesn't sound patronising, but I'm really proud of you.'

'That means a lot to me, Bridg.' He blew out the breath he hadn't realised he'd been holding. 'I'm really glad you came.'

Tender green eyes met his. 'I wouldn't miss it for anything, sugar.'

His groin tightened at all that Southern coming his way, but he commanded himself to behave.

'Would you like the tour?' Anticipation rolled through him like an itch he couldn't scratch.

'Lead on.' She smiled.

He offered her his arm and she took it. She felt good tucked into his body. He didn't want to let go of her.

He took her around, showing her the pieces he'd chosen for the show. Many of them she'd seen at his place. A few were new and she exclaimed excitedly over them, making him feel quite accomplished.

Their progress was slow since patrons regularly stopped Connor to ask him about his work or offer their compliments. Finally, they made it to the last piece. A crowd surrounded it. Connor politely pushed through to the front, making sure Bridget's view was unobstructed, and waited for her response.

Bridget was stunned speechless. Nothing could have prepared her for the sight hanging in front of her.

Connor had taken the image he'd drawn at their first picnic and blown it up to life-size proportions. She gazed out from the canvas with a look in her eyes that could best be described as tortured yearning. It was as if he'd seen into her soul and put it on display.

He'd seen what she'd not wanted to acknowledge. That he'd understood what she'd refused to was evident in the painting's title: *Yearning to be Whole*.

Tears welled in her eyes. She didn't know what to say. She'd pushed him away and he'd been right there the whole time just waiting for her to see it. She'd been a class-A idiot.

'Hey.' He tipped her chin up. 'What's wrong?'

She started to respond, but became highly aware of the people surrounding them. Taking his hand, she led him to Mona's office. Once inside, she shut the door.

'Bridget –' he began.

She cut him off with a kiss. Wrapping her arms around his neck, she clung to him and poured all her pain and sorrow at pushing him away into it. He matched her fervour. His tongue duelled with hers even as he gripped her ass and pressed her tightly against him.

When she finally broke the kiss, they were both panting and breathless.

'Hell, I'll paint you every day if that's the response I'll get.'

She laughed and felt all her tension drain away.

'It wasn't the painting, even though it's gorgeous.' She took his hand and pulled him over to the chairs in front of Mona's desk. 'It was how you saw me. How you knew I wanted more.'

She looked away from his all too knowing eyes and smoothed her skirt.

Meeting his grey eyes again, she said, 'I'm so sorry, Connor. Everything you said was right. I did keep you at a distance. I was comfortable in my box, as much as it chafed, and I didn't take any risks.'

Grabbing his hand, she continued, 'I'd like to change that.' She was reassured when he squeezed her hand in return. 'If you want to try, that is.'

Connor was silent, his eyes suddenly unreadable, and she began to doubt whether or not she'd get her man after all.

When he finally spoke, his voice was soft. 'I owe

you an apology. I was demanding something from you that I wasn't even doing. It was hypocritical.'

He brought her hand to his mouth and kissed it.

'I love you, Bridget. I want to be with you, but I guess I'm asking how you see this going?'

Hope flared in her chest. He was willing!

Tears welled and she couldn't stop them. 'I don't want any barriers between us. I've been seeing a rape counsellor and I've been talking with Evan and other experienced people about the kinkier stuff. But I only want to be with you. I don't want to be with anyone else. I want to try these things with you.'

Tears flowed unchecked and she felt ecstatic at this second chance. He tugged her into his lap and held her close. She breathed him in, taking in the scent of soap and clean skin, the warm hardness of his chest and the steady thrum of his heartbeat.

She sighed contentedly. 'I love you, Connor.'

She felt him grin against her hair. 'There's no way you're getting away now.'

She chuckled. 'Oh really. How do you plan to keep me?'

Squeezing her tighter, he teased, 'Maybe I'll just have to tie you down and keep you in my bed.'

'Hmm.' She snuggled in closer, nipping his neck. 'That might work, but what if I don't cooperate?'

A deep laugh rumbled in his chest at her flirting, 'Maybe I'll have to spank you if you're bad.'

She grinned into his neck. 'Promise?'

His cock leaped under her hips and she laughed.

Pulling back, he tipped her chin so that their eyes met. His had deepened to a charcoal grey and were filled with heat. 'Are you serious, Bridg?'

She nodded, 'Yes, darlin'. I'm dead serious. I want you to do all that to me, Connor.'

He put her out of her lap and tugged her towards the door.

She laughed harder. 'Connor, what are you doing?'

He grinned that lopsided grin she loved so much. 'We're leaving. I've got a lot of time to make up for.'

She was laughing so hard she could barely speak, but managed to force out, 'What about your show?'

He stopped short and she almost ran into him.

'Shit!' He raked a hand through his hair. 'I guess I can't run out on my own show. But, woman, you are not getting away from me again. Understood?'

She rose up on tiptoes and brushed a kiss across his lips. 'I'm all yours, sugar.'

His grin melted her heart. 'Damn straight!'

Taking her hand, he pulled her back out into the crowd.

Chapter Thirty-two

She was magnificent. Naked and on her elbows and knees, her ass in the air, Bridget looked resplendent. Her skin was cherry red from the spanking he'd given her and her pussy glistened in the low light.

He dipped his fingers into her core and then brought them to his lips, sucking her moisture from them. She was tangy and ripe, but, as much as he wanted to bury himself inside her, he wasn't near done with her.

He'd returned everything he'd bought to Victor, so he was improvising. He'd found a scarf shoved in his closet that had been a present years ago and he'd bound her wrists together.

That had been a tense moment. He'd thought she'd balk then, but she'd locked eyes with him until her breathing had calmed down. It had tested all of his self-control to take it slow with her, but ensuring her re-entry into this was uneventful was crucial and he didn't want to fuck it up. Spanking her had been sublime and she'd nearly come as he'd played with her clit in between strikes, but he'd backed off. He wanted her mindless when she finally came.

'Roll over, baby,' he directed.

She obliged and he kissed her deeply, enjoying her

taste and her soft submission. He was going to ensure she didn't regret giving him this gift.

Bridget felt the cracks in her mind filling in. As ironic as it was, with each strike, she'd felt more at peace. When Connor had bound her wrists, images of Trent had threatened to overwhelm her, but staring into Connor's eyes, so filled with love for her, had kept her grounded.

Right now her butt was on fire and the cotton of his sheets abraded the tender skin. She arched and moaned under him, thrusting her breasts in the air, silently begging for more.

She got it.

He smacked first one nipple then the other. Pain, sharp and hot, radiated across her breasts before fading into a pleasant sting. He leaned over and sucked gently on her nipples, soothing the tender buds before striking them again.

She cried out, amazed to feel her clitoris pulsing. She arched and writhed as pleasure filled her. Inside she began to coil, like a string being pulled tight. Her pussy pulsed; she wanted him inside her.

'More!' she demanded.

'Shh,' he murmured. 'We'll take this slow. There's no need to rush.'

He set up a rhythm, first spanking her nipples and then soothing them with his tongue. Soon she was squirming under him, begging him to finish her.

Her skin felt alive. She could feel each tiny hair; each nerve-ending. This is what she'd wanted. This was what Trent had stolen from her all those years ago. The freedom to be who she was. To be free and uninhibited with a man she loved.

No more. It was hers again and she was owning it.

Connor moved between her legs and penetrated her slowly. She revelled in the feel of his skin against hers. Her body was so sensitised she was almost overcome with these new sensations. The tension in her belly grew even tighter.

He filled and stretched her, slowly fucking her. He took her to the edge again and again, but didn't let her fall over. The tension became unbearable. She needed to come. She felt like she'd come apart if she didn't.

'More, Connor!' She thrust against him. 'Harder. Please!' She didn't even care that she was begging.

He drew her knees up over his arms and began to pound into her. His balls were slapping the skin of her ass where he'd spanked her and that small edge of pain intermingled with the pleasure of his possession sending her over the edge.

Bridget came in waves of intense, soul-stealing pleasure. They wrapped around her, suffusing her body in an ecstasy so deep her vision went black at the edges. It was several seconds before she realised the screams she was hearing were her own.

She shuddered and twitched in the aftermath as Connor increased his pace. She luxuriated in the burn and stretch of his cock deep inside her. She was going to be sore and she would love every second of it.

Connor groaned and she felt the warm, hot jets of his semen filling her.

Later, as they lay entangled in each other's arms, she knew she'd finally been made whole.

The story continues in…

UNSETTLED

.

Chapter One

Wade Stalls whipped his pick-up into a parking spot and checked his reflection in the mirror. Today was the day. He wasn't waiting any more. He'd let this go on too damn long.

Slamming the door, he locked the truck and headed across the street. Pushing open the door to the café, he was assaulted by the aromas of coffee and pastry. This was normally where he caved in. He'd tell himself he was going to do it. He'd get in line, order his coffee, and watch his plans fall apart in front of his eyes. Every. Single. Damn. Time.

Not today.

He wasn't getting in line today. He wasn't waiting passively. He was going to seize the bull by the –

His chest squeezed and the breath in his chest dissolved. Scanning the café, he saw no trace of his quarry. With his plans derailed, he was at a loss. The adrenaline that had been sustaining him began to fade.

With no better course of action presenting itself, Wade placed his order and took up residence at a table that afforded him a complete view of the establishment. Another alteration for him. Usually, he'd be so frustrated by the time he'd gotten his coffee, he'd just leave. He didn't think he'd ever taken the time to sit down.

He'd never really noticed how packed the café was. Or how everyone seemed so happy. The tables were filled with students and couples. Everyone was chatting, and not just with each other. They talked among tables like old friends.

She'd done well for herself. He was proud of her. She, on the other hand, treated him like he had the plague.

For the life of him, he couldn't figure it out. He didn't think he'd ever done anything to her to warrant it. And, God knew, he wanted to do things to her. Lots of things. Lots of dirty, erotic things that put those full, luscious lips to use.

He shifted in his seat, acutely aware he was getting a hard-on in public. That was not acceptable. He hadn't come here to indulge his fantasies of her. He did that often enough in private.

He'd come to confront her once and for all and to ask her out. He was tired of being a chicken-shit coward around her. He wanted her. Hell, he'd wanted her as far back as high school, but she'd been too young. His conscience hadn't allowed him to go there. She wasn't too young any more, though. Nope, she was all woman now and it was time for him to man up and remember he had a pair.

Glancing at his watch, he wondered where she was. Her schedule was usually as routine as his. He counted on seeing her every morning. He'd come early today just to be certain, but he had a job site to get to and he made a point of always being on time. He'd developed a reputation as the man to turn to for contracting in River Rock and he ensured he did what it took to keep it.

Frustrated at having his plans thwarted, Wade picked up his coffee and stood. He turned toward the exit and felt his legs give way at the sight that greeted him. With a hard thunk, he landed back in the chair. Paralysed, he could do nothing but watch.

His Mona was being kissed by a huge linebacker of a man. It was a tender kiss, full of restrained passion. The man's hunger for her was evident. When he broke the kiss, Mona wrapped her arms around him and hugged him tight. When they parted, regret was evident on both their faces. Clearly, they couldn't stand to be parted from one another.

All the clichés about hearts shattering came back to him in that moment as a wave of grief washed over him that was so intense he almost cried out.

He'd waited too long.

He'd lost her.

Mona watched Irving leave and cursed herself for a fool. He was a good man. Funny, kind, sexy as hell, and great in bed, but she just hadn't been able to get her heart in line with her head. It wasn't fair to stay in the relationship when she knew there was no future. She was in love with another man and, despite all her attempts to erase him from her heart, he was dug in like a tick.

The problem was that she fell apart every time she was around him. The instant he appeared, she went from successful, grown woman to that 14-year-old girl who'd first seen him across the concourse in high school. She'd been so tongue-tied she'd barely been able to stutter her name when he'd introduced himself. He'd run the other way when he'd found out she was a freshman and had kept his distance ever since.

She, on the other hand, had pined for him from that moment forward. Every boy paled in comparison. Every man just didn't measure up.

She blew out a disgusted breath.

She really needed to get a grip. It was time to grow up and move on. She was wasting her time. He didn't want her. He never had.

She pushed open the door to the café and entered without watching where she was going. She slammed into a rock-hard chest and had to grab a handful of cotton to stay upright.

Large, warm hands cupped her lower back, bringing her into full contact with a long, lean body. Her breath caught in more than mere surprise at the feel of him.

Looking up, she almost fainted at the sight of Wade staring down at her. He looked gorgeous and sexy and absolutely devastated.

He looked as if someone had died.

'Wade?' She tugged out of his arms to put distance between them as she felt all the usual tension and giddiness welling inside her.

'Sorry.' His voice was gruff and strained.

He didn't say anything else, just pushed past her and left the café. Mona watched him as he crossed the street and got into his F-150. You'd have thought someone was chasing him, he moved so fast.

What in the hell had happened to hurt him so badly?

With a determined shake of her head, Mona turned and went to tackle the paperwork she'd been putting off. She hoped that, whatever had happened to him, he'd be OK.

See where it all began:

Claire Ryan and Evan Lang are two people stuck in the past. Claire holds herself responsible for her abusive past and Evan can't get over the death of his wife and submissive. Together they have a chance at new life and new love, but will they let themselves have it?

Awakening – Book One of the Chrysalis Series

Winner of the New Writing Competition at the Festival of Romance 2011

If you enjoyed this book, please tell a friend and support an independent publisher.

www.xcitebooks.com

Please scan the QR code to join our mailing list

or visit:

www.xcitebooks.com

Please review me – thank you!

Printed in Great Britain
by Amazon.co.uk, Ltd.,
Marston Gate.